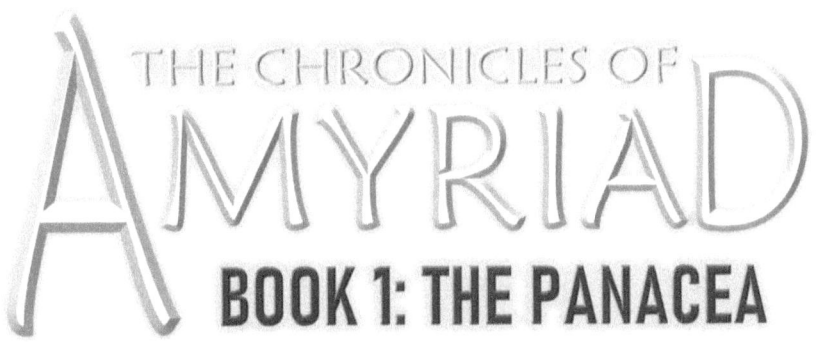

THE CHRONICLES OF AMYRIAD

BOOK 1: THE PANACEA

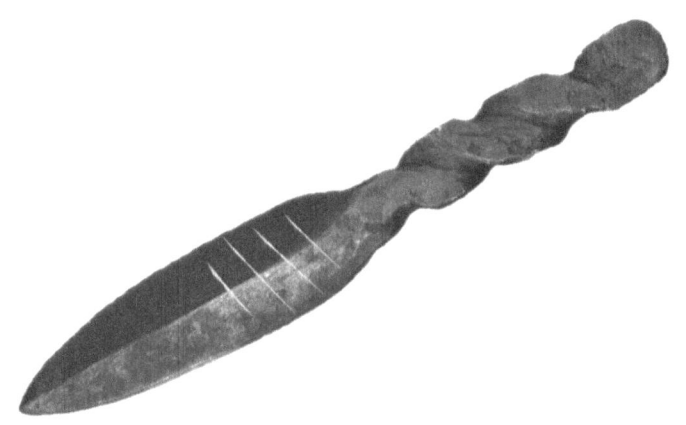

S.R. JENSEN

AMYRIAD
ADVENTURES

THE CHRONICLES OF AMYRIAD

BOOK 1: THE PANACEA

Cover design and layout by S.R. Jensen
Flaming animal and weapon images from www.stock.adobe.com
Map © 2020 by S.R. Jensen, created using Other World Mapper

Published by Amyriad Adventures, LLC, Rigby, ID 83442

AMYRIAD ADVENTURES

ISBN (Paperback): 978-1-7355199-0-6

ISBN (eBook): 978-1-7355199-1-3

Library of Congress Control Number: 2020914960

www.srjensenbooks.com

www.amyriadadventures.com

For Amy

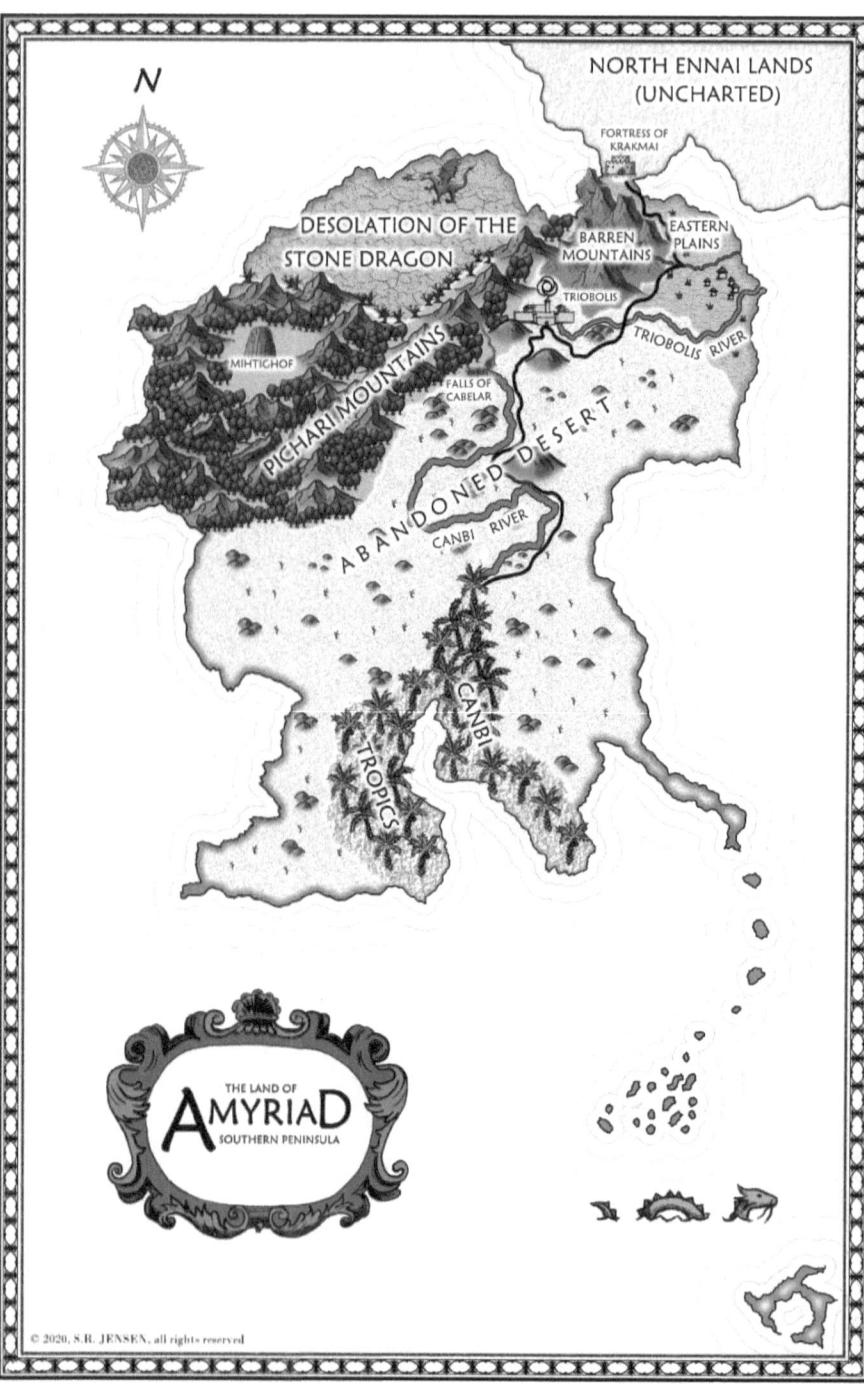

N

NORTH ENNAI LANDS
(UNCHARTED)

FORTRESS OF
KRAKMAI

DESOLATION OF THE
STONE DRAGON

BARREN
MOUNTAINS

EASTERN
PLAINS

TRIOBOLIS

MIHTIGHOF

PICHARI MOUNTAINS

TRIOBOLIS RIVER

FALLS OF
CABELAR

ABANDONED DESERT

CANBI RIVER

CANBI

TROPICS

THE LAND OF
AMYRIAD
SOUTHERN PENINSULA

CONTENTS

CHAPTER 1: BLOOD

Peltrin's silver-blue eyes scanned the forest. His dark hair ruffled in the breeze as he smiled confidently. There was plenty to smile about. Assassin was his favorite assignment and his targets would be arriving any minute.

He shifted slightly to improve blood flow to his left arm and leg. Thanks to his years of training, the noiseless movement was automatically timed to be in sync with a soft gust of wind that wafted through the leaves around him.

A plump rabbit munched on the grass in a clearing only a few paces away, but even the wary rodent didn't notice the stealthy intruder.

Near the rabbit was a patch of late spring daffodils.

Every flower has a meaning, Peltrin thought. He didn't believe the old saying, but he had heard it so many times the thought was automatic. Daffodils stood for new beginnings. He found it entertaining that he had unwittingly plotted two deaths in a meadow filled with these particular flowers.

Off to his right, he could just see his cousin Berin. Berin was muscular, full-bearded, and nearly a full head taller than Peltrin. Though he looked much older, Berin was only seventeen, less than a year older than Peltrin.

Peltrin sighed as Berin shifted loudly, cleared his throat, and cracked his knuckles. Berin's inability to wait silently was exactly why Peltrin had placed his cousin as far as possible from the place where the trail emerged from the trees.

Sensing someone behind him, Peltrin glanced over his shoulder. Just up the hill, he could see a dark figure peering down at him through the trees.

Small-boned with curly black hair and dark skin, the poorly hidden figure was clearly of the Canbi race.

"Don't mess this up for me, Soyem," Peltrin muttered.

Only two Canbi who lived nearby. Bensil, the healer, was so old his hair had turned white. The watcher was Soyem—the younger of the healer's two apprentices. Soyem was thirteen years old and tended to be a bit reckless.

Aralis, the healer's other apprentice—who was about Peltrin's age—was probably with Soyem. She, however, was much better at hiding. Unlike the Canbi healer and his younger apprentice, Aralis was Ennai.

The healer's apprentices were far enough away they wouldn't cause him any problems, Peltrin decided. He turned his attention to other, more pressing matters.

***

"Come out from behind the tree," Soyem said excitedly. "You have to see this! Peltrin and Berin are going to kill them any minute now."

"Quietly," Aralis chided in a low whisper. "We shouldn't even be here." She wasn't one for a lot of talking.

Aralis had long, dark brown hair, brown skin and particularly long limbs. Standing at her full height, she was easily head and shoulders taller than Soyem.

"We live in a tiny town in the Pichari mountains," said Soyem, rolling his eyes "These fights are the only interesting thing that ever happens around here. Besides, you're never that opposed to coming. They're easily the best-looking guys around…besides me, of course."

Aralis scowled but didn't deny Soyem's accusation. She silently rolled over to where she could see Peltrin better. She couldn't see Berin well from her current position, but she had let Soyem talk her into this kind of thing before. Berin, looked like quite the warrior, but Peltrin was where the real action would be.

BLOOD

Peltrin looked at the rabbit again. Come to think of it, the rabbit would make a nice stew. Maybe he had time to shoot…

His thoughts were interrupted by something pulling on his leg. He looked down to see a large yellow-bellied marmot.

"Lieutenant Rockchuck, reporting for duty, sir!" the rockchuck said with a smart salute. "I've been scouting the perimeter. Two enemies approaching."

"Good work, Lou," Peltrin whispered. Listening carefully, he could hear voices. He considered telling the rockchuck his report was a bit late, but decided against it. The Lieutenant took his job very seriously.

"What's your plan, sir?" asked the Lieutenant.

"Bow first…then throwing knives. I should be able to kill them both at a distance, but I have a tomahawk and a sword for up close fighting if I need them."

"That's it?" the Lieutenant said flatly, unimpressed. He was obsessed with planning everything down to the last detail. "That's your master plan?"

"What's Berin's plan?" asked Peltrin.

Lou sighed, "Yell a battle cry and charge, swinging his ax like a madman."

"Will he wait until after I shoot, or is he planning to ruin the element of surprise?"

"I was able to convince him to wait until after you make the first move," said Lou, "I can only hope he follows through. It would be best if you kill both of them with long-range weapons. These men are experienced fighters."

Peltrin nodded his head in agreement. Just then he heard the voices again and turned his focus to the upcoming confrontation. He could feel his adrenaline ramping up, but he wasn't nervous. He and Berin did this sort of thing regularly.

From the volume of the voices, Peltrin guessed he had just a few more seconds before they entered the meadow. He used the time to get into his final position, nock an arrow to his bow, and ensure his knives were easily available.

Peltrin's stomach tightened and his eyes narrowed as the two men came into view. Like Peltrin and Berin, they were both Pichari. They had light skin, dark hair and beards, and prominent noses. They also had silver-blue eyes, which was rare even among the Pichari. Their eyes, more than anything else, made it clear these two were brothers. Each of them carried a large wooden shield on his back.

One of them was big, almost freakishly so. He carried a massive, double-bladed ax over his heavily muscled shoulder. Though the man carried the weapon lightly, Peltrin knew the ax would have incredible momentum. Peltrin's tomahawk and short sword would be no match for it, certainly not in the hands of that giant.

The second man, though dwarfed by his enormous brother, was still taller than average for a Pichari. He was lean, and his nose was even more prominent than his brother's, making him look almost like a bird of prey. Peltrin forced himself to remain calm as the smaller man's keen eyes flitted back and forth, scanning the trees and underbrush for trouble.

Peltrin labeled the brothers Bear and Hawk.

Hawk would be first to die, the bow over the smaller man's shoulders made the decision easy. Bear would likely be a tougher target to kill but he had no shooting weapons and a man that size wasn't likely to be quick. In this terrain, Peltrin expected he could easily stay out of the giant's reach and kill him from a distance.

"Beorn, wait," Hawk said, stopping his companion, "look!" Peltrin nearly panicked as the smaller man pointed directly at Peltrin's hiding place.

"It's a rabbit," Bear said with a distinct lack of interest.

BLOOD

Peltrin was able to breathe again…barely. He glanced over at Berin. Thankfully, his cousin had held his position as well.

"It's dinner," Hawk replied, removing his bow from his shoulder and retrieving an arrow. He moved a few paces to Peltrin's right to avoid being directly upwind of the rabbit. The wiry man nocked an arrow to his bow and moved a few paces closer.

Peltrin glanced in Berin's direction again. Berin tended to get impatient when Peltrin delayed the attack. Berin was poised for action. True to his word, however, he remained concealed behind the large boulder.

As Hawk moved toward the rabbit, Bear moved out of the trees as well until they were well into the clearing, within easy range of Peltrin's bow and knives. Peltrin considered striking but decided against it. If he waited only a few seconds, Hawk would still have his bow ready, but he wouldn't have an arrow in shooting position.

"Skinned and boned, it's barely a mouthful," Bear muttered impatiently.

"For you, maybe," Hawk answered, "which means it's practically a feast for anyone else. I'd rather have it as a stew anyway."

I saw it first, Peltrin grumbled to himself silently. This gave him another reason to wait just a few more seconds. If Hawk succeeded in shooting the rabbit, Peltrin and Berin would kill the brothers and have the rabbit for their own.

Hawk moved slowly toward the rabbit. Its ears perked, but it continued to munch on the greens.

Peltrin tensed as the perfect moment approached. Hawk would shoot the rabbit. Peltrin would shoot Hawk. Bear would charge like a raging bull and Peltrin would put three arrows into him before the giant got close enough to use his ax.

Berin would be angry Peltrin had taken all of the fun, but Peltrin did that often. It was a natural advantage of being skilled with distance weapons.

"What about Peltrin and Berin?" Bear called. "No telling when they might pop out and attack."

"They'll be ahead, hiding in those rocks," Hawk answered, nodding up the trail.

Without moving, Peltrin smiled internally. Hawk was right. The boulders ahead were a perfect spot. Berin had wanted to stage their attack there. Peltrin had guessed—correctly, it seemed—that their targets would be on high alert as they approached the rocks. He had also guessed they would not be as careful in this quiet little meadow. On any other day, it was just another meadow in the forest. Today, it would be a place of death.

Finally satisfied with his position, Hawk raised his bow. Peltrin poised for action, taking advantage of the distraction to slowly draw his own bow and take aim.

Then the wind changed.

The rabbit tensed as its nose confirmed what its ears had suspected—people! It bolted into the bushes straight towards Peltrin.

Still hoping for his rabbit stew and guessing where the rabbit would flee, Hawk quickly adjusted, firing directly at Peltrin's leg.

Relying entirely on instinct, Peltrin twisted out of the way. He felt the arrow graze his pants as he spun aside.

Peltrin's arrow flopped uselessly to the ground and his bow snapped to the no-draw position with an ominous crack. Peltrin groaned internally. It was a sadly familiar sound. The bow had dry-fired. He knew he could no longer rely on the weapon.

"It's them!" Hawk shouted, shrugging his shield off his back. Peltrin glanced at Bear, but it was clear the giant hadn't caught on yet and probably wouldn't for several precious seconds.

"Focus on the plan! Stick to the plan!" Lou chanted from somewhere in the bushes.

BLOOD

Everyone has a plan until something unexpected happens, Peltrin thought to himself. He sometimes wondered why he bothered to plan at all.

Ignoring the huge man and the marmot, Peltrin focused on the most immediate danger. Hawk had already produced a new arrow and was about to nock it to the string. Peltrin flicked his wrist, sending a knife in Hawk's direction.

Peltrin's aim was off, which wasn't surprising considering the situation, but still he muttered under his breath. He didn't miss often, even in this type of surprise situation.

The knife served a purpose, however. Hawk dodged, which distracted him from nocking his arrow to his bow.

"What a lousy throw," Lou groaned. "Any plan is useless if you can't execute."

Still ignoring the animal, Peltrin sent knives two, three, and four in quick succession. Hawk, amazingly, dodged all three. Peltrin paused before throwing his fifth and final knife. He doubted the wiry man was quick enough to see each knife coming and dodge appropriately every time. It was far more likely he was just dodging from side to side as quickly as he could. Sure enough, Hawk began to dodge again while Peltrin was still holding the last knife.

Peltrin's hesitation was short but it was enough to see which direction Hawk's next dodge would take him.

Peltrin made his final throw, smiling to himself as he watched the knife connect and heard a satisfying thunk. His grin widened as he heard Hawk's anguished cry. It was, perhaps, his favorite sound in the world.

Altogether, the death of Hawk had taken less than five seconds.

"Nothing better than blood for breakfast," Lou cheered. "That's what happens when you get the plan right."

"That doesn't make any sense," Peltrin grumbled. It was almost time for dinner and Lou rarely ate meat, much less blood.

Finally, Bear realized what was going on. He pulled his shield off his back and charged, roaring a terrible roar. Berin, realizing it was his turn, roared and charged as well.

Peltrin rolled his eyes. Huge muscular men like these two looked like great warriors, but all they ever did was yell and charge.

Peltrin let the tomahawk fly. The deadly weapon caught Bear right in the forehead, just as he was about to engage with Berin.

"Come on!" Berin protested. "You have to stop doing that, Peltrin!"

Peltrin smiled at his cousin. "You're welcome," he said with a smile.

Peltrin then turned around to see that—impressively—Hawk had successfully killed the fat rabbit. He picked it up, holding it aloft as he jumped up into the air, hooting his victory to the trees.

After his little celebration, Peltrin glanced up the hill and waved at Soyem and Aralis. Soyem was jumping up and down, his face aglow with excitement. Aralis had come out of hiding as well. The two waved back and then disappeared into the trees, probably to resume looking for herbs in the forest, as they often did.

"That makes three times today I've killed both of you," Peltrin laughed. "This is getting too easy."

"No one likes a bragger, son," said Hawk. He put his large wooden shield down on the ground, placed a foot on it and wrenched Peltrin's fifth knife out of the center. "You know the old Ennai saying: 'Excessive boasting can make the victorious less honorable than even those they defeated.'"

"We're not Ennai," Peltrin countered, "We're Pichari. Besides, I'm not bragging. I'm just stating the obvious."

"I'm pretty sure that counts as bragging. What do you think, Beorn?"

"Bragging," Beorn answered, "no doubt about it, Perwin." He lowered his heavy shield, resting the bottom edge on the ground. The tomahawk was still embedded in his heavy wooden helmet.

Peltrin's father, Perwin, smirked. It was a look that came easily to his hawkish face, "the final vote is two to one, my boy. Lou doesn't count."

"Hey!" the lieutenant protested.

"You still lost…again," Peltrin wasn't going to give up his gloating easily.

"He's the man with the master plan," hooted Lou.

"Is this how you raise your son, Perwin?" Beorn shook his head gravely.

"Berin is a worse bragger than I am," Peltrin pointed out.

"Hey!" Berin protested. "the only reason I'm not bragging with you right now is you never gave me the chance."

"Don't hide behind your cousin, son," Beorn taunted, taking off his helmet and dropping the shield. "If you want me, come and get me."

Father and son both dropped their axes and charged each other. Peltrin and Perwin smiled as they watched the heated wrestling match.

Eventually, Beorn got the better of his son and they both stood up, breathing heavily and laughing.

"Bragging is definitely an issue with both these boys," Perwin said to Beorn, picking up the conversation where they had left off. "Don't take it personally, though, it's only one of the many follies of the rising generation."

"Oh, please," Peltrin groaned.

"Not this again," moaned Berin, rolling his eyes.

"Absolutely," Beorn agreed, catching on to the joke more quickly than usual. He retrieved his shield and hefted it to its usual location on his back. "Too much play, not enough discipline."

"We parents tend to be too gentle-hearted," said Perwin as he collected the other throwing knives. "Back when we were young, looking at your parents wrong meant a spanking. Bragging like this called for nothing less than a sound beating."

"Grandpa Thettlemar never gave you any beatings," Peltrin laughed. Their Grandpa Thettlemar had died when the boys were young, but they still had faint memories of the huge, kind man.

"Besides," Berin added, "you're both getting old and soft. It probably wouldn't hurt, even if we were bored enough to just stand here and wait while you tried."

Beorn grunted and feinted in their direction. Peltrin, Berin, and Lou simultaneously yelped and jumped well out of reach. The brothers laughed heartily at their expense.

"When are we going after thieves again?" asked Peltrin. After 'killing' his father and uncle multiple times in the last few hours, he was feeling ready for anything.

Because of their military experience, Perwin and Beorn served as policemen for the little town of Aldayin. Their volunteer work consisted of little more than occasionally driving off roving thieves and gangs. It had only been the last year or so they had allowed Peltrin and Berin to come along. Not surprisingly, both boys had proven to be quite adept at dealing with the generally untrained thugs.

Perwin walked over to where Peltrin had been hiding, "You need to make yourself a new bow before you can join us again, son," he said. He picked up the ruined weapon and looked it over disapprovingly. It was still mostly intact, but one arm had a large crack and some prominent splinters.

Peltrin scowled but didn't argue.

"Not a bad little mouthful of a rabbit you got there," said Beorn, trying to lighten the mood again.

"Spoils of war," Peltrin answered, holding it up and smiling again. "One day you'll be as good as I am. You'll understand better when it happens."

"It was a waste of an arrow," said Lou.

"I'm pretty sure the rabbit belongs to me," Perwin said.

"Not unless you want to admit to Mom you almost shot me today," Peltrin answered with a grin.

There was a short silence. "Nice shooting, son," Perwin said with a laugh. "You had better get your prize back home to your mother."

"Yes!" Peltrin pumped his arm. "Race you!"

Perwin and Beorn watched as the boys and the marmot ran off. Neither of the brothers tried to run after them.

"Looks like all this training is paying off," Beorn said. He picked up his helmet, which he had taken off during the wrestling match. It was still impaled with the tomahawk, but he put it back on his head anyway.

"We live in a time war," the wiry older brother answered. "I hope they will never need these skills for an actual battle, but you know the world we live in. Even little Pichari towns like Aldayin get attacked sometimes. Aramir wants everyone and everything in Amyriad either subjected or destroyed, including us."

"Especially us," Beorn agreed. "He will never forget what Father Thettlemar did to him."

Perwin nodded. "He will not have forgotten what we did either."

"These boys are getting good," Beorn muttered. He looked cross-eyed up at the tomahawk still embedded in his helmet.

"You were supposed to stay behind the shield," Perwin chided, reaching up and pulling out the weapon with a jerk.

"How can I charge the boys if I hide my face behind a shield?" the larger man protested, "all they have to do is step to the side and watch me crash into a tree."

[11]

"Crashing into a tree is safer than coming out from behind the shield," Perwin answered, brandishing the weapon.

Beorn laughed and clapped his brother on the shoulder, "point taken."

They continued chatting amiably as they walked home. Most of the discussion centered around the boys' training. The topic had become something of an obsession for both of them.

"Good luck with Nirani," Beorn said as they parted ways. "She's going to have a thing or two to say about you nearly shooting her boy."

"I think we already agreed the rabbit is his," Perwin answered.

"If I know Nirani," Beorn said knowingly, "she'll know whether you tell her or not."

"True," Perwin admitted with a wry grin, "but a man can hope." Perwin reached down to the ground and picked several purple hyacinths.

"Good idea," said Beorn. Maybe that will help.

"It's nothing unusual for me to give her a few flowers," Perwin said a little defensively.

"It isn't that you're giving her flowers," said Beorn. "It's that you're giving her those flowers."

Perwin looked at the flowers he was holding. He knew Beorn was right. Purple hyacinth typically represented a plea for forgiveness. 'Every flower has a meaning' was one of Nirani's favorite sayings.

Perwin watched as his brother went home. The two brothers lived next to each other, with barely a stone's throw between their houses.

Beorn's wife Besla was waiting on the front porch for him with a smile on her face. She was a very large woman, a perfect match for her very large husband. Beorn put his arm around her as they went into the house.

Perwin could see several pies on the window sill of the tiny house. Besla was particularly fond of making pies. Beorn and Berin were particularly fond of eating them.

BLOOD

Perwin walked into his house to the smell of the early stages of rabbit stew. Their home was cozy and attractive, but simplicity reigned supreme. A counter along one wall served as the kitchen. A bed where husband and wife slept together occupied a far corner. Most of the rest of the house was a small sitting area. There was a ladder near the door leading up to Peltrin's small loft where his mattress and few possessions occupied most of the space.

Perwin's wife Nirani was at the counter, cutting vegetables for the stew. Like her husband, she was also Pichari. She was medium height and thin, with long, dark hair, light skin, and hazel eyes.

She didn't respond when Perwin walked into the house. Not a good sign.

Nirani threw some carrot tops and onion stems out the window and Lou cheered. The oversized yellow-bellied marmot lived in the woodpile behind the house. Peltrin's mother wouldn't allow the rodent to enter the house, but she had long since given up on getting rid of it. She just didn't have the heart to send him away.

Perwin walked over, put the purple hyacinth on the counter, and put his arms around Nirani from behind.

Nirani craned her neck to give him a quick kiss—without a smile—and then continued working as if he wasn't there. She pushed the flowers away.

"Not a bad rabbit Peltrin shot there," Perwin said casually, eying the rejected flowers.

"Waste of an arrow," Lou called from outside.

"So, he tells me," she said casually. "But you're both lying."

Perwin glanced over at his son, who shrugged, his expression wide-eyed.

"He was also doing his best to hide a new hole in his pants," she said conversationally.

"Um…" Perwin searched for something to say but came up short.

His wife turned around in his arms and looked him in the eyes. "Did Peltrin come very close to getting hurt during training today?"

"Well…"

She didn't bother to wait for an answer. "Do you honestly still believe all this training is worth the risk?"

"I…" He searched for something to say. The right words probably didn't exist.

"I know what you're going to tell me," she said angrily. She turned around in his arms to continue her work on the stew. "But don't. I don't want to talk about it right now."

He continued holding her silently for a moment, unsure of what else he should say.

"Peltrin was amazing today," Perwin said, finally letting go of his wife. He decided shifting the attention to his son was probably the best strategy.

"Did he?" she sounded more tense than interested.

"I got Beorn with a tomahawk," Peltrin bragged, "If he hadn't been wearing a helmet, his brains would have been all over the place!"

Perwin bowed his head and sighed.

"Was that before or after your father nearly shot you in the leg?"

"After," Peltrin answered absentmindedly "but I did an amazing dodge so I didn't get hurt, and he killed the rabbit, which was pretty amazing because the rabbit had just gone into the bushes right next to me, and he had to guess where it went, and he still killed it even though he couldn't see it when he was shooting."

Perwin rolled his eyes, then tried to look apologetic as his wife gave him a look.

"So…the, um, corn is coming along well," Perwin was reaching desperately for another topic—any other topic. He pushed the purple hyacinths towards his wife.

"I suppose," his wife answered, rejecting the flowers again. "Wouldn't it be nice if you and your brother didn't get Peltrin and Berin killed. Then the boys could help with the harvest."

"What do you mean?" asked Perwin a little defensively.

"It's bad enough you have them waving weapons at each other all of the time. Lately, you've even been taking him on your police rounds, which no one pays you for. They have been fighting criminals for no other reason than your so-called training!"

"You don't need to worry about me, mom," Peltrin inserted, "last time, there were three guys who tried to sneak up behind me and Berin. I knocked out all three of them before Berin even got a chance to do anything."

"Peltrin's easily the best fighter in Aldayin," affirmed Lou from outside the window, "Besides Perwin and Beorn, of course. He's proven that over and over again, even at his age."

Nirani looked to be on the verge of tears. She grabbed the hyacinth and threw them on the floor. She then stomped out of the house and towards the cellar.

"Not another word about training," Perwin ordered his son. He picked up the flowers and put them back on the counter. He then scooped up the broken petals and tossed them out the window.

"These taste terrible," Lou complained.

"But…" Peltrin protested

"When she gets back, we're talking about the corn."

"Fine," Peltrin huffed. He clearly would have preferred to continue bragging.

Later that night, after Peltrin had finally been persuaded to go up to his loft, Perwin and his wife sat together on the edge of their bed.

"I went along with your corn distraction," said Nirani, "but we need to talk about this training."

Perwin just nodded his head, unsure of what to say next.

"I understand why you want these boys trained," she said quietly, "and I agree with you, but are you sure this is the safest way to do it?"

She touched his hand softly. He inhaled a deep breath. The edges of his mouth twitched upward and he sat up a little straighter.

She smiled to herself. They had been married for nearly twenty years. Lately, she particularly enjoyed seeing how her touch still affected him.

"I hope so," he said softly. "I'll try to do it as safely as possible. But Beorn and I are the only remaining sons of Thettlemar. We've been able to hide quietly for years, but the day is coming. I am sure of it."

He took her hand and looked in her eyes, "Aramir has a lot of minions out hunting for us. Out here it will probably be devastors—or something like them. Peltrin and Berin need to be ready when it happens."

She shuddered at the mention of the fell creatures. They had encountered Aramir's servants before. Hopefully, the boys didn't remember.

"I know," her answer was soft. Perwin hadn't been a war hero when they were first married, but she had known his strength and his natural ability with weapons. More importantly, she had known his heart. The fact that he had become great soon after the war broke out had been no surprise to her. The fact that they would spend most of their lives hiding from the wrath of Aramir probably shouldn't have been a surprise either.

"I'll never be comfortable with you teaching these boys to fight," she continued. "But at the same time, this training helps me believe it when I tell myself to not be afraid for them. I know it's better they have the ability to protect themselves."

"They are surprisingly good, for their age," said Perwin, letting go of her hand and putting his arm around her. "No one can guarantee anything these days, but they are already much safer than they would have been."

Blood

"I hate to even think about it," she said sadly, glancing up at Peltrin's loft. "It makes me want to run away and hide them under a mountain."

She leaned into him, placing her head on his shoulder, "I want to believe there is someplace in Amyriad where Aramir can't find us. I just can't handle the thought of Peltrin and Berin being attacked again."

Perwin didn't answer for a moment. "Me too," he admitted.

As he felt her relax in his arms, Peltrin glanced towards the counter. Sometime, when he hadn't been looking, Nirani had placed the purple hyacinth in a vase with some water.

THE CHRONCILES OF AMYRIAD

CHAPTER 2: DEVASTOR

The knife embedded itself deeply in the stump with a solid, satisfying thunk.

Peltrin came forward to inspect his work. At ten paces, three out of the five knives were stuck firmly in the wood. A fourth knife had been on target as well, but it had hit a hard knot and had fallen out almost immediately. The fifth had missed altogether and was embedded in the ground.

After inspecting his handiwork, Peltrin turned to compare his results to Berin's. The huge boy hated practicing with throwing weapons. According to him, fighting from a distance took all of the fun out of it. Berin was practicing at a shorter distance than Peltrin but had succeeded in only one out of his five throws. He looked more than a little frustrated.

Peltrin then turned to watch Perwin and Beorn, who were sparring. Beorn was wearing full armor, though it seemed a bit tight around the waist. Perwin was wearing only shoulder guards, arm guards and a helmet. The smaller man preferred the increased speed and freedom of movement the lighter armor provided.

Nearby, Peltrin could see a bucket of smelly yellow powder they had collected from a nearby hot spring. The brothers would dip their practice weapons in the bucket before sparring. Whenever one brother struck the other, it would leave a yellow mark. The yellow marks were a way of telling who had struck whom and where.

Beorn stepped forward, swinging his enormous wooden sword down like an ax splitting firewood. Perwin also stepped forward, quickly placing himself too close to his brother to be in any danger from the sword. Beorn, whose movements were more subject to momentum, continued his swing, pounding his bulging arm onto the smaller man's shoulder.

The power of the blow forced Perwin to his knees where he grunted in frustration. With rattlesnake speed, Peltrin's father pulled a large wooden knife out of his belt and struck Beorn on the breastplate. The knife left a yellow streak on the armor.

Beorn struck back, first with his fist, then with his knee. Perwin ducked the punch, then slid gracefully sideways to avoid the knee. He slipped behind the giant, striking Beorn's back twice with his wooden knife before moving safely out of range. Each blow with the wooden knife left a bright yellow streak on Beorn's armor.

Peltrin returned to pulling his knives from the stump. Before he turned away, he was proud to see Beorn had at least four or five yellow streaks for every one of Perwin's. Beorn was far bigger and stronger than anyone else Peltrin had ever seen, but even he was no match for his brother's speed and skill.

"Our enemies all cowered at the sight of your uncle," Bensil had once told Peltrin, "but it was usually your father who killed them."

After he had removed the last of the knives, Peltrin stopped to watch again. For a moment he imagined what it would be like to be one of them. Based on his current size, it was unlikely he would ever have Beorn's height and strength. But to have his father's skill, that would be spectacular!

"Not bad," Perwin said as they paused for a drink of water. Both men were breathing heavily and sweating profusely. "But you're slowing down. I think you have to accept the fact that you are getting old and fat."

"You know it's not fat," Beorn protested, "I only look fat next to a skinny little runt like you."

"Maybe I am a skinny little runt," answered Perwin. "But as it happens, I am the skinny little runt who has killed you at least a dozen times in the past forty-five minutes."

"A dozen times!" Beorn blustered, "it was no more than three, and that was only because I had to hold back so I didn't chop your head clean off your shoulders."

"It was three times in the last five minutes," answered Perwin, "and there was never any need to hold back. I had time to take a nap between your every attempt."

Peltrin laughed as the two brothers continued to banter. They insulted each other endlessly, criticizing each other's build, ability, strength, and technique. Even with the yellow powder, they were never able to settle on how many times they each would have killed the other had the fight been real.

Finally, Perwin came over to see how Peltrin was doing. "Good work today, son," Perwin said, he looked pleased with his son's progress.

"I do good work every day," Peltrin answered. "That's why I'm better than both of you combined."

"Oh, really?" said Perwin, as he and Beorn chuckled. "What makes you think you're that good already?"

"Spar with me and I'll show you," said Peltrin, an aggressive glint in his eye.

"I'd be happy to," answered Perwin. "As soon as your drills are done."

"Come on," Peltrin complained, "those drills are so boring." He had grown to hate the series of fighting positions, kicks, punches, and weapons drills. His father and uncle insisted he and Berin do them three times a day, every day.

"They're nothing like a real fight," Berin agreed.

"They are if you are doing them correctly," answered Perwin. "If you do them right, those drills teach you muscle memory. With good muscle memory, your body will continue to do those moves well, even when you are tired or disoriented, which happens a lot in a battle."

"I'd rather be sparring," said Berin.

Or doing the forest attack scenarios," added Peltrin. "Or chasing off a band of thieves. Even hunting is better than that. And hunting, we all know, is also excellent practice."

"We'll keep doing all that," Perwin said with a laugh, "but you still have to do your drills. And do them right, or they aren't doing you any good at all."

"Mom knows you almost shot me yesterday," Peltrin said sadly as he picked up another knife. "She probably won't let me do the forest attacks, or help drive off thieves, or even hunt anymore. The drills are the only thing she's okay with me doing."

"She wants you trained every bit as much as I do," Perwin answered. "You…"

"Then quit stalling," Peltrin interrupted with a mischievous grin. "Let's skip the drills and get on with the good stuff."

"No matter how good you can eventually become," Perwin replied, "You have to start with the basics. You will have to punch and kick tens of thousands of times if you want to be good at hand fighting. Weapons are no different, if you want to be great, you will have to drill the basic moves of each weapon tens of thousands of times."

"It's so boring," Peltrin complained, thinking of all the hours he spent every day on the endless drills.

"Every man in Amyriad would love to have your father's skills," inserted Beorn, "but very few are willing to work hard enough to even come close."

"Speaking of practice," said Perwin. "Why don't you start throwing at that stump over there."

"Which one?" asked Peltrin. There were at least a dozen stumps in sight.

Perwin took one of Peltrin's knives and threw it. The four of them watched as the knife sailed high overhead end over end until eventually it came down and impaled a large rotten stump, surrounded by rhododendrons. "Walk toward it until you think you are at a distance of about thirty paces, then start throwing."

Peltrin nodded and sullenly walked away. Back to the endless repetition…again.

It wasn't the furthest Peltrin had ever successfully thrown a knife before, but thirty paces was definitely outside of his comfort zone. He looked back at his father and uncle—he had their full attention. Berin was watching as well. Peltrin pulled out a knife. It was one of his practice knives. They were functional but unattractive. The lumpy black pieces all had broken tips and damaged edges from Peltrin's many long hours of practice.

Taking the handle in his right hand in the familiar hold, Peltrin launched the knife into the air. Though thirty paces was not as far as his father could throw, it pleased Peltrin to see he had estimated the distance well. The knife descended, end over end, and sank deep into the soft wood, immediately next to the knife Perwin had thrown.

"Nice throw," called Beorn.

"Well done," shouted Perwin.

Berin scowled but muttered his approval as well.

There was a motion in the trees. Peltrin was fairly certain Soyem and Aralis, had seen his throw as well. He smiled to himself. He liked the fact that the two of them—particularly Aralis—had seen his success.

Peltrin pulled out two more knives, holding one in each hand. Again, he launched one into the air. Like the first, the second knife sailed through the air in a beautiful arc, flipping end over end.

This time, however, Peltrin's wrist had twisted slightly just before release. The error was small enough that, at five or ten paces, it might have still worked. At thirty paces, however, it was just enough that the flat of the blade struck, rather than the sharp edge. The third knife struck the first two, driving them nearly to the ends of their handles into the soft, moldy wood of the stump.

Then the stump exploded.

From Peltrin's perspective, the stump had all but disappeared in a shower of slivers and dirt. In place of the stump was a hairy, muscular, mole-like creature a little more than half Peltrin's size.

The creature had pointed teeth and long, thick claws. Its body was almost completely covered in thick, brown fur, much like a monkey but with stout hands and thicker arms and legs. Its body was tube-like, presumably adapted to digging tunnels like a common ground mole. It's bony, rat-like face looked primitive, as if the creature had been taken from a time long ago. It was bleeding from its shoulder and was absolutely furious.

At thirty paces, Peltrin couldn't see the eyes well, but he saw the teeth and claws and immediately turned and fled, dropping the knife he had been holding.

Enraged, the wounded creature gave pursuit. It ran on all fours, quickly closing the gap between them. Saliva dripped from its snarling mouth as it moved to a standing position and leaped for Peltrin's neck.

Peltrin saw something flash in the corner of his left eye. The snarling was replaced with a howl and the creature slowed. The snarl slowly diminished in volume and increased in emotion until it was little more than a pitiful, high-pitched moan.

Peltrin continued to run for a while before he chanced to look back. It wasn't until that moment he realized he had been screaming. The strange gigantic rat...mole...whatever it was, had stopped running, its clawed hands were covering its face. Blood was running down its left cheek, presumably coming from its eye.

Beorn and Berin reacted immediately together. Raising their weapons, they charged the creature and roared.

The lieutenant entered the clearing. He had found a patch of wild strawberries that morning and had spent the entire afternoon looking for more. He looked at the creature but held back. Lou was larger than most rockchucks, but he was no match for this creature.

Seeing the two men charging, the creature howled in fury and agony and fled. Beorn and Berin followed in hot pursuit.

Perwin had another knife in hand, but he had been too distracted looking at Peltrin and had missed the opportunity.

"Are you hurt, Peltrin?" Perwin demanded, placing a hand on his shoulder.

"I'm fine," Peltrin answered.

"You're sure?" his father insisted. "It didn't injure you at all? Not even the tiniest scratch?" Perwin turned him around and looked him over. Perwin touched the back of Peltrin's neck, when he withdrew his finger, there was blood on it. Peltrin's blood.

"The eyes!" Perwin cried in fear, "what color were the eyes?"

"I don't know," Peltrin answered, confused. He had been injured from time to time in his training, and his father had never reacted like this before. Peltrin couldn't understand why a retired war hero was falling apart over a little scratch.

"Are you sure?" Perwin asked desperately.

"I'm fine," Peltrin answered, suppressing a laugh.

Beorn and Berin returned, chests heaving from the running. "We lost it once it left the clearing," Beorn admitted. "Lou is still following. We didn't get close enough to see the eyes."

"It's a good thing I'm not seriously injured," Peltrin mumbled to himself. He didn't understand why these two couldn't handle a few drops of blood. Berin, at least, didn't look concerned.

"What made you run?" Berin asked Peltrin, confused. "I've never seen you run from anything before."

Peltrin struggled to answer. All four of them knew Peltrin had often stood his ground in front of armed men. Wolves, bears, moose, even mountain lions didn't scare him, as long as he had a weapon in hand. But something about this particular creature had awakened a feeling of fear unlike anything else he could remember.

"I don't know," Peltrin finally admitted. He had no other answer.

"We'd better make sure it ends here," said Perwin. All four of them jogged to the place where the creature had disappeared into the trees.

Not long after they reached the trees, however, the trail disappeared.

The lieutenant jumped down from a tree branch and marched over to join them. "It took to the trees," he declared. "Once in the trees, it was quite fast. I wasn't able to follow. I never did get a good look at the eyes."

"Took to the trees?" Perwin mumbled. "That's odd."

"I thought devastors live only underground," said Beorn.

"They do," Perwin answered, "that's why they have such tough claws. They use them for digging. I've never heard of one climbing a tree."

"This one can," Lou insisted. "And it can climb like you wouldn't believe. It was jumping and swinging from branch to branch like a squirrel."

"We'll never find it now," Beorn huffed loudly, looking at the dense foliage above.

Peltrin considered pointing out that, with Berin and Beorn's stomping and loud voices, any hope they had of finding any game in the area was long gone.

"You're probably right," Perwin admitted after scanning the trees one last time. "We'd better get home."

"What was that thing?" Peltrin asked, surprised their daily training was ending early.

Berin only shrugged.

"They're called devastors," Perwin answered. "They're basically oversized ground moles."

"They have an incredible sense of smell," said Beorn, "and they are much faster and more agile than their annoying little cousins."

"You don't see them much around here because the wolves hate them," explained Perwin." This one must have been particularly careful and clever."

The men and boys re-entered the clearing, but Lou lingered at the edge. He claimed he was going to look for more berries. Peltrin suspected the marmot was actually going to scout the area for more enemies.

As Peltrin and Berin walked ahead to retrieve their practice knives, Perwin pulled Beorn aside and they exchanged knowing looks.

"Tell your family to start packing," Perwin said quietly enough the boys didn't hear. "More will be coming soon. We'll leave tomorrow morning."

Beorn nodded.

Berin headed over to where he had been practicing and began picking up his knives. Peltrin had expected a severe teasing from his cousin for his cowardice, but the bigger boy appeared to have surprisingly little to say.

Peltrin went over to find his knives. The two he had thrown and the one his father had thrown were still near the stump. Looking at the stump again, he could see it hadn't actually exploded. It was split into two large halves with a few handfuls of smaller pieces lying around. Now that it was open, he could see it had been mostly hollow.

As Peltrin searched for his knives, Perwin and Beorn continued to hover at the edge of the clearing, talking in low voices.

"You don't think it was a white-eyed devastor?" asked Beorn.

"Not likely, unfortunately," answered Perwin. "The eyes must have been black or red. I don't believe a white-eyed devastor would ever take to the trees. Climbing trees is completely against their nature."

"How do you think Aramir convinced them to do it?"

"No idea." Perwin looked over at his son. "All we can do now is hope the eyes weren't red. Usually, the black-eyed devastors are sent out first and the red-eyed devastors follow, so we have reason to hope he will be okay. I looked at the scratch but I can't see the early signs of the poison well enough to be sure. Nirani has a better eye for that. She should be able to tell right away."

"You put out one of its eyes with a knife," said Beorn. "Couldn't you see what color the eyes were while you were aiming? The red in their eyes glows like embers in a fire."

"Not enough to see at that distance in full daylight," Perwin answered regretfully. "Trust me, I was looking. I couldn't see the eyes well enough. I had to aim for the shadow under its brow."

Peltrin glanced over at his father and uncle. They were talking quietly enough he couldn't hear what they were saying.

He sighed. They were probably talking about what a coward he was. Most likely, they were debating how they were going to train him to not scream and run the next time a strange creature showed up.

I do just fine against people, Peltrin thought to himself defensively. It's not like weird creatures with huge teeth and claws come exploding out of stumps every day. The creature had been terrifying, but part of him suspected it was more than that. His body had reacted before he had consciously figured out what he was looking at. It was as if he had encountered devastors before.

By now Berin had finished retrieving his knives and was trotting back to the others. Peltrin cleaned the bloody knife his father had thrown at the creature by wiping it on the grass. He then moved to join them when he remembered the knife he had been holding when the creature had first appeared.

It took more time to find that one. After wandering around for a while, he finally saw it lying on the ground, half-hidden under some smashed down grass. He looked it over for damage. A small piece of the tip was broken off and it wasn't quite perfectly straight, but that wasn't unusual for a well-used throwing knife.

The knife did, however, have some unique white scratches. It appeared the devastor had stepped on the knife, gouging it with its claws as it ran after Peltrin. The marks were deep and white, contrasting sharply with the rest of the black knife. He put it away quickly. Looking at those white marks on the black steel knife reminded him of the shame of running away.

After Peltrin finished retrieving his knives, the four of them walked for some time without speaking. Peltrin's usual cockiness was nowhere to be found. He found that, without it, he didn't have a lot to say. Eventually, Beorn and Berin had hurried ahead—something they had never done before—so Perwin and Peltrin were walking alone.

"I don't get it," said Peltrin. Finally breaking the silence. "You hit it right in the eye. How could it still be alive?"

"It probably wouldn't be," his father said, frowning a little, "but I don't think it was a clean hit."

"So, you missed?" Peltrin asked, grinning slightly. Perwin's flawless marksmanship was a huge source of pride.

"It was running," Perwin protested a little defensively, "and jumping for your neck. I hit the eye I was aiming for. It just glanced off the bone instead of going all the way in."

Peltrin sensed his father was unusually shaken and he left off the teasing sooner than he normally would have. "I know, Dad. It was an amazing throw."

He looked down at his feet as he continued to walk, "I have some decent skills, but what good does it do anyone if I just run away?"

Perwin turned to face his son, putting his hands on the boy's shoulders and looking him in the eye. He hesitated slightly as their positions reminded him his boy was nearly as tall as he was. "You're no coward, Peltrin. You've proven that over and over again."

"After what happened today, I'm not sure you can always count on me," Peltrin pointed out. "It's dangerous for all of us. We can't go into a fight wondering if I'm going to run away."

"We all know we can count on you," Perwin insisted. "What happened today does not define who you are. Everyone does things they aren't proud of. If one mistake makes you a failure, then everyone is a failure. Don't believe it."

"It's as if I've seen that thing before," said Peltrin, looking down. "I was afraid of it before I even knew what it was."

Perwin looked at his son curiously.

"It's not possible though," Peltrin went on. "I would surely remember something like that. I think what it really means is I'm just not meant to be a fighter."

"If you don't want to be a fighter," Perwin said seriously, "there's nothing wrong with that." His eyes seemed to pierce Peltrin's soul. "What good people do to live their lives every day is just as important and heroic to me as anything you could do on a battlefield. My father, Beorn, and I were farmers until Aramir's army attacked our town. We didn't have a choice in the matter. My brother Aiden was the only one who had joined the King's Army before the attack on our hometown. Your grandfather never asked to be a hero, a farmer was all he ever wanted to be."

"I just hate being afraid," Peltrin looked down. He had no memory of his uncle Aiden. Perwin didn't bring up his dead brother very often. "It happened so fast. In less than a second, my fear transformed me from a good fighter to a cowering weakling."

"I've been there, too," Perwin admitted. "But don't make any decision out of fear. I'm happy with whatever you want to do with your life. Just be sure you make that decision based on what you want to be, not based on what makes you afraid. Courage isn't about whether or not you are afraid, son. It's about what you do when you are afraid."

"I ran, screaming like a little girl," Peltrin said bitterly.

Perwin laughed, releasing his son's shoulders and resuming the walk, "Almost everyone runs the first time they are taken by surprise by a creature like that. You're no coward, Peltrin. Overcoming this fear is just a matter of practice and realizing what you really want."

Just then, Lou appeared at their feet.

"The area is clear," said the lieutenant, his tone businesslike. "There are no signs of more devastors. I sent Bensil's apprentices to tell the healer what happened. Soyem is excited he might get a chance to see a devastor—idiot. Aralis is smart enough to realize the danger, I think we can trust her to get word to the healer."

"Good work, lieutenant," said Perwin.

"You have some work to do, Peltrin," Lou went on. "You have more than adequate training and you had a weapon in hand. You must learn to execute in the crucial moment or none of the rest will ever matter. This likely won't be your last encounter with devastors so we need to incorporate this into your training. I think we need to capture one of these creatures and…"

Moving quickly, Perwin slipped his foot underneath Lou's belly and launched him into the air.

"Ungratefuuuuu…" the marmot howled as he crashed into the brush.

"Go back to the house," Perwin yelled after the marmot. "Let us talk alone for a minute."

Perwin continued talking to Peltrin. "The first time you overcome fear like that, it will be because you want something. Something so important you refuse to give in to your fears, no matter how bad they are. The second time will be easier. Eventually, you will find yourself doing what needs to be done—every time—regardless of the fear you feel. The fear is still there, just as real as it ever was, but it no longer controls you."

"Thanks, Dad," Peltrin said, his eyes were still down. "After what just happened, I think I'll stick to farming."

Perwin didn't answer, but his brow was furrowed. It was clear he didn't agree.

It's the right answer, Peltrin told himself. Until today, Peltrin had been growing confident in his skills, but Lou was right. All the skills in the world were pointless without courage. Someday, Perwin and Beorn might have to return to battle. If that happened, Berin would want to go with them. Someone would have to stay home and take care of Mother and aunt Besla and the farm. Peltrin would be that someone.

"It is," Peltrin repeated to himself again. He only hoped that, eventually, he would believe it.

As they approached the house, Perwin picked a few rhododendrons.

"Wash" called a stern voice from inside the house. Perwin and Peltrin looked at each other in shock. They had approached in complete silence and Perwin hadn't even stepped on the first porch step.

"Peltrin, clean that mud off the porch and both of you leave your shoes outside." Neither of them had noticed Peltrin's shoes were covered in mud or that he had left a muddy footprint on the first stair.

They both shifted sideways to look through the window. There was no glass. Glass of any kind was difficult to come by in Amyriad. Sheets of glass large enough and smooth enough for a window would be worth a fortune. The wooden shutters could be closed if needed, but they were currently wide open. Nirani's back was turned and she continued her work.

"How does she do that?" Peltrin whispered.

"I don't know." Perwin mouthed.

"How a wife and a mother know what her husband and son are doing is a secret you'll have to figure out some other time," she called. "For now, go wash up so you can get in here and help me finish."

There was a short pause, then her face appeared at the window. She looked at the flowers in Perwin's hand. "What happened to Peltrin?"

Peltrin wondered how she always knew before they even walked into the house if he was hurt in any way, even if it was only a tiny little scratch on his neck.

"Did Lou tell you what happened?" asked Perwin.

"Lou is sulking in the woodpile. All I heard was the word "ungrateful" over and over again."

Peltrin told her the story. She listened intently and calmly, though her face paled considerably when he said "devastor."

"Let me see the scratch," Nirani demanded. After a quick look, she disappeared into the house, quickly returning with a bandage. "Take your shirt off, Peltrin."

"Mom, it's barely a scratch," he complained.

"Take it off!"

Peltrin complied, taking off his shirt and turning so his mother could get a better look. Nirani looked at the scratch carefully, poking at it and at the skin around it.

"It isn't bad," she said finally, giving Perwin a look that seemed to put him at ease. "You'll be fine but we need to make sure it doesn't get infected. No telling what nastiness that creature got its claws into before scratching you."

"Everyone was worried about the color of the eyes," Peltrin said as she worked. "Why does that matter? And why have I never heard of devastors?"

"There are few in this area," said Perwin, repeating what he had said before. "The wolves make sure of that. I'm surprised we encountered one so close to our home. As for eye color," he looked at his wife, who gave him a nod.

"The white-eyed devastors are fiercely territorial," he went on. "They are frightening, but not terrible. They are usually no more dangerous than a bad-tempered badger."

It was the first time Peltrin heard someone refer to a bad-tempered badger as "not terrible."

"Red-eyed and black-eyed devastors, on the other hand, are far worse. They are not natural. Red-eyed devastors are created by Aramir, and black-eyed devastors follow them. You can think of the red-eyed devastors like a queen bee, and black-eyed devastors like the rest of the hive."

"Do they run around in packs together?" asked Peltrin.

"Not always," said Perwin, "but they often do, which makes them far more dangerous than a solitary animal. But even if they are alone, you need to be especially careful if they have red-eyes.

"Why?"

"They are poisonous," Nirani explained, "one scratch and you will die at sunrise on the fifth day. A cure for their poison has never been found, and there is no way to delay it."

She made a coughing sound and Peltrin turned to look at her. She looked particularly upset—like she was on the brink of bursting into tears. Peltrin wondered if she had known someone who had been poisoned.

"I didn't know Aramir has the power to create an animal," Peltrin said incredulously.

"He doesn't," said Perwin, "though he would probably love it if people believed he did. All he can do is corrupt. Aramir takes a white-eyed devastor from the wild. Through some horrible combination of magic and torture, it becomes poisonous and its eyes turn red. It then recruits other wild devastors, somehow taking control of them and making their eyes black."

"There," Nirani said. "You can put your shirt back on now."

Peltrin quickly put his shirt back on. Nirani washed her hands in a bucket and then buried her face in her hands. Perwin quickly stepped in and surrounded her in his arms.

"You never saw the eyes?" she asked, her face still covered.

"I couldn't see it well enough myself," answered Perwin. "I threw that knife on a prayer. I've never been so afraid in my life."

She leaned into him, still covering her face. "It wasn't many years ago you and your brother led the Pichari armies. You fought in battles where thousands died, some of them died horrible deaths. You want me to believe you have never been more afraid than you were today?"

"I've been afraid for my own life many times," he said thoughtfully. "It's awful, but I've learned to cope. Being afraid for the fate of an army you are leading is much worse. But today I knew if it had been a red-eyed devastor, Peltrin would soon die. There would be nothing I could do. I also knew, if that were the case, it meant we had been discovered and it wouldn't be long before you were in danger. Being afraid for my wife and son is, by far, the worst fear I have ever felt."

"You're the best there is," she said. It wasn't her pride speaking. It was the truth, pure and simple. "I'm so glad you were there. Even a white-eyed devastor might have killed him had you not been there. What I don't understand is how it can live after being hit directly in the eye."

Perwin grew defensive, "I threw that knife from more than twenty paces. It had to pass within inches of Peltrin's face and come down behind his shoulder. They were both running as fast as they could, and I was running towards them."

There was a long pause. "I'm glad it was you," Nirani finally said. "There was no other way to save him, and I wouldn't have trusted anyone else with that throw. I just wish it would have died then and there. I don't like knowing it's still out there."

Peltrin's father furrowed his brow. "I think it lived because the knife only grazed its eye. It was pointing more down than straight when it made contact. Given the downward direction the knife was traveling, my guess is it passed through the front portion of the eye—the eye was definitely damaged—but it must have glanced off of the bone below the eye rather than going in."

"I didn't want you to describe it in detail." She looked annoyed, but not angry. "I'm going to have enough trouble sleeping tonight without visualizing the blood and gore."

"There wasn't much gore," Perwin answered thoughtfully. Peltrin could see a hint of a smile on his father's face. "Now blood…there was certainly plenty of blood. Head injuries, you know, can…" His speech ended in a short "oomph" and a laugh as she slugged him in the gut.

"I'm no soldier," she said. There was a light warning in her voice "I don't want to hear about it."

"You could have fooled me," he said, still smiling, "that punch was better than most…" there was another "oomph" and another laugh.

"Enough!" It was clear that, as far as she was concerned, the joke was over.

Perwin knew when to take his wife seriously, he stopped.

THE CHRONCILES OF AMYRIAD

CHAPTER 3: POISON

Peltrin eventually was able to break free from his parents and wander outside. He quickly walked around to the side of the house where there were no windows. After all of the attention from his parents, he was relieved to finally be away from them for a moment.

He looked up and watched as the edge of the sun approached the tops of the Western mountains. With the exception of hunting, they always came home well before dark, he wondered if creatures like devastors were the reason why.

He could still hear his parents talking, but they were too distracted now with each other to pay any attention to him. Sometimes he complained when they were like that, but secretly he liked it. Peltrin was perfectly aware of how lucky he was to have grown up with the security of having two people in his life who would always be there for each other, and for him.

Not far away, he could see Berin splitting firewood. He raised the ax over his head as if it weighed nothing. He then let it fall, effortlessly splitting the log in two. Peltrin considered going over to talk to Berin but decided against it. He didn't want to talk right now, not even to his best friend.

Peltrin pulled out a knife and looked at it in his hand. There were several more in his pockets and his clothes. He was trained to use them, but rather than use the knife to defend himself, he had dropped it and run. He had survived, but that did not change the fact he was a coward. It occurred to him that, given his family's history, Aramir was probably going to send devastors after them again. He needed to be able to fight them, even if he didn't go to war.

Just then, there was a flicker of movement on the edge of the forest. The ground around the two houses had been cleared and leveled. Nothing could approach unnoticed this early in the season when the corn was just beginning to sprout. There was something, however, hiding on the fringe.

"Berin," called Peltrin.

The large boy turned and waved, smiling.

"Did you see that?" Peltrin pointed to the trees.

Together they turned and looked. Peltrin held a knife in his hands. Berin still held the woodcutting ax. The world around them held its breath.

Determined to not be the coward again, Peltrin stepped toward the movement. He stopped after only a single step. A slight breeze came from behind, ruffling their clothes and carrying their scents across the field. When it reached the fringe of the trees, the leaves and branches moved unnaturally.

Then the devastors charged.

There were no fewer than twenty when they first emerged, and more continued coming out of the trees. Their huge teeth and claws flashed in the late afternoon sun as they raced recklessly towards the houses. The alarming creatures moved with disturbing speed as they pummeled the ground, kicking up dirt behind them.

Berin, as usual, had little regard for strategy. Yelling at the top of his lungs, he charged them, swinging the ax from side to side.

Peltrin's strategy wasn't well thought out either. All pretenses of bravery fled to the wind and Peltrin ran to the house. His legs found unnatural speed and he entered the doorway several seconds before the creatures. "Devastors," he shouted, "hundreds of them."

Perwin glanced at the weapons cabinet near his bed in the far corner, so close yet hopelessly out of reach. "The loft," he shouted.

Outside, Beorn's battle cry rang out, joining his son's.

POISON

Peltrin, wasting no time, scrambled up the ladder. Already, the first of the foul creatures were in the doorway, their eyes black as night. They hesitated at the sight of Perwin, but only for a second. Now Peltrin could hear aunt Besla—Peltrin's aunt and Berin's mother—screaming. Their house was under attack as well.

Nirani snatched a frying pan. She tossed the steaming contents in the face of a devastor about to come in through the nearest window. Scalded and helpless, the creature fell back, clawing its face and howling in pain. Still holding the pan, she hurried up the ladder behind her son.

By the time Perwin reached the base of the ladder, there were several in the house. More were at the doors and windows.

Giving up on the idea of getting up to the loft himself, Perwin tore down the ladder, bringing it crashing down on two of them. They didn't try to get up.

Perwin grabbed a set of cooking knives from the counter as the devastors surrounded him.

There was a short hesitation and time stood still. It gave them all—humans and devastors alike—a moment to take in what was about to happen.

Then the battle started. Perwin, who had led tens of thousands of men into dozens of battles, fought as never before. His speed was surreal. Everything in his reach became a weapon.

Four devastors fell to the kitchen knives, a chair ended two more. Peltrin knew those knives were too thin for throwing and were poorly balanced, but Perwin used them as if they had been made for the task.

Another devastor was crushed under a second chair, two more fell to the shattered remains of the chair's leg. The poker for the fire ended three more, but they continued pouring in through the door and windows. They were seemingly in endless supply.

[41]

Perwin's movements continued. There was no ridiculous waving around or unnecessary acrobatics. Every movement resulted in blood, many resulted in death. His fighting that day was a perfect study in economy of motion.

As Perwin swept the rug out from under three devastors and flashed it through the air, confusing several others, Peltrin came to himself enough to remember he was still carrying his throwing knives. One of them was already in his hand.

Cautiously, he approached the edge of the loft. The flurry of motion below was sickening to watch. He didn't see any with red eyes, but there had to be at least one somewhere nearby. One of the devastors looked up and hissed, its black eyes glaring. Peltrin drew back in fear.

Already, Perwin's clothes and face and hands were drenched in blood. It was impossible to tell how much of it was his own but, despite his almost inhuman performance, he was not unscathed. The seasoned warrior finally made it to the weapons cabinet and withdrew a short sword and a tomahawk—his favorite weapons.

Despite the paralyzing fear, Peltrin couldn't help but notice Perwin's fighting style changed significantly when he fought devastors. Against Beorn, Perwin was always working to get close, negating the reach and momentum advantages of the heavy weapons Beorn favored. He would dodge and deflect, waiting for the perfect moment to get in close for a quick kill stroke.

Against the smaller devastors—who moved in quick, aggressive motions with their dagger-like claws—Perwin stretched his arms wide. He used the tip of his blade and the full reach of the tomahawk to keep them at bay. He favored long, sweeping slices, rather than a single, end-all blow.

The strategy seemed to be working. Though irrationally aggressive by nature, the devastors were forced to keep their distance. The floor was covered in the blood and littered with the bodies of those who didn't. Now that Perwin had his favorite weapons, his enemies were dying as quickly as they could enter the house.

Then the red-eyed devastors appeared. Peltrin's eyes were drawn immediately to them. Unlike the others, they didn't appear to be completely out of their minds with aggression. There were four of them. They moved deliberately, staying outside of the fight zone Perwin dominated. Sniffing the air, they looked around the room, searching for their targets.

One, in particular, had a severely mangled face, no doubt due to Perwin's skill. It had separated itself from the frenzy and looked around, sniffing the air. Eventually, it looked up. Its glowing red eye locked with Peltrin's. Peltrin immediately knew it was there for him and him alone.

It began climbing the wall, never looking away. Another locked eyes with Nirani and also started to climb. The remaining two moved towards Perwin.

"Perwin," Nirani shouted, "It's here for Peltrin."

"Peltrin, use your knives!" his father shouted.

Peltrin's hands went weak and one of his knives fell to the floor below. One of the devastors kicked it aside disdainfully, gouging the knife with its claws. Peltrin looked at the dark knife in the corner, which now had white claw marks. He now owned two knives scarred by his cowardice.

One of the red-eyed devastors reached the edge of the loft. Nirani sprang into action. Screaming and crying, she used the frying pan to beat at the creature with surprising fury. Her attack was less coordinated than Perwin's surgical precision, but what she lacked in technique she made up for with pure determination.

Peltrin continued to back away.

"Peltrin, your knives!" Perwin yelled again, rage filled his voice as he continued to fight. Two more fell to his sword and another lost its head to the tomahawk. Perwin looked as if he could go on like this for hours. He continued to move with lightning speed. The only injuries he had sustained so far appeared minor. As long as he didn't get poisoned, he would heal.

Peltrin turned to the red-eyed devastor with the mangled face. He looked directly into the horrible red eye as it moved towards him. At this short distance, he could easily put out the second eye without endangering himself in the slightest, but he was completely immobilized.

As Nirani continued to fight with the frying pan, a tomahawk appeared in the creature's back. The creature's head and shoulders jerked backward involuntarily. Then those horrible red eyes closed and it fell limp to the ground.

Nirani screamed. While she had been occupied, Peltrin's red-eyed devastor had crept in. With a lightning-fast move, it had reached through the guardrail and gashed her leg. She fell to the ground with surprise but was quickly back on her feet again. Blood flowed from gashes in her leg but she ignored it as she resumed her attack.

"Peltrin, help your mother!" Perwin's voice was desperate.

Peltrin was still immobile. His whole body shook and he was drenched in sweat.

"Perwin, this one is here for Peltrin!" Nirani cried out.

She was right. The devastor's eye was fixed on Peltrin.

Nirani continued to fight with the frying pan, but she was beginning to tire. Eventually, it would get through.

"Perwin!" she screamed again.

Throwing caution to the wind, Perwin threw his sword at the creature. The sword went completely through its body, pinning the creature to the wall. There it hung from the sword, dead.

This left Perwin in the center of the room without a weapon. The circle around him collapsed immediately as the devastors claimed their prize. Left and right the claws tore at his body as two red-eyed devastors and at least a dozen black-eyed devastors collapsed on him. Mercilessly, they shredded his clothing and flesh. Perwin collapsed into a ball, doing his best to protect his neck and vitals.

Just then, Beorn came crashing through the front door, ax in hand. He was covered in blood. Judging by the injuries crisscrossing his entire body, much of it was his own.

"They're dead!" he cried in anguish. "Besla and Berin are dead!"

Seeing the creatures tearing at his brother, he flew at them in a rage. They scattered, momentarily confused.

Perwin—who somehow had escaped fatal injury—seized the moment. He rushed to one of the dead bodies and withdrew his tomahawk. Leaping in the air, he withdrew his sword from the devastor pinned to the wall. The ruined body fell to the floor lifeless.

Then the two brothers fought side by side. Together, they fought even more effectively than they fought separately. They formed a wall, bringing immediate death to any who wouldn't turn and flee.

Then a hiss drew Peltrin and Nirani's attention away from the horror below. A single enterprising black-eyed devastor had found its way to the roof and shimmied through a small opening under one of the eaves. It was now in the loft and completely focused on Peltrin.

"Use your knives, Peltrin," Nirani whispered. Then she said in a louder voice, "Now, Peltrin!"

Frozen in fear, Peltrin did nothing as it leaped for his throat.

Crying out, Nirani attacked. Armed with nothing but the frying pan she was still holding, she beat at it again and again. There was no technique, no strategy, just pure and simple determination and desperation. The fear was plain on her face as tears streamed down her cheeks, but she pounded with everything she had to give.

Hoping to overcome her by sheer force, the devastor gave up on Peltrin and jumped for her throat. Rolling onto her back, she kicked it over the railing. Perwin cleaved the creature in two midair and immediately resumed fighting alongside his brother.

Outside there was a mighty howl. Peltrin crouched low to look out the door and window. Wolves had entered the clearing around the houses and devastors were falling by the dozens. Two of the wolves towered over the others. One of them looked large enough to be a horse. With the coming of the wolves, devastors were no longer entering the house.

A few seconds later, Beorn swept his ax and relieved his last two opponents of their heads. There was a brief moment of silence as all four survivors took a moment to try to process what had just happened. The change seemed too sudden to be real. In less than half an hour, they had gone from normal life, to absolute horror, to silence.

Chapter 4: Aftershocks

Y ou're sure there's nothing more to be done?" asked one of the neighbors.

With the help of the neighbors, the houses had been cleared of the dead devastors and, as much as possible, the blood had been cleaned from the floor. The bodies of Berin and his mother Besla had been moved into their house where they would be safe until the burial the next day.

"Thank you for coming so quickly," answered Perwin from his bed, "but the wolves have agreed to guard the clearing around the house tonight. You should see to your own families."

It took some time to convince them but eventually, at Perwin's urging, the friends and neighbors nervously hurried home to lock their doors and sharpen their weapons.

Soon, only Bensil and his two apprentices remained. Like Soyem, his young apprentice, Bensil was of the Canbi race. He was small and thin-boned, particularly now that he was getting older. His hair was white and curly, though it had been jet-black when he was younger. He had dark skin and round dark eyes that glittered when he smiled. Typical of the Canbi, Bensil smiled a lot.

But even Bensil wasn't smiling today. His hands and eyes moved with amazing precision, considering his age. Beorn, who had lost a lot of blood, had been treated first. Now that the worst of Beorn's bleeding had stopped, the huge man was lying on a makeshift mattress on the floor.

After Beorn, the ancient little healer had focused his attention on Perwin. Perwin couldn't help but wrinkle his nose. Bensil had a bit of an odor. It wasn't too bad if he was on the opposite side of the room, but it could be quite overpowering when he was up close. Beorn, whose mattress on the floor was only a few feet away, was covering his mouth and nose.

"These four scratches are poisoned," the old healer muttered as he wrapped Perwin's forearm, "probably four marks from the same hand." He continued searching for and treating the worst of the wounds, mumbling and muttering as he went.

Peltrin sat on one of the two remaining chairs. Though the night was warm and he was near the fire, he wrapped his arms around himself to keep from shaking. His entire body was drenched with sweat as he stared blankly into the fire.

Soyem had tried unsuccessfully to talk to Peltrin. Soyem was several years younger than Peltrin and had only recently been taken on as an apprentice. Though they appeared to be of the same race, Soyem was taller than the old healer and his skin wasn't quite as dark. Unable to get any response from Peltrin, the small-boned boy watched with a sick look on his face as the old healer worked on the men.

Peltrin was dimly aware that his mother was sitting on the other remaining chair, only a few feet away. The older of the two apprentices, Aralis, was sitting at her feet. Her long legs were crossed and her arms rested on Nirani's lap. She looked up at the distraught mother with soft brown eyes, listening intently as Nirani spoke of what had just happened and struggled to compose herself. How an Ennai girl was apprenticed to a Canbi healer in a Pichari village was quite a mystery. Only Bensil knew the whole story, and he refused to tell anyone.

In contrast to her amazing courage during the actual fighting, Nirani had completely broken down as soon as it was over. Tears poured down her cheeks and much of what she said wasn't even comprehensible. As soon as she had arrived, Aralis had rushed over to Nirani, taking her in her arms.

AFTERSHOCKS

The woman and the girl had held each other for a long time as Nirani cried. Unlike many of the neighbors, there was no fear in Aralis' eyes. If anything, the girl looked protective. As she held Peltrin's mother in her arms, her eyes scanned the trees through the door, as if daring the devastors to return and face her wrath.

Later, Aralis had long since finished putting a poultice on Nirani's leg, but she continued to hold her hands as Nirani talked. Thanks to Aralis, in less than an hour, Peltrin's mother went from hysterical, to frantic, to somewhat reasonable.

Were it not for the terrible circumstances, Peltrin would have been happy to see Aralis. They were about the same age and had become friends, of sorts. Peltrin was fairly confident around girls his age, but Aralis spoke little so the relationship was growing very slowly. Despite her near-silence, Peltrin had the distinct impression he would grow to like her even more as they got to know each other better.

He glanced over at his father and uncle. Both brothers were pale and were visibly getting weaker. Neither was even trying to sit up anymore. The frail old healer opened his bag for the hundredth time and turned and muttered something to Aralis.

The tall, slender girl nodded and looked at Nirani, who released her hands. Aralis stood and ran out the door into the dimming light.

Peltrin stood and walked to the door as Aralis left. Part of him felt like he should go with her to keep her safe. He probably would have except that he had no confidence in his ability to protect her. He watched through the door as she practically flew across the clearing.

She seemed to be built to run. Her long arms and legs pumped in automatic natural rhythm as her long, dark hair waved behind her. She hesitated at the edge of the trees, looking uncharacteristically uncertain. One of the large wolves barked and two wolves joined her. Her face relaxed and she resumed running with one wolf in front of her and another behind.

Peltrin felt his mother's hand on his shoulder. "How are you doing?" she asked.

"I'm fine," he said, shrugging her off. "I'm the only one who didn't get hurt, remember?" He walked back to his chair, sat down, and stared into the flames again.

Aralis was gone only a few moments. She handed Bensil the requested herb and returned to listening to Nirani. Though she had been running hard, only a few seconds went by before her breathing slowed. The only remaining evidence of her run was a slight glow of her brown skin.

Soyem decided to try to talk to Peltrin again. "There were a bunch of dead devastors around Berin's body. Did you kill any?"

Peltrin felt his face harden.

"I've seen you train," Soyem went on, "I'll bet you could have killed a lot of these devastors. With your throwing knives alone, you could have…"

"Soyem, don't talk about the attack unless Peltrin wants to talk about it," Bensil interrupted sternly.

To Peltrin's relief, Bensil and Aralis had no interest in pressing him for his version of the attack. His mother, though she had talked nonstop, had said nothing about his failure to do anything to help. So far, neither the healer, nor his apprentices, nor any of the neighbors knew of Peltrin's cowardice.

"None of these wounds are fatal in the traditional sense," Bensil said as he bound up the last of Perwin's deeper injuries. "You did a good job of protecting your vital areas. Even taken together and considering the loss of blood, all of you would be fine in a matter of weeks, were these not devastor wounds."

"Part of it has to do with how they fight," explained Perwin. "They rarely go straight in for the kill. They are more inclined to use the tips of their claws to slice you from arm's length."

"Well, whatever the reason," Bensil said dismissively. He clearly wasn't interested in the fighting techniques of devastors. "These are not injuries that would normally kill two healthy, strong men such as yourselves. That is, as long as they are properly treated so they do not get infected."

"What about the poison?" asked Peltrin quietly. Aralis looked at him but he looked away. He didn't want anyone to look at him right now. He already knew the answer, but he couldn't help but ask. Maybe the old healer had learned of a cure Peltrin's parents didn't know about.

"Yes, well, the fact that these were caused by devastors changes everything." Bensil looked very tired. Emotion and strain showed on his face and crept into his voice as he continued. "All devastor wounds, poisoned or not, take longer to heal than one would expect.

"As for the poison…well…it isn't often I have to admit defeat. In all my years, I have never found anything—or even heard of anything—that will extract, counter, or slow the effects of this poison. One of Perwin's old friends—an Ennai man named Valdor—thought he found a magical cure, once. But in the end, his wife and daughter died as well."

"He visited us not long after that happened," said Perwin. "And I have seen him a few times since. He completely fell apart when they died. I hear he is still living in the same house but I doubt he'll ever be the same."

"I've searched so long," Bensil said sadly. His head hung a little lower and his shoulders looked as if they were carrying something very heavy.

"We knew there was nothing to be done about the poison," said Nirani kindly. She looked exhausted, but she was finally starting to talk normally again. "You are the most skilled healer anyone could hope for. Thank you so much for coming so quickly and for doing all that could be done."

The old man's face lifted a little. "I think you are all familiar with how the poison works, so you are aware your time is limited. I'm so sorry to say it, but I don't know any way to make the message gentler."

"Yes, we know…sunrise of the fifth day," Perwin said. He looked excessively tired, to the point that Peltrin wondered if his father would be able to keep his eyes open much longer.

"The symptoms you exhibit will depend on the extent of the poisoned injuries," Bensil explained. "You," he nodded towards Nirani, "only received a few small scratches so you probably won't notice any symptoms at all. Though it is possible you might feel some unusual fatigue and see some mild hallucinations on the last night.

"Each of you two, however," he looked at Perwin and Beorn, "has a large number of poisoned wounds. You will likely feel very weak and have difficulty breathing as soon as tonight or tomorrow. Your hallucinations may start as early as tomorrow. You men are strong, but even for you these symptoms are unavoidable."

"All of this was avoidable," Peltrin broke in miserably.

There was an uncomfortable silence.

"How so, Peltrin?" asked Perwin.

"Twice in one day," Peltrin said. His voice was shaky and his usual confidence was nowhere to be found. "I had the weapon in my hand and an easy chance to kill a devastor. You two have been training me for years. All I had to do was throw the knife. They were less than ten paces away. I never miss at that distance." Peltrin hung his head. He was barely holding back the tears of shame.

"There's a big difference, son," said Perwin, "between missing an opportunity and being the guilty party. None of this is your fault." Perwin's voice was weaker than usual, but there was no hesitation or doubt.

"What does it matter?" Peltrin persisted.

"Aramir deranged the minds of those creatures and sent them to kill us," Perwin explained. He paused for breath. "He and he alone is guilty."

Even the devastors themselves are not responsible for this, much less you. The truth is you are not to blame."

"I get it," said Peltrin, a hint of anger in his voice. "You don't want to blame me for what happened. But the truth is two people are dead. The truth is you three will be dead in five days. And the truth is I could have stopped it. I had everything I needed. I had the knowledge, I had the training, I even had the weapon in my hand. The only reason I failed, the only reason they died, the only reason the rest of you are going to die, is because I was afraid." Too ashamed to be in their presence anymore, Peltrin stomped out of the tiny house.

Perwin tried to get up and failed. "Call him back," he said. "He doesn't understand what I was trying to say."

"Give him a moment," said Nirani, placing a hand on Perwin's shoulder. "He needs time to think about everything that happened today."

At her touch, Peltrin took a deep breath and stopped straining. "But he's thinking about it wrong," he insisted weakly.

"Which is why he needs time," Nirani was returning to her natural, perceptive self. "You are the same way. You often need time to think things over before you are ready to listen."

Perwin looked up at his wife and sighed his resignation. It didn't matter how badly he wanted to say something to Peltrin. He lacked the strength to get up.

"Eventually, he will need to hear exactly what you want to say," she assured him. "Just wait until he's ready. His shame is not rational, but it is just as real as any of our injuries. Just as much as any of us, he needs time to heal."

"You're probably right," said Perwin. "I worry, though, that the time he needs before he is ready to listen is more time than the rest of us have left to live."

"Is that how it happened?" Soyem asked Bensil quietly enough the others couldn't hear. "Was Peltrin really so afraid he didn't even try?" He had seen Peltrin training from time to time and was secretly jealous of his size and skills. He knew Peltrin had fought thieves and gangs of men on several occasions. The short Canbi boy couldn't imagine that Peltrin, a boy he admired so much, would be afraid of anything.

Bensil shot him a glare. "We are healers, Soyem," he snapped. "It doesn't matter why it happened. It doesn't matter whose fault it is, and it doesn't matter if someone is guilty."

"All that matters is the information we need in order to administer proper treatment," Soyem recited. This was something he struggled with from time to time.

Outside and alone, Peltrin took a deep breath of the evening air. He still felt shaky and unsteady after everything that had happened. The sun was gone and the sky was darkening but it wouldn't be fully dark for another half an hour. There was a large pile of devastor bodies in the ruined cornfield not far from the house.

He could see Lou by the pile of bodies. The marmot was upright, walking on his hind legs and waving his front legs in angry gestures. The lieutenant appeared to be telling the foul creatures exactly what he thought of them. From time to time, Lou would walk over to the pile and angrily kick one of the bodies. For all the world, the overweight marmot looked like an angry two-year-old child throwing a tantrum.

"Perhaps we should stay the night," Peltrin heard Bensil offer.

"You might as well go home where you can sleep comfortably," Perwin answered. Peltrin was near the window but he had to strain to hear his father. Perwin was talking so quietly and stopping for breath regularly. "With the wolves patrolling the fields around the house, we're in no danger of dying tonight. Besides, we have no place for the three of you to rest."

"The sun has already set," said Bensil after a short hesitation, "the light is fading and it will be dark soon. Even with the wolves on guard, I'd like to be home when that happens. We'll leave you with the herbs you need for tonight and we'll be back to check on you in the morning."

He and his apprentices, always ready to move quickly from one place to another, were ready to leave in a few minutes.

Aralis looked at Nirani, "I wish we could have been here sooner. Tell Peltrin we hope…I mean, we will…I mean, we think…."

"Thank you, Aralis," said Nirani, embracing her one more time. "Thank you for caring."

Peltrin reentered the house only a few minutes after Bensil and his apprentices had left. It was clear from the look on her face that his mother wanted to talk, but Peltrin didn't. He immediately went up to his loft without saying a word.

Peltrin was so tired he hoped he would quickly fall asleep, but sleep was impossible to find. Every time he closed his eyes, he would see some portion of the battle. Usually, he relived the parts where he could have helped if he hadn't been such a coward.

When he finally slept, Peltrin dreamed of another attack. He was lying in an unfamiliar bed, surrounded by devastors. One had red eyes that held him completely paralyzed. The eyes were filled with a fury and a hatred he had never before imagined. He felt young, inexperienced, helpless, and vulnerable.

Just as they moved to attack, Peltrin's grandfather Thettlemar came into the room and a fight ensued. Peltrin's grandmother—Thettlemar's wife—was there as well.

THE CHRONCILES OF AMYRIAD

CHAPTER 5: THE RED MIRROR

C onsult the mirror!"

Peltrin awoke with a start. His heart was pounding and he was drenched with sweat. He looked around for his grandparents, then he shook his head and rubbed his eyes. His grandparents had died ten years ago, he reminded himself. The dream couldn't have been real. But something about the dream seemed too familiar to have been just a dream. It felt more like a memory.

"The mirror calls your name! Consult the mirror."

Peltrin jumped at the sound, confused. The voice had come from directly above.

There was a flurry of motion and Peltrin ducked, covering his head. A bat landed on the railing of the loft. Its eyes were glowing the same red as the red-eyed devastors.

Peltrin snatched a knife and poised for action. After the attack, he had decided he would always sleep with a weapon handy, just in case.

"I am not here to harm you," the bat said in its high-pitched voice. "You have been summoned. You must approach the mirror."

"What mirror?" He glanced at the knife he was holding. It was a black throwing knife with white claw marks. He wished he had chosen to sleep with a different weapon. He didn't like how the claw marks reminded him of his cowardice.

He then looked the bat directly in the eyes. He was surprised to see that, while the bat's little round eyes glowed the same red, they didn't affect him like the red-eyed devastors. He felt none of the terror he had felt earlier.

"The mirror is hidden," answered the bat. "I was sent to be your guide. The way is difficult, but such is the price if you seek the cure."

"There is no cure," said Peltrin, remembering what he had heard earlier. "Everyone but me dies at sunrise on the fifth day." It occurred to Peltrin that someone poisoned just after sunrise would have almost a full day longer to live than someone poisoned just before sunrise. He couldn't help but feel angry Beorn and his parents had been poisoned in the evening.

"The mirror can teach you how to prevent the cursed death," the bat insisted. "But you must go tonight. There is much to be done if you want your family to live."

"Why do your eyes glow red like the red-eyed devastors?" Peltrin asked.

"The same venom runs in my veins," the bat answered.

"Then you would be dead," said Peltrin.

"The red-eyed devastors live with the poison," the bat pointed out. "Consider it proof of the wisdom and power of the mirror. I am a sentient being, like yourself, yet the poison does not kill me. What's more, I retain power over myself. The mirror has elected that you may have the knowledge to preserve your family, even as I have been preserved."

"Where is the mirror?" Peltrin asked, "and why haven't I heard of it?"

"It is near, in the cave."

Peltrin dug into his memory. He knew of two caves in the mountain south of his home. The first was to the southeast and was filled with ice. The second was to the southwest and had a steady flow of wind coming out of it. He and Berin had explored a little ways into both caves more than once. He could travel to either cave and back in less than an hour.

Was it possible there was a mirror in one of those caves that could give him a cure for his family? He didn't even know what a typical mirror looked like. But then again, his family had been poisoned by a creature he had never heard of before and he was talking to a bat with glowing eyes. It was hard to know what to believe anymore.

Was it worth the risk? He was about to be left without any family at all. Maybe he should consider anything that might cure them, no matter how strange, to be worth the risk. Besides, their current predicament was his fault, it would be justice rightly served if the bat led him to his death.

"I should wake the others, first," Peltrin decided. His brain felt addled. Normally, he tended to be bold and overconfident. After everything that had just happened, he found himself unsure of everything—particularly himself. Even worse, he still couldn't stop thinking about the attacks. The distraction seemed to interrupt his every thought.

"You may if you like," conceded the bat. "Though you should ask yourself what the purpose would be. Your father and his brother can barely get out of bed, and your mother has difficulty walking. The path to the mirror is difficult, none of them can help you."

"I can't just sneak away and leave them unprotected."

"Are you their protector?" asked the bat. "How effective are you at fighting devastors?"

Peltrin lowered his head. He had done nothing to defend himself in the morning, and he had done nothing to defend his family in the evening. His presence wouldn't make his parents and uncle any safer. If the wolves failed again, his family would die regardless of whether Peltrin was there or not.

"You're sure the mirror can stop the poison?" asked Peltrin. Even knowing he might not be able to protect them, he still didn't want to leave them alone. The possibility of a cure, however, might be worth the risk.

"The mirror will provide you with the information," answered the bat. "After that, you will be required to seek out the cure alone. Look at me, and the color of my eyes, as evidence."

Peltrin didn't want to say it aloud, but the color of the bat's eyes, more than anything else, made him question whether he could trust the animal.

"Will we make it back by sunrise?" Peltrin asked.

"Easily, unless you cause delays."

Peltrin was still debating waking up the others. He knew they would be upset if they woke up in the morning and he was gone. His mother, in particular, would be frantic.

If he woke them up, however, he was certain his mother wouldn't let him follow a red-eyed bat to a cave—not even for the possibility of a cure. After the horrible events of the previous day, she probably wanted to barricade the window and door and not let anyone out of her sight for the rest of her days.

Thanks to Peltrin, those days were numbered—literally. If he was to go at all, it would have to be in secret.

Was it worth it? Should he risk his own life in the hope that he could save theirs?

He thought about how he had left Berin to fight alone. He thought about how his mother had been poisoned by the devastor that was coming for him. He thought about how his father had thrown his weapons away, leaving himself exposed, to protect Peltrin.

"Let's go," he said quietly. "Show me the way."

Peltrin crept silently down the ladder. Normally his father was a light sleeper. Any movement in the loft and Perwin would be awake and alert, often with a weapon in his hand. But that wouldn't be a problem for Peltrin tonight, thanks to Perwin's injuries and Bensil's herbs.

As he left, Peltrin could hear all three adults breathing steadily. His parents were sleeping on their usual bed in the corner. Beorn on his makeshift straw mattress on the floor.

Peltrin crept outside, opening and closing the door silently. The night was a little chilly, but not terribly so. The stars sparkled in the sky with perfect clarity. The moon was just past full, so he had ample light to guide him as he tiptoed down the porch stairs and into the field.

The next obstacle was the lieutenant. But there was no sound from the woodpile as Peltrin crept away.

As Peltrin entered the forest, he took a deep breath of the strong scent of pine. He was dimly aware of the wolves as they patrolled the fields and the woods. Their patrolling didn't give him as much confidence as he would have liked. Only hours before, dozens of devastors had made it past the wolves and to the houses.

Peltrin remembered hearing a rumor that Bensil had an agreement with the wolves around Aldayin. It was the reason the wolves never bothered the people or the livestock of the village. He wondered if killing devastors was something the wolves did entirely on their own or if that was part of their agreement with Bensil.

As he walked, Peltrin continued to relive the attack on the house over and over again. Often, he would jump at shadows. Doing his best to keep from losing his courage altogether, he continued to follow the glowing eyes through the forest. He found himself constantly questioning whether he should be doing this. What if the bat was lying?

There was a dark corner of Peltrin's mind that hoped it would be dangerous, that the bat was actually leading him to a lair of devastors. After failing Beorn and his parents—causing their inevitable deaths—that little corner felt it was only right he should die with them.

He did his best to suppress the self-doubt, but he found he couldn't shut it out completely. It was a confusing and frightening change from his usual overconfidence.

Peltrin followed the bat to the left once they entered the forest. So, we are headed to the ice cave, Peltrin thought to himself.

As they approached the cave, the opening was little more than a shadow on a shadowy cliff. It was twice Peltrin's height and wide enough for four men to walk in, shoulder to shoulder. Peltrin knew it became smaller not far in.

Peltrin hesitated a little, but eventually he entered the cave. He could always just come back out, he told himself. As they entered, Peltrin was surprised to see the glow in the bat's eyes increased in intensity. It wasn't bright, but he could see well enough to avoid falling and hurting himself. He generally wasn't afraid of the dark, or caves. He generally wasn't afraid of heights, spiders, mice, or dozens of things people are often afraid of.

Being afraid of devastors made him useless as a fighter.

Peltrin shook his head, trying to drive the foreign thoughts from his mind. It felt as if the thoughts were being placed there by someone else. Somehow, entering the cave had made the source of the thoughts even more powerful.

The temperature dropped quickly as he went deeper into the cave. After scrambling over the boulders for only a few minutes, he slipped and nearly fell on a flat, smooth area. Looking closely, he saw that he had reached the ice. He was in an open room about the size of his house where the entire floor was covered in a smooth sheet of ice. Ripples of ice covered the walls. This was the furthest he and Berin had explored in this particular cave.

Carefully, he continued. As he walked, eventually it became clear he was walking along a frozen stream. When the ground was sloped, he sat and slid down the ice, using his feet to keep from running into rocks.

A few minutes later, the cave opened into an enormous cathedral-like room. The dim lights from the bat's eyes cast surreal shadows on the wall and ceiling above. Like the smaller room he had entered earlier, the entire floor was a flat, smooth sheet of ice. There were hundreds of frozen waterfalls of all sizes around the walls. High above, the ceiling consisted of massive stalactites made of ice and stone.

The bat flew to the other end of the room and then down into the floor. Peltrin stared for a moment, confused until he realized the ground dropped away.

Peltrin walked gingerly to the edge of the drop-off, trying his best not to slip on the ice and inadvertently fall off the edge. There, he stood at the top of a frozen underground waterfall. Once he went down, there would be no coming back this way. Peltrin was a good climber, but he had neither the gear nor the experience for such a climb. For the first time since he had entered the cave, he hesitated.

The bat flew back up, hovering near his face. "You can slide down," the bat assured him. "The mirror has indicated it intends for you to survive the cave."

There were so many reasons this was a bad idea. The bottom was deep, beyond the dim glow of the bat's eyes. What's more, there was every likelihood the bottom would be covered with sharp rocks and jagged ice.

"You have destroyed your family," the bat reminded him. "In exchange for hope, you can risk your own death. Alternatively, you can be completely assured of the deaths of everyone you care about."

Peltrin's shoulders slumped and he signed. The bat was right, of course.

"Remember your failures yesterday," the bat prompted. "Will you fail them again?"

Some part of Peltrin knew the bat was manipulating him, possibly to lure him to his death. But the words of the bat matched exactly the words he was hearing in his head. Somehow the bat seemed to know exactly what he was thinking. For a moment, he was suspicious the bat might be the source of the dark thoughts.

As if strengthened by the bat's words, the dark part of his mind became more powerful. He thought for a moment about death. In the silence and darkness of the cave, it was easy to imagine death as unending silence and darkness. Perhaps it would be relaxing. Maybe it was peaceful. Maybe he wouldn't feel pain anymore. Maybe…he wouldn't feel anything anymore. With all of the shame that currently consumed him, he liked the idea of a numb nothingness that just went on and on forever.

"Is the thought of death so frightening you will not risk it even to save your family?" asked the bat.

Against his better judgment, Peltrin made a conscious decision to let the little dark part of his brain take command. He stepped forward into the darkness.

There were a few seconds of weightlessness, then he was sliding down a steep, smooth, icy slope. The slope eventually flattened until he slowed to a stop.

"I guess I'm committed now," Peltrin mumbled to himself as he worked his way to his feet. The rush of adrenaline had cleared his head a little. Now that he had done it, he was instantly filled with regret. Silently he vowed to never let the darkness take over again. He had survived the fall, but he had a distinct feeling the darkness couldn't be trusted. He felt certain that, eventually, it would destroy him if it could.

The bat flew ahead. Peltrin started to follow—but then stopped, catching his breath. To his right, he felt cold and darkness.

I'm in a cave filled with ice, Peltrin reminded himself. Everything is cold and dark. Yet he couldn't shake the feeling that a particular patch of darkness was different from the rest. He forced himself to continue, but pressed himself against the left wall, as far away from the feeling as possible.

It was only then he realized he had brought no weapons with him. It was a somewhat shocking reminder of just how distracted he was. For a moment he reconsidered the foolishness of what he was doing. But he knew the thought had come too late. There was nothing he could do. He had no way of getting back up the ice waterfall. No matter what he thought, how he felt, or what he wanted, he was fully committed now.

Recognizing he had no other choice, he followed the little red eyes deeper into the darkness.

As he went deeper, the temperature in the cave increased just enough for water to flow. Eventually, the frigid water was everywhere. It trickled between the stones he walked on, it leaked from the walls. In some places, if he pressed his ear to the icy cold rock, he could feel and hear what seemed to be a river inside solid stone.

Peltrin had the distinct impression that this portion of the cave was not a place intended for humans. He crawled on his belly, scrambled up chimneys and down walls and crevices. Sometimes streams crossed his path, sometimes the path itself was a stream.

From time to time he would feel the same presence he had felt just after sliding down the ice waterfall. Each time he tried to convince himself it wasn't real, but deep down he knew that wasn't true. Somehow, something in the cave produced darkness that was more than a simple absence of light. It also produced a cold that was more than the absence of heat. It was as if darkness and cold emanated from something. Could it be alive? Was there such a thing as a creature that created darkness and cold?

It was at those times that the dark part of Peltrin's mind nearly took over. He began to suspect the darkness was the source of the thoughts. It would make sense that the thoughts were being placed there by something else. But how could it get into his mind?

Occasionally, when he didn't feel the ominous presence, he would pause to take a drink. The water was cold but remarkably tasty and refreshing.

Natural shafts and tunnels went in all directions. Left to himself, Peltrin would have had no hope of finding his way back again. Not that it mattered anyway. Hope in general was soon to be a thing of the past. All hope was scheduled to expire at sunrise, just a few days away.

Peltrin shook his head to expel the foreign thought.

The bat flew on and Peltrin continued to follow. After a while, the walls drew closer until, reaching side to side, Peltrin didn't have to fully extend his arms to reach the opposing walls. There, he found himself at the top of a drop-off. Far below, he could hear a stream flowing.

Placing his hands and feet on the opposite walls, he started to make his way down.

"Stay high," the bat commanded. "The way narrows as you get lower. You'll eventually be unable to move as you approach the bottom."

Grudgingly, Peltrin worked his way up until his head was near the ceiling. It was still more than a little disconcerting to listen to a bat whose eyes glowed like a red-eyed devastor. But, as far as he could tell, the bat appeared to be leading him somewhere. He could only hope it was somewhere he actually wanted to go.

Here, in this precarious position, he asked himself for the hundredth time: did he trust the bat? No, trust was too strong of a word. He didn't have any way to know for sure whether the small animal was trustworthy. For the moment, however, he believed the bat did not intend to lead him to his death. Not today, anyway. Even the dark little corner of his brain seemed convinced of that.

This portion of the cave was the most difficult so far. The attack had left him emotionally and physically exhausted. He hadn't had a full night's sleep, and the cave so far had also been incredibly taxing.

"One slip," he said to himself, "and it could all be over."

But it turned out that wasn't true. Peltrin did slip, and he caught himself. The one advantage of being in a crack that narrowed at the bottom was, if he did slip, there was likely to be an opportunity to catch himself before he fell far.

How long was this cave? How long had he been in here? It felt like hours had gone by, but in the stillness and darkness of the cave, it was impossible to be sure.

Finally, the cave widened again and the bat instructed him to make his way down to the stream below. Peltrin let out a steamy, shuddering breath as he let himself down into the water. The steam from his breath lingered in the air, glowing red in the odd light from the bat's eyes. He had to make a conscious effort to keep his teeth from chattering. The temperature near the water was freezing and the ice-cold water was up to his knees. Near the water, ice crystals laced the walls.

As he continued, the water deepened until Peltrin was up to his waist and the ceiling lowered until he could barely stand up straight. Peltrin paused to look ahead, shivering. He couldn't see how deep the water was, but he could see the ceiling dipped low, nearly touching the surface of the water for quite a distance. He hesitated, watching as his breath billowed in red clouds in front of his face. As cold and exhausted as he already was, he wasn't sure what his body would do if he had to submerged himself in the freezing water.

"You must move forward," the bat insisted in a shrill voice. "There is no other way."

Lacking options, Peltrin ducked his head and moved forward. To his dismay, the water was too deep to crawl in and the ceiling was too low for him to stand upright. As it was, he shuffled neck-deep in the freezing water in an awkward half-kneeling, half-standing position. It was almost impossible to keep his chin above water without knocking his head on the low ceiling. After the third time hitting his head on the sharp rocks above, he felt a trickle of blood coming down his face. All the while, the freezing water sucked what little remained of his energy.

Though it felt like an eternity, it was only a few minutes later that Peltrin emerged from the water. He immediately fell to the ground, gasping for breath. His entire body was shaking violently from cold and exertion. He closed his eyes and tried to steady his heartbeat. His breathing came in short, uncertain puffs. Most of his upper body and all of his lower body ached with a dull, paralyzing numbness.

The numbness in his body sapped what little remained of his willpower. He cringed as a sudden crushing feeling of depression and shame washed over him. He had no will to fight the darkness. It took over and all of the horrors of the past day and night came crashing down on him like a waterfall.

Since the first sight of the first devastor, everything had been a blur of fear and shock. But now the memories emerged with perfect clarity. The images flashed through his mind: the log exploding, the eyes, the teeth, the claws, Berin chopping firewood and then fearlessly shouting and charging, the contrast of his parent's selflessness and courage against his own cowardice, the agony in Beorn's voice when he cried out that his wife and son were dead.

At some point in all of the flashing images, tears began to flow. Peltrin cried for Berin, his cousin and his best friend. He cried for aunt Besla, who had always been a second mother to him. He cried for his parents and uncle, who soon would be dead as well. The crying went on and on until he thought it would never stop. Eventually, it did, but only because he just physically couldn't cry anymore.

Eventually, Peltrin sat up slowly. He took a deep, shuddering breath and shakily did his best to wipe his face and nose on his clothes. His clothes were still soaking wet so the action did very little to help. As he wiped his face again, Peltrin tried to remember the last time he had cried. It had been years. He was glad this had happened in a cave where no one could see him.

He looked up; suddenly aware the bat had been perched on a nearby rock. Its glowing, unblinking eyes were fixated on him. It appeared to have been watching him intently the entire time. It looked supremely satisfied, as if it had just eaten a huge feast.

"Your pain," it said breathlessly, "is absolutely exquisite!" The little creature sounded almost happy.

The comment bothered Peltrin deeply. It sickened him to the point that, even here deep in the cave, he was tempted to kill it, or at least to part ways with it. It felt like the bat had somehow been feeding on his pain. He was deeply bothered by the fact that it had been watching him during such a personal moment. It bothered him even more that it seemed to have gotten some kind of twisted enjoyment from his intense suffering.

"I haven't cried in years, you flying rat," he grumbled. "Don't expect to ever see it again." Forcefully, he expelled the darkness from his mind and vowed it would never take over again.

Insulting the bat made him feel a little better. It was something he would have done automatically before yesterday's events muddled his mind. He was sure now there was something very wrong with the animal—or with whoever or whatever was controlling it. Peltrin still hadn't fully ruled out the possibility that Aramir was behind this.

"Let's keep moving," Peltrin grumbled. "You smell like an old carcass." The bat's smell wasn't strong, but again, the insult made him feel a little better. As much as he now hated the bat, he had to admit to himself that he wasn't sure he could ever find his way out on his own. Now that he was thinking more clearly, he wanted very much to be with his parents and Beorn again.

He got up and jumped up and down, stamping his feet and slapping himself to get the blood moving again. After a short while, he was still shaky and uncomfortable, but the worst of the numbness was gone and he was able to continue.

The next leg of the trip was surprisingly uneventful. The cave widened and, other than a few places where Peltrin had to scramble over some loose rock, was relatively free of obstacles.

Peltrin knew the mirror the instant he saw it. It was a pool of water in the floor, just large enough that he could have laid down in it. The water dimly glowed the same hue of red as the eyes of the bat. Looking in the mirror, he could see himself. His reflection in the reddish glow gave the appearance of someone gazing up from the depths of a pool of blood.

"The mirror knows what you seek," the bat said. "You may approach."

Peltrin approached the mirror hesitantly. He could distinctly feel the source of the darkness and the cold hidden in the shadowy wall behind the mirror. Though he couldn't see anything suspicious, he knew without a doubt the presence was there. He had a distinct feeling he was being manipulated. He wondered if he had been led into a trap.

Even with those thoughts, however, Peltrin continued forward. Now that he was finally here, he needed to hear what the mirror had to say.

"Welcome, young one," the mirror said. The voice of the mirror gave Peltrin the chills. It was unlike anything he had ever heard before in his life. It made him want to scream and run. It was somewhat deeper than the bat's voice, but somehow, they sounded connected. Peltrin glanced around. The bat was behind him but the new voice came from the direction of the water. Peltrin half expected to see another bat. It would explain the voice, but not the glowing water.

"My parents and uncle have been poisoned by devastors," said Peltrin, not knowing how else to begin.

"I know your need," answered the mirror, "and I have an answer."

"But what is the price?" Peltrin asked. He cursed himself for coming this far without ever thinking to ask. Of course, there would be a price.

"A price will be paid," answered the mirror, "but not today."

"But what is the price?" Peltrin repeated. He didn't like the idea of owing a debt without knowing what it was.

"To heal your family," the mirror said. "You must go to the Fyllcarcern. There you will find the panacea."

"What's a panacea?" asked Peltrin. He had never seen the Fyllcarcern, but he had heard of it. It was a unique multicolored mountain hidden deep in the Pichari Mountains. The rumor was that it resembled a huge monolith, with a flat top and sheer cliffs all around. He had heard that it was only a few day's journey from Aldayin.

Panacea, however, was a word he had never heard before.

"The panacea will purify all poisons, cure all diseases, and heal any injury. You will find it at the top of the Fyllcarcern."

"But no one can climb the Fyllcarcern," said Peltrin. "It's impossible."

"It has been climbed before," the mirror answered, "the man's name is Valdor. He is old and weak now, but he was once a hero of great renown. In his younger days, he went in search of the panacea and reached the top of the Fyllcarcern."

"Valdor," Peltrin repeated to himself. Somehow the name seemed familiar. Was that the name Bensil had said earlier? Didn't his father and Beorn know someone by that name?

"You must avoid Valdor at all costs," the mirror instructed. "The man failed in his attempt to obtain the Panacea. Any advice he would give you—and even his very presence—will ruin any chance you have for success."

"You should also know the Fyllcarcern is protected by a creature known as the guardian," the mirror continued. "You must not trust it. The guardian will do its best to deceive you. It will weave strange stories to confuse your mind. It will tell you that you are not allowed to climb. It may even tell you the panacea does not exist. But if you can get past the guardian and climb the Fyllcarcern, the panacea will be yours."

"But how does the panacea work?" asked Peltrin, "and if it will cure anything, why aren't people trying to climb the Fyllcarcern every day? And what is the price? You still haven't told me the price."

"The price will be paid," the mirror answered smoothly. "The last instruction I give you is critical. You must perform this mission alone. If anyone comes with you, the Fyllcarcern will deny you, and you will fail. Go now. Go Secretly. Don't even tell anyone where you are going."

Peltrin thought about that for a moment. The idea of a Panacea seemed too good to be true. And something didn't feel right about leaving without telling anyone.

"That is all the information you need to save your family," the mirror concluded. "Your audience has ended." The red in the mirror began to fade. Eventually, the glow was gone and there was nothing left but a pool of water.

"Your audience with the mirror has ended," repeated the bat. "Now I will lead you out of the cave."

Peltrin once again wanted desperately to part ways with the bat. Looking around, the darkness reminded him that he was in too deep…literally. He nodded and turned away from the mirror.

Just after Peltrin rounded the corner, a large section of the wall shifted and a pair of large multifaceted red glowing eyes appeared.

A minute later, the bat hesitated.

"Wait here," the bat instructed.

Out of Peltrin's sight or hearing, the little bat returned to the mirror and bowed to the multifaceted eyes.

"You didn't slay him," the bat said quietly. "Does this mean we can indeed use him for our cause?"

"Now that I have seen him up close, I am sure," answered the voice of the mirror. The multifaceted eyed blinked. "I cannot yet fully control him, but he can hear the thoughts I place in his head. His greatest utility will be only after his family has perished and his quest has fully broken him. He must attempt this mission and fail. Watch him as he tries. Make sure he fails."

"If he succeeds?" asked the bat.

"If he follows any of our instructions, he cannot succeed," answered the darkness. "If he rebels, we'll use other methods to ensure he fails before he faces the Fyllen. Even I do not want him to release the Fyllen. Given the chance, the creature would destroy all of Amyriad, including us."

"Our success is inevitable, thanks to your power and wisdom," the bat replied, bowing again. It then returned to Peltrin.

Peltrin resumed following the little red glowing eyes through the maze of tunnels. It bothered him the bat had left him alone in the darkness. It was a stark reminder of how helpless he was without its guidance.

The way out was much less difficult than the way in. The only real obstacle was a wall nearly three times his height. There were enough handholds and footholds that he was able to manage the climb, but his arms and legs were shaky with cold and exhaustion.

Less than an hour after consulting the mirror, Peltrin exited the cave and the bat disappeared into the trees. He recognized the place. It was the wind cave. He never would have suspected the ice cave and the wind cave were connected. As he breathed deeply and watched the rising sun peek over the distant mountains, Peltrin felt something glimmer in his heart. It was so different from anything he had experienced recently that it felt almost completely unfamiliar.

It was hope. It was thin and fragile, but it was hope nonetheless.

THE CHRONCILES OF AMYRIAD

CHAPTER 6: QUESTIONS

This is very unlike Peltrin," Nirani insisted. "I can't imagine why he would wander off in the middle of the night. Especially after what happened yesterday." Peltrin's mother was pacing back and forth. She limped severely but seemed completely unaware of the pain.

Perwin and Beorn were awake and alert, but lying down. Their condition had not improved through the night.

"He was seen leaving by both of the wolf brothers," old Bensil confirmed, "along with several other wolves in their pack. Peltrin was following a bat with red glowing eyes. It led him into a cave. He appeared to be going of his own free will."

Bensil had come to check on the progress of the three injured people. His apprentices Aralis and Soyem, along with several neighbors, were digging graves for Berin and Besla. Per Beorn's instruction, the graves would be next to his house, near the place where Berin had been chopping firewood.

"But why didn't they intervene?" Nirani asked.

"He didn't appear to be in danger," said Bensil. "By their nature, wolves tend to avoid close contact with humans. By our agreement, they left him alone."

"I knew it," said Beorn from his mattress. "You do have an agreement with the wolves."

"Yes, yes," said Bensil, waving his hand dismissively.

"It concerns me the bat had red glowing eyes," Nirani said. She couldn't have cared less at the moment about Bensil's unique agreement with the wolves. "Could it be a servant of Aramir?"

"I wish I could say it was impossible," answered Bensil, "I have never heard of such a thing. But Aramir's methods for creating and controlling his minions is something I don't understand. I have no idea if he could make it work on other animals."

"Peltrin is smarter than that," Beorn insisted, attempting to sit up and then lying back down. "He would never just leave in the middle of the night, following some strange creature he'd never met."

"Last night," Bensil mused, "Nirani said something that struck me. Shame can be like an injury. It requires healing. You know Peltrin better than anyone else, but right now I don't think even you can predict what he would do. He isn't acting as he normally would."

"I want him here now," said Nirani. "Once he gets back, I don't want any of us to leave this house."

"Leaving the house isn't an option for me and Perwin, anyway," Beorn pointed out. There was more than a hint of bitterness in his voice.

"All of this is more than a boy his age should have to deal with," said Nirani. She didn't appear to have heard Beorn. She was getting frantic, exactly as Peltrin had predicted. "What if he is trapped or hurt somewhere in the cave? What if he needs our help? You two can't even get out of bed, and I won't be able to help him, even if I can get there.

Nirani looked ready to explode. But just as she opened her mouth to speak again, Peltrin burst into the house. Nirani caught him up before he was three steps past the door.

"Don't you ever do that again, Peltrin," she commanded, squeezing him tightly, "ever."

"I know where to find a cure, mom," Peltrin managed. He returned his mother's embrace only briefly, clearly focused on sharing his message. "I think there's a chance you all might live!"

QUESTIONS

Nirani released him, looking him over from head to toe. "Your head is bleeding."

Peltrin touched his hair. Though he hadn't been paying attention to it, by now, it was thick with drying blood.

As Bensil cleaned and bandaged his head, all four of the adults barraged him with questions.

"I can't tell you where I went or what I learned," Peltrin insisted. "All I can tell you is the bat led me to something that told me how to find the cure. The more I tell you, the less likely it is I will succeed."

"Then you're not going," Nirani insisted. "Anything that tries to convince you to sneak away from your family and keep secrets from those who love you is not trying to help you."

"But I have to try," Peltrin insisted. "All three of you will die if I don't.

"That is exactly why we can't have you doing anything foolish," said Perwin, "You are the only one of our family who wasn't poisoned. As long as you are safe, there is hope."

"The only reason I wasn't hurt was because you threw away your weapons, and because mother got between me and the devastors, and because Beorn showed up to help after the others died. I can't just sit around and do nothing! That's no way to pay you back."

"The best way to pay us back," answered Perwin, "is to stay alive and safe. If I had died yesterday, I wouldn't have regretted a single thing. These few remaining days are a gift. Why would we not spend them together?"

"But they said I can't tell you," Peltrin protested. "And if I do tell you, you probably won't let me go." He glanced at the bloodstains that still covered the floor. It was a stark reminder that his home would never be the same.

"Give us a chance, Peltrin," said Bensil, his eyes were kind. "Tell us your story. If you want to leave there is no one here with the ability to stop you. I know you were told not to tell, but what does your heart tell you. Do you honestly believe keeping a secret from us will improve your chances?"

"The part about not telling you felt wrong," Peltrin admitted. "But what if I'm wrong?"

"It's entirely possible you will be wrong in telling us," Bensil conceded. "But it is also entirely possible you will be wrong in not telling us… correct?"

"I guess," Peltrin murmured.

"You have no evidence either way?"

"All I know is what they told me," he admitted.

"In the absence of hard evidence, what better guide could you have than your own heart?" asked Bensil.

"But how do I know I can trust my heart?" asked Peltrin. He felt weak and vulnerable asking such a question. Until yesterday, confidence had been as much a part of him as his arms or his legs.

"We trust your heart," answered Nirani. "Far more than we trust a stranger."

"That goes for all of us," confirmed Perwin.

Sighing, Peltrin gave in. It took only a few minutes to tell them what had happened. He didn't say anything about the dark thoughts or the dark presence, and he skipped the part where he had cried on the floor of the cave. He wasn't sure how to describe the darkness and the crying was too embarrassing to talk about, even with his family.

Peltrin let out deep breath of relief when he finished. In a way, he was relieved they had persuaded him. He hadn't felt right about keeping it all a secret from them.

"I don't know," Nirani repeated. She had said those words, or something similar, several times during Peltrin's story. "I'm excited about the possibility of finding a cure, but I'm not convinced we can trust the bat or the mirror."

"The idea of a panacea seems too good to be true," Perwin said skeptically. "I would have been far more inclined to believe if the mirror had promised something specifically for the devastor poison. That alone would be a miracle. People who promise too much and ask for too little are typically lying, usually because they want something from you."

"But it didn't ask for anything," Peltrin pointed out.

"That worries me as well," said Perwin, "the mirror made it sound like you would eventually pay a very steep price. The mirror also seemed fairly confident the payment was unavoidable."

"Why did you have to go in through all the ice and water?" Beorn asked. "Couldn't the bat have led you in through the wind cave?"

It was a valid question. The way out after consulting the mirror had been far easier than the way in. Come to think of it, Peltrin was reasonably confident he could make it back to the mirror without the bat if he ever wanted to.

"Maybe it was some sort of test?" the boy guessed.

"I wish I understood its motivation," Perwin mused. "I just don't understand what the bat or the mirror stand to gain. If they wanted you to succeed, they should have given you more information. But if they wanted you to fail, why bother to tell you anything at all?"

There was a long pause as everyone tried to guess at the possibilities.

"Peltrin, your father and I need to talk in private," Nirani said finally. "Beorn and Bensil can stay, but we need you to wait outside."

"What? No!" he protested. "You only say that when you want to think of a way to say no." Peltrin was beginning to think the mirror had been right. Now that he had told them, he might not be able to go at all.

She didn't bother to answer verbally. She just gave him a look and Peltrin stomped out the front door.

"He's not leaving," said Nirani, immediately after Peltrin closed the door. "We're all staying here together."

"I think the mirror assumed we wouldn't know Valdor's story as well as we do," said Perwin. "Beorn and I have a history with Valdor that goes back to when father was still alive. I don't know everything that happened at the Fyllcarcern, but I know it ruined him. Years have gone by and he still hasn't fully recovered."

"I hadn't thought of this before," said Bensil, "but knowing Valdor's story is also how we know the Fyllcarcern might have the power to cure the poison."

Nirani gave him a look that made the old healer cringe.

"I'm not advocating for him to go," the little Canbi said defensively, "That's your decision, not mine. I'm just saying there is a real possibility it might work."

"Perhaps," said Perwin, "But it's not worth the risk. If Peltrin were poisoned as well, I would be in favor of him going. As things are, the three of us know we are going to die, but at least we die knowing that Peltrin is going to live."

Nirani choked and covered her face. Perwin saw her reaction and wished there was something he could do to comfort her.

Unable to get out of bed and go to his wife, he continued. "It isn't logical for him to risk his life for the very small possibility he might be able to save the rest of us. He isn't going to die; we should keep it that way."

"Peltrin needs to go." said Nirani.

They all looked at her in surprise. Even Perwin wouldn't have guessed she would ever consider letting Peltrin go. She was still covering half her face. A stray tear leaked between her fingers.

QUESTIONS

"I want him here," she clarified. "But this isn't about what I want. This is about what is best for him. Sitting around and waiting for all of us to die would be horrible."

"But that is exactly what we did when my parents died," said Perwin. "As I remember, it was good for all of us."

"Thettlemar died of devastor poison?" asked Bensil.

"Aramir sent devastors for Peltrin and Berin years ago," Perwin explained. "They were spending the night at their grandparents' house. It was pure luck that Thettlemar walked into the room at exactly the right moment. Father took on ten of those monsters with his bare hands. Two of them had red eyes. Mother heard the commotion and came to help. The boys were okay, but my parents were both poisoned."

"Peltrin and Berin didn't remember, thank goodness," said Nirani.

"How could they possibly forget something like that?" asked Bensil.

"They were only six years old," said Beorn. "The next morning, they were both very confused. The experience had been so strange that neither of them believed it was real. They both told us it was a bad dream and we decided not to correct them."

"Our last few days with your parents were different," said Nirani. "We didn't feel responsible. Peltrin believes he is the reason we are all going to die."

Perwin looked at his wife. "I don't understand, Nirani. I know he wants to go, but why would we let him take the risk?"

"I want him here," she said again, coming over to the bed and taking his hand. "But not if it's hurting him. In a way, it would be like dying with us. I don't even want to say this, but I think we need to think of it that way. I think we need to make this decision as if Peltrin were poisoned."

Perwin was silent for a long time. He looked closely at his wife, searching for further explanation. "If we are thinking of it that way, then he should go."

"I don't think he should go alone," said Nirani. "I know the mirror told him he could only succeed alone, but that's ridiculous. I don't believe it for one minute."

"The three of you can't go," Bensil pointed out, "and the rest of the town is boarding up their windows and doors. They are terrified for their own families."

"They're in no danger," Beorn grumbled angrily. "Don't they know a red-eyed devastor only has a single target at a time?"

"They know you were targeted," Bensil answered, "But they don't know why. I am the only one here besides you who knows your past. As far as they know, Aramir is now targeting ordinary farmers. They have no idea Aramir has been searching for you for years."

"Can you use your agreement to send the wolves with Peltrin?" Perwin asked. "If more of Aramir's servants are sent, they might be sent after him. Aldayin will be safe enough without the wolves. We can barricade the doors and windows until he returns."

"Perhaps," said Bensil, "as it happens, they viewed this attack as an embarrasing loss on their part. They are more willing than usual to be helpful right now."

"How do you do that?" asked Beorn.

"Do what?" Bensil looked genuinely confused.

"Keep the wolves in your debt." Beorn waved his arms emphatically as if it were the most obvious question in the world. "They promise to never hurt the people or the livestock of Aldayin, they promise to hunt devastors, now you're sending them off on missions. How do you do it?"

"They are not mine to command," clarified Bensil, "they are wild animals. All wolves generally avoid humans. Devastors and wolves have always been natural enemies. Avoiding the livestock requires some self-control on their part, but they are proficient enough hunters that it doesn't present much difficulty for them. Also, the agreement benefits them greatly."

"But what do you do for them?" Beorn persisted.

"Keeping their secret happens to be part of the agreement," answered Bensil.

"But you're sure they would be willing to go along for protection?" Perwin asked.

"I can't make any promises until I have spoken with them," said Bensil, "but I do think it is very likely. I would like to go with him myself. I would except I have patients who need me here. At the very least I can send my apprentices."

"I would like that very much," said Nirani. "Aralis was wonderful for me yesterday."

"She is a very good listener," Bensil agreed. "and she is quite accomplished as a healer. She has other skills as well, though she tends to keep them to herself."

"Other skills?" asked Perwin.

"They are hers to share, not mine," replied Bensil. "To be honest, I don't think she knows I am aware of these skills. Suffice it to say that, although she is accomplished as a healer, it is possible her heart will take her another way.

"Soyem will, perhaps, be less useful than Aralis, but he is strong enough and competent enough that he won't be a burden. He is a good boy and he looks up to Peltrin. He's fairly certain some adventure will make his life infinitely better. It will be interesting to see if anything changes when he gets a dose of exactly what he thinks he wants."

The other three all nodded their agreement.

"If they're going to do this," said Perwin, "they should go to Valdor first, no matter what the mirror says. He isn't what he used to be. He's certainly broken in many ways, but I am certain he is still a good man."

"I think you're right," Nirani said, "I'm not convinced I trust the mirror, but going to the Fyllcarcern feels necessary. Going to Valdor first feels right as well. Do you know anything about the guardian, Bensil?"

"Not much," Bensil confessed, "from the little Valdor told me after his wife and daughter died, it sounds like the guardian is some sort of shapeshifter who protects the Fyllcarcern. I have no idea if it will be any more helpful or trustworthy than the mirror."

"I don't think there's much more to be said," said Perwin after a short pause. "We can talk about this for days, but if he is to have any hope of success, Peltrin and the others need to leave this afternoon." He looked at his wife, "are you sure we are thinking of this the right way? I'm only in favor of them going because, as you suggested, I am thinking of this as if Peltrin's life were in danger as well as ours."

"Yes," she said. She still looked unhappy about the idea but there was no hesitation in her voice.

"Shall we tell Peltrin, then?" asked Perwin with a sigh.

The others all nodded their heads.

"Yes!" said Peltrin, pumping his fist as he walked in the door uninvited. "Um…I mean…what did you decide?"

"No worries, everyone," Lou called from the front door. "I'll be with him every step of the way. Success is inevitable!"

"Stop pretending, young man," Nirani scolded Peltrin. "We all know that you and the lieutenant were listening by the kitchen window for the last half of the conversation."

"Did you know that?" Beorn asked his brother quietly.

"I had no idea," Perwin answered under his breath.

"Since you already know," Nirani went on, "you might as well start packing. I'll get some food together."

QUESTIONS

"Perfect!" cheered Lou, "a mission without proper supplies is a mission guaranteed to fail. Nirani is second to none when it comes to food preparation, we all know that!"

Nirani couldn't stop the corners of her mouth from turning up a little as she continued talking to Peltrin. "You will need to leave right after the burial. The day will already be half gone by the time you three get on your way."

"The mirror told me to go alone," Peltrin reminded them. "Lou and Aralis and Soyem can't come with me. The wolves can't protect me. I can't get help from Valdor, either."

"Absolutely not," Nirani countered. "I don't care what the mirror said. I refuse to let you go alone."

"But…" Peltrin protested.

"No!" Nirani didn't even wait for the Peltrin to finish. Her face was set in stone.

"Your mother's right," said Perwin. "We will only allow you to go if you agree to let the others help you and if you promise to go to Valdor's house along the way."

Peltrin hesitated. He wanted to point out, as Bensil had, that his parents and Beorn were injured, and no one else in Aldayin was even close to Peltrin's level of skill as a fighter. If Peltrin decided to go alone, there was no one to stop him.

"I'll let them come with me," he said finally. "And I'll go to Valdor's house before we go to the Fyllcarcern."

The tension in the room eased. The adults all knew Peltrin would keep his word.

"If you leave soon after midday," said Bensil, "you can get to Valdor's house by tomorrow and to the Fyllcarcern by the next day. The way isn't difficult to find. I'll give Aralis a map and provide her the necessary directions."

"They just finished digging the graves," said Peltrin, his eyes watered slightly. "We can start the burial any time now."

Beorn coughed and cleared his throat several times.

"Then we should go on with the burial right away," said Bensil. "As soon as it is over, I'll tell Aralis and Soyem to get their things together and I'll consult with the wolves about whether or not they would be willing to provide protection."

"Tell Aralis and Soyem to come here when they are ready," Nirani instructed, "I'll have food ready for them and I have some things I need to speak with Aralis about before they go."

"What things?" asked Beorn curiously, lifting his head a little.

"None of your business things," she answered, giving him a stern look.

"Right," he said, setting his head back down again.

Burials in Aldayin tended to be short, simple affairs. This was normal among the people who lived in the hidden towns of the Pichari mountains. There was no singing or long speeches and there were no ceremonial burial clothes or rituals. To the Canbi, the lack of emotion was cold-hearted. To the Ennai, the lack of ritual was disrespectful. To the Pichari, it was an appropriate way to remember their loved ones.

Once the bodies were placed in the graves, each person had an opportunity to say something. Beorn only blustered, completely unashamed, as tears poured down his face. He and Perwin had been helped outside and were sitting on the ground. Several people, including Perwin and Nirani, spoke of Berin's courage and strength and Besla's kindness and thoughtfulness. Peltrin, afraid he might cry in front of everyone and embarrass himself, was among those who chose not to say anything.

Finally, the bodies were buried and the short service was ended. Many paused to give the survivors a few kind words of comfort. Several people laid pansies on the graves.

QUESTIONS

"Every flower has a meaning," Peltrin mumbled to himself. Pansies typically represented thoughtfulness and remembrance. They were common at Pichari funerals.

After getting instructions from Bensil, Aralis and Soyem went back to Bensil's house to prepare to leave. Aralis was ready in minutes, but Soyem had to pack his bag three separate times. He just couldn't fit everything he "needed." Finally, Aralis packed his bag for him, leaving the majority of his things scattered on the floor.

"What about the rest of my stuff," he protested.

"You don't need it," she answered sternly. "Go. Now."

They had been apprentices together long enough that Soyem knew better than to argue.

By the time they arrived, Peltrin was already packed. He wore his short sword and a tomahawk on his belt. He also had several throwing knives hidden in his clothes. His bow was still broken. Despite Lou and Perwin's urging that Peltrin take Perwin's bow, Peltrin decided to go without.

Peltrin's pack included everything he would need, as well as most of the food the three of them would need for the short journey. There was also a large pocket on the outside of his pack for the lieutenant to ride in. Soyem was relieved he didn't have to carry the animal. The large yellow-bellied marmot was a significant portion of the weight in Peltrin's pack.

Nirani gave packets of food to Soyem and Aralis. Aralis noticed her packet of food was easily larger than Soyem's but decided not to say anything. Even with the lightest pack, he was likely to be the slowest. Soyem noticed that the food made his pack really, really heavy. Luckily, Aralis had anticipated that Soyem would need room for food and had left enough open space for his share.

"What about the wolves?" asked Nirani.

"They have agreed," answered Bensil.

"I still want to know how he does that," grumbled Beorn.

"The two largest wolves can talk," Bensil explained to Peltrin, ignoring Beorn, "but don't be surprised if you don't see them often. Also, it is more likely they will wander around the forest, rather than stay close to you. Rest assured they will be there if you need them."

"Do we need to tell them when we are leaving?" Peltrin asked

"I told them who to watch for and which direction you would be going. They watch all of the comings and goings in Aldayin much more closely than you realize. For ordinary wolves, knowing when you leave and where you are as you travel would be a menial task. These two are the greatest of their kind, in every possible way."

"What do you mean by, 'in every possible way?'" Nirani asked.

"Larger, stronger, more effective hunters, more cunning, and so on," answered Bensil. "It may sound like bragging, but it's the simple truth. Fang is the size of a small horse. Fangmort, Fang's older brother, is somewhat smaller but he is still much larger than any ordinary wolf, and is even more cunning than his brother."

"Doesn't sound like they will be entertaining as traveling companions," said Perwin, "but I can't imagine better protectors."

"There is also a small pack of wolves who follow their orders," said Bensil. "If you see an ordinary wolf wandering around, don't be alarmed. Remember, these two wolves agreed only to ensure your safety. Be very careful if you try to ask for anything more. They are not bound to obey you. There is nothing more offensive to them than the idea of becoming domesticated."

"I thought wolf packs were all about territory," said Beorn, "what happens if they encounter another pack?"

Bensil chuckled, "typically the lead wolves, or alphas, challenge each other. Can you imagine any ordinary wolf challenging Fang or Fangmort? These two brothers can go where they like without fear."

QUESTIONS

"Can Fang and Fangmort climb trees?" asked Peltrin.

"They cannot," Bensil admitted. "Now that they know devastors can climb trees, the wolves will be watching. But if they detect anything in the trees, they will have to wait for the creatures to come down."

Peltrin looked like he wanted to ask more questions but Perwin cut him off. "It's time for you to go," he said. "Time is so short. We can't afford to sit here talking all day."

Nirani and Aralis came back into the house. Nirani had discretely pulled Aralis aside and talked to her alone while the others discussed the wolves.

Nirani put her hand on her son's shoulder, "Peltrin, I am concerned about the scratch on your neck. It isn't big, but I think it will get infected if we're not careful. I've asked Aralis to check it and change the bandages regularly."

Aralis nodded her head. She looked as if the idea bothered her for some reason.

"Would you like me to look at it?" offered Bensil. "If it needs special attention, I may be able to demonstrate something for Aralis that she hasn't learned yet."

"It's just a scratch," Nirani answered. "I'm sure it's well within Aralis' abilities."

"I could help!" offered Soyem.

"Not this time," Nirani answered. "I don't doubt your skills, but I gave Aralis some special instructions. It is a little family secret I'd prefer she didn't share."

"Oh really?" Bensil looked extremely interested.

"Of course, I'll share it with you later," she said.

The old man's face brightened. The idea of some new herb or technique to add to his impressive store of knowledge always made him excited.

"Do you know what the family secret is?" Soyem asked Peltrin.

"I have no idea what they are talking about," said Peltrin.

Soyem felt a little better. It seemed a little silly that only Aralis could know the family secret. It would have been much worse if Peltrin knew the secret and Soyem was alone in ignorance.

"All secrets should be known by the leader," said Lou from Peltrin's pack. "Someone needs to tell me what is going on here.

"Very well, then," Perwin said, "come here, lieutenant."

Peltrin took off his pack and put it on the floor. Lou scurried out of the pocket, across the floor, and up into the bed, where he sat on Perwin's shoulder.

Nirani leaned in close as well.

"Peltrin's confidence is low after what happened yesterday," Perwin said softly.

"I understand," the lieutenant answered loudly and importantly.

"Your orders are to do anything you can to remedy the situation," Perwin was talking quietly enough that only Nirani couldn't hear. "Don't tell any of the youths about your role in resolving the issue."

"Of course, sir, you can count on me." The lieutenant gave a salute with one of his front paws. He then scurried back over to Peltrin's pack and into his pocket.

"That has nothing to do with what I told Aralis," Nirani said quietly to Perwin as Peltrin moved away."

"I didn't think so," said Perwin, giving her a wink. "But it seemed like a good idea, and it will keep Lou from pestering Aralis."

"I hope it really turns out to be a good thing," Nirani answered quietly, "it's hard to guess what Lou will come up with."

Peltrin was anxious to get out the door so the farewells were quick. A quick embrace from Nirani and a few words from each of the others and they were out the door. Nirani and Bensil stood at the door and watched until they disappeared into the trees.

Old Bensil was smiling as they disappeared.

"You seem happy to see them go," said Nirani. She had tears in her eyes.

"I'm happy to see them together," said Bensil, "though I certainly wish it were under better circumstances. Peltrin is Pichari, Aralis is Ennai, and Soyem is Canbi. They represent each of the three races of Amyriad. It pleases me to see them together, completely unaware of the social problems between their races in places like Triobolis."

"It is a nice thought," Nirani agreed, smiling a little herself.

"Also, Soyem and Aralis are both orphans," Bensil went on, "their parents were victims of the war that Perwin, Beorn, and Thettlemar fought in so many years ago. It also pleases me to see them living their lives so well despite the struggles of their past."

Nirani nodded her agreement and the two of them went back into the house.

"Are they gone?" asked Perwin, as Bensil and Nirani reentered the house.

"Yes," answered Nirani, showing more than a few tears she had been holding back.

"Then we need to start making preparations," said Perwin. "Once the wolves are gone, we will be vulnerable. The three of them, on the other hand, should be quite safe."

"Are you expecting another attack?" asked Bensil.

"We are not dead yet," said Perwin. "And we are extremely vulnerable."

"But there's nothing more to be done here," said Bensil, "I don't mean to be insensitive but, unless Peltrin succeeds, you three will be dead in a few days. It seems like Aramir should focus all of his energy on Peltrin."

"I think it's a good idea to assume Aramir doesn't know the extent of our injuries," said Perwin. "And I doubt he suspects Peltrin is off to search for a cure. If I were in his place, I would assume we were sending Peltrin somewhere where he would be better protected. Even if he does find out we've all been wounded, patience has never been one Aramir's stronger attributes."

"I can stay to help," offered Bensil.

They all looked at the thin, shriveled old man who had never been trained in any form of fighting. There was a slight pause.

"If we are attacked," said Nirani, "you could get injured or killed, or you could be trapped here in the house with the rest of us. With both of your apprentices off with Peltrin, Aldayin will be left without a healer.

Bensil's shoulders slumped. "I don't suppose I would be much help anyway," he admitted. There are two babies to be born any day now, a farmer with a broken arm, and a small boy with a fever. Who knows what else will come up in the next few days?"

"Just give us what herbs we need to get by for these next few days," said Perwin, "and then you probably better leave. It would be better if the devastors don't even catch your scent."

"Of course," said Bensil. "I have nothing for the venom, as you already know, but it would be wise to dress those wounds regularly to prevent infection and help them heal faster." He began digging things out of his bag and placing them on the table.

"Perhaps I can give you something you can use for your secret family remedy," Bensil looked hopeful.

"Not today," said Nirani, "But I promise you will have it. If nothing else, Aralis has permission to share it with you when they get back."

"Very well," he said, disappointed. "My scent won't be a problem though, there are a number of herbs with odors animals detest. I use several of them regularly."

"That explains the smell," Beorn mumbled, referring to the terrible odor that always followed the old man wherever he went. Beorn thought he was talking quietly but, as usual, he wasn't.

"It explains why rodents don't disturb my herbs," Bensil answered a little defensively. "It also explains why I can go from house to house in the middle of the night without fear of being attacked by animals."

"Never mind that," said Nirani, giving Beorn a look. "There's nothing wrong with using your skills to keep yourself safe. But for now, you need to get going, and I need to get to work."

CHAPTER 7: DECISIONS

Inevitably, the funeral was still heavy on their minds as Peltrin, Aralis, and Soyem began their walk in somber silence. Lou had quickly fallen asleep and was breathing loudly from his large pocket in Peltrin's pack.

It took less than an hour to pass through the sparsely spaced houses that made up the town of Aldayin. The fields, normally littered with people and work animals, were empty. The shutters to every house were closed and locked.

"Not a lot of excitement here today," mumbled Soyem. "Not that Aldayin is ever an exciting place, but at least there's usually people around."

"They're afraid," said Aralis. Her eyes were scanning the forest. She looked intense and surprisingly unafraid. Her face looked to Peltrin more like the face of a hunter than the face of the hunted.

"They're safe," said Peltrin. "Aramir won't be sending devastors after anyone else."

"Everything is back to the usual boring," said Soyem. "It's just a matter of time before everyone figures it out."

High in the trees, a bat with glowing eyes watched as the three youths entered the forest. It watched them for a few moments, and then silently flew away.

It was only a matter of minutes before the conversation fell flat. Peltrin didn't feel like talking and Aralis, as usual, had little to say. Not long after they left Aldayin and entered the forest, however, Soyem was getting uncomfortable. He was the first to break the silence.

"Peltrin, why are we going to the Fyllcarcern?"

Peltrin didn't know where to begin. The adults had been skeptical of his story about the cave. He suspected Soyem and Aralis would be the same.

"Bensil said it was because of something you learned from a cave," Soyem prodded, "and now we're supposed to go to some old guy named Valdor, and then to the Fyllcarcern. But that's all we know."

"I don't want to talk about it right now," said Peltrin, still deep in thought and mourning. "Besides, I'm not sure I should tell you. I was supposed to do this alone."

"Keeping information like this to yourself would be ill-advised," said Lou sleepily. "We must be united in purpose. We cannot do that if there are secrets between us."

"It's not a secret," said Peltrin. "I just don't want to talk about it right now."

"Please," said Aralis quietly.

Peltrin looked at her soft brown eyes and relented. He took a deep breath and told the story exactly as he had told the adults. Again, he left out the thoughts, the cold darkness, and the crying.

"Where is the bat now?" asked Soyem when Peltrin had finished. "You would think it would stick around to help."

"I don't think we need the bat anymore," said Peltrin, feeling a little defensive. The instructions from the mirror had given him hope. Not enough to totally hide his shame, but enough he was able to function again. He didn't like that the adults, and now Soyem, were doubting whether the bat and the mirror were trustworthy.

"But why did it tell you and not the others?" Soyem persisted, "and why did it drag you through the whole cave ordeal? Why couldn't the bat just talk to the mirror and then bring you the message? It's not like the message was long and complicated. Why…"

"I don't know!" Peltrin shouted. Soyem cringed. Peltrin felt a little guilty, but not enough to apologize. They resumed walking in silence.

DECISIONS

Over the next few hours, Soyem and Lou made several more attempts to start a conversation but Peltrin and Aralis had refused to join in. Soyem even attempted singing a song, but his less-than-impressive singing voice, combined with comments and cold stares from the others, had ended the song rather quickly.

They had been traveling in the forest for hours before Peltrin first detected the wolves. It was little more than a shuffle in the bushes well away from the trail. Peltrin glanced in that direction only to catch a flash of grey. He didn't see much, but what he did see was far larger than any ordinary wolf. He wondered which of the two brothers this would be. From Bensil's descriptions, he guessed it was fang, the larger of the two. Fangmort, Bensil had said, was somewhat smaller and more cunning.

"Why do you keep looking at the ridge?" asked Aralis some time later. She caught Peltrin looking at the ridge to their left for the fourth time in as many minutes.

"There are people up there," said Peltrin. "I think they are watching us." He had considered lying so she wouldn't be afraid, but he doubted she would appreciate that.

"Why would they be watching us?" asked Soyem. He sounded concerned.

"No idea," Peltrin answered honestly. "I've seen at least three, but there's probably more. For all I know, there could be hundreds of them hiding on the other side of the ridge."

"Could they be a scouting party for an army?"

"I doubt it," he said, furrowing his brow and looking at the ridgeline again. "They're pretty sloppy. I saw the first one because he was standing up on top of the ridge right out in the open. It's more likely they are a group of thieves."

"Do you think they will try to rob us?" There was a slight grin tugging at the corners of his mouth. "I'm kind of hoping they do."

"How could that be a good thing?" Peltrin asked, surprised.

"I've seen you train," he answered, "and Bensil has told us about what you and your family do to keep Aldayin safe. It won't go well for them."

"Put me down!" Lou insisted. "We need intel."

Peltrin put the pack down. He made a show of retrieving his canteen, just in case someone was watching. Lou slipped out of the pocket and disappeared into the grass.

"Aren't the wolves supposed to protect us?" asked Soyem.

"From devastors," said Peltrin, "I don't know if they agreed to protect us from people. Either way, it doesn't hurt to send Lou out to take a look. I'd like to be prepared just in case the wolves decide it's not their job." Part of Peltrin hoped the wolves would let him deal with the people. After his repeated failures yesterday, he was looking forward to a fight he could win.

"Try not to look at the ridgeline," Peltrin instructed the others a few minutes later. He'd noticed Soyem stop to stare at least four times. "If it turns out they are thieves, it would be better if they think we don't know they are watching us."

Aralis didn't look up directly, but she continued to watch the ridge closely out of the corner of her eye.

Soyem struggled to follow the instruction.

Peltrin considered leaving the trail and disappearing into the woods to make themselves more difficult to follow, but he was certain it would slow them down too much. Getting the panacea and returning on time was the only thing that mattered.

"It will be dark soon," said Aralis, several hours later. "We need a place to sleep and firewood."

"Let's keep going," said Peltrin, a little surprised that Aralis had broken the silence. Until now, she had been content to let Soyem do most of the talking. "We'll get there sooner if we travel after dark."

"In the dark?" Aralis looked horrified. "Why?"

"We won't get there until tomorrow either way," Soyem added.

"And dinner," Lou called, emerging from the bushes. It was the first they had seen him in hours. "Delaying dinner would be unacceptable. Definitely thieves, by the way. I counted six, though I can't guarantee there aren't others."

"Another reason to keep going," Peltrin insisted. "It will get us away from the thieves. Besides, we need to get there as soon as possible. We can give up a little sleep to get there sooner."

"The sooner we get there, the better," Peltrin insisted. "we can give up a little sleep to get there sooner."

"Bensil and your mother sent us to keep an eye on you," said Aralis. "You need to sleep."

"Fine," Peltrin conceded. He had never seen Aralis so insistent before. "When it gets dark, we'll stop for sleep. But we're not stopping until then, and we're not going to bother with firewood. It will take too much time."

"We need a fire," said Aralis with finality.

"We need food," Lou reminded them.

"The wolves are watching out for us," Peltrin insisted. "If anything, a fire and hot food just makes us more vulnerable. It will draw the attention of other things that might be roaming the forest." By "other things," they all knew he was referring to devastors, as well as the potential thieves.

"We must have a fire," Aralis insisted.

Peltrin noticed something in her eyes. "Are you afraid of the dark?"

"No," she ducked her head slightly and looked at the ground.

"Liar," said Soyem with a smirk. "If you won't admit it yourself, then I'll tell him."

"Don't you dare!" said Aralis, anger building.

Soyem moved behind Peltrin. "She's not afraid of the dark if she is in the house or next to a fire," he explained.

Aralis took a step forward and Soyem cowered a little lower behind Peltrin.

"But she is terrified of being in the forest at night. Even if someone else is with her."

"Stop!" she stepped forward angrily.

Peltrin didn't immediately respond. He was a bit surprised. When he suggested walking at night, he had expected Soyem to protest. It hadn't even occurred to him that Aralis would be afraid of the dark.

"She won't even go with Bensil when someone needs a healer in the middle of the night."

Aralis' face was filled with fury, "one more word…"

"Let's get some firewood," interrupted Peltrin, "we'll camp for the night."

Aralis' face softened and Soyem stopped cowering. They both turned and looked at him in surprise.

"We crossed a stream not long ago," Peltrin said, "it should be right over there. Let's see if we can find a flat spot away from the trail and near the water."

Not long ago, Peltrin would have continued to insist. But he couldn't disregard someone else's fears anymore. Not after experiencing for himself how terrible fear can be.

Aralis continued to glare at Soyem from time to time as they prepared for the night, but he didn't say anything more.

As soon as Peltrin put his pack down, Lou jumped out and disappeared into the bushes. "Get dinner going," Lou ordered, "I've been smelling it all day and I'm ready to eat."

"Where are you going?" asked Peltrin.

"To fulfill my mission," the marmot answered energetically. "The leader's got to do what the leader's got to do."

DECISIONS

"Wolves…pssst…hey wolves," Lou called after he was well out of earshot from the youths.

"What's this?" asked a gravely, rough voice. "Has Peltrin's pet escaped?"

Two large wolves emerged from the bushes. One was twice the size of any ordinary wolf. The other was nearly as large as a horse.

"This forest is a dangerous place for woodchucks," warned Fangmort, the smaller of the two.

"I hear there are wolves in the area," said Fang. "I'd hate for Peltrin's juicy little groundhog to get eaten."

"I'm not a woodchuck or a groundhog," Lou protested nervously. "Actually, woodchucks and groundhogs are the same thing. I am a yellow-bellied marmot. Sometimes people call us rockchucks." He stood on his hind legs and picked up a small rock.

"You can call yourself whatever you want," said Fang, coming closer. "What I want to know is whether or not I would call you…tasty." He finished the sentence with a toothy grin, only inches from the lieutenant's face.

"Not that I've ever understood why," Lou went on nervously. "I've never seen a woodchuck chuck wood, although I have been known to occasionally chuck a rock, so maybe the name isn't completely wrong in my case."

By now, Fangmort had approached as well and the two wolves were circling.

"Anyway," Lou said, trembling a little. "I'm just here to make sure we're clear on responsibilities. Since we are all here to keep the kids safe."

"Does the pet have responsibilities?" asked Fangmort mockingly.

"Of course he does," answered Fang. "He's here as a meal. It saves us the trouble of looking for a snack."

Lou cleared his throat nervously. "Um…well…no. I just wanted to be sure you knew that you are only responsible for devastors or other magical-type beings. If anyone else were to come along—ordinary people, that is—you are supposed to let me and Peltrin handle them."

"We promised the old man we would keep them safe," said Fang. "If anything happens to them, we don't get our reward."

"Yes, well, the old man told me to tell you that your agreement only applies to devastors and other such magical beings." Lou was stuttering a little, but he was putting on a decent show.

Fangmort moved in close and sniffed. "You're either very afraid or you are lying," he said. "It's hard to tell with a woodchuck."

"I'm a rockchuck…and I'm telling the truth," Lou asserted.

"Very well," said Fangmort. "We won't bother with the people."

"Great," said Lou, scampering away. "By the way, I counted six people. How many people have you seen?"

"There's a group of six who just came down from the ridge," Fangmort confirmed. "They smelled of trouble."

"Perfect!" said Lou as he ran back toward the camp for all he was worth.

Later they sat around the fire, eating hot stew. Nirani had packed all of the ingredients such that Peltrin only had to boil water and add the different ingredients at prescribed intervals. Peltrin didn't mind helping in the kitchen, but he was certainly no expert. He was particularly pleased when the stew turned out to be excellent.

They were sitting contentedly, mopping up the last of the stew with flatbread when Peltrin's head snapped up. The others looked at him questioningly.

"Lou," said Peltrin.

Lou disappeared into the forest, taking another flatbread as he left.

DECISIONS

Aralis and Soyem stared at each other wide-eyed, wondering what was going on.

Lou reappeared a few minutes later. "There's six of them," he said quietly. "They're looking for us but they went right past the spot where we left the trail."

"Do you think they'll find us," asked Aralis.

"They should have found us already," Peltrin answered, feeling a little guilty for his carelessness. "We didn't even try to cover our tracks and we're camping near the trail with a fire. We should have been easy to find but it looks like they don't have any idea what they're doing."

"Where are the wolves?" asked Soyem, "aren't they supposed to be protecting us?"

"I think they're still around," said Peltrin. "There are some huge fresh wolf tracks down by the stream. But they're holding back. I think they're letting us handle these people on our own."

"Not their responsibility," said Lou. "They are on magical creature duty only."

"What do we do?" asked Soyem, concern in his voice. His earlier confidence in Peltrin seemed to have faded a little.

"I'm not afraid to fight people," Peltrin assured him. "I've helped tracked down and deal with thieves before. Some of them were pretty good." He didn't mention the fact that he had never done that without his father and Beorn. It would just make them nervous.

Soyem seemed very relieved at the reminder that Peltrin had done this before. Peltrin looked at Aralis, but she didn't look afraid, she looked calm, and maybe even a little excited. Again, she reminded him of a hunter, waiting for its prey to arrive.

Peltrin looked around the area. The fire made their position obvious. Any minute now the intruders would pass through the trail of smoke. As incompetent as they were, Peltrin couldn't imagine they would miss the smoke and the smell of stew."

"Aralis, you sit by that tree over there," said Peltrin, pointing to a large tree. "And Soyem, you sit over there." He pointed to a large bush. The two complied.

"Okay good. Lou, I need you to spy on the thieves. Let me know just before they get here."

Lou stared hard at Peltrin.

"Relax, Lou," Peltrin said. "I'm making a plan right now. I'll take care of these six the same way we did the last group."

"That will work." The marmot saluted and disappeared into the bushes.

Peltrin started visualizing dozens of possibilities. He wasn't used to doing this by himself. He also wasn't accustomed to having two people to protect.

Changing Aralis and Soyem's positions eliminated several situations he didn't like. In particular, it made it impossible for the thieves to immediately grab Aralis or Soyem from behind and force Peltrin to put down his weapons.

"Most likely," explained Peltrin, "only one or two will come into the firelight at first. The others will probably try to sneak up on us"

"How do you know?" asked Soyem.

Peltrin ignored the question. "If you hear me say 'wait,' Aralis will go there," he pointed to another tree, "and Soyem will go there," he pointed to another bush. He then identified third positions for both of them and had them repeat back the instructions.

"But when do we attack?" asked Aralis.

"Don't attack," instructed Peltrin. "If you attack, there's a chance you will get hurt. There's only six, and more than likely they are all untrained.

The most important thing for you two is to stay out of reach. When I'm ready to attack, I'll say 'now.'"

"Then what do we do?" asked Soyem.

"Stay still," answered Peltrin. "That's when I'll be throwing knives or something. The last thing we need is for you to move into the line of fire."

"So that's your plan?" asked Soyem, "Move when you say 'wait' and stay still when you say 'now?'"

Peltrin nodded his head, ignoring Soyem's skepticism. The best plans were kept simple, he reminded himself. The instructions were simple, but they went over them again, just to be sure. Soyem was skeptical, but Aralis seemed willing to go with Peltrin's plan.

Lou came back a few minutes later shaking his head. "They're right over there," he said, "and they're ridiculously sloppy. If you listen closely you can hear them arguing."

They were silent for a moment. They could hear dim voices in the still night air.

"What do we do now?" asked Soyem, fear mounting. Aralis looked focused but unafraid.

"Just talk, and pretend you have no idea they are coming," Peltrin answered. "And don't forget the instructions."

They stared at each other for an awkward moment. They were all obviously thinking about the thieves. It was surprising how difficult it is to start a conversation when they couldn't talk about what they were all thinking about.

"Why are you afraid of being in the dark in the forest?" asked Peltrin.

Aralis gave him a warning look, not answering.

"No, really," Soyem said, "it doesn't make any sense, especially if someone like me is around. You are probably the fastest runner I know. If a bear or mountain lion or something attacked, you would outrun me, and I would get eaten."

Peltrin smirked and Aralis rolled her eyes.

"It may surprise you to know," Soyem went on, "that being with me is better protection than being with Peltrin."

"What, how?" asked Peltrin, a little offended.

"Well, you two are both fast," explained Soyem. "So, if something big and scary comes after you and you both start running, who knows who is going to turn out to be fastest, right? So, if Peltrin turns out to be faster, then Aralis gets eaten. With me, Aralis gets away safe every time. There you have it, I'm the better protector."

They all laughed.

"I don't really need protection," said Aralis, though she looked more amused than offended.

"I mean, Peltrin's bigger than I am, and he can fight better" Soyem went on. He was clearly enjoying being the center of attention. "But if whatever attacks is really big and scary, it doesn't matter how tall you are, and it doesn't matter how well you fight."

Peltrin and Aralis laughed at him again.

"I have dreams," Aralis said quietly. "I see through the eyes of a predator. Alone in the dark, we are so weak…so vulnerable."

Peltrin could think of many words to describe Aralis. 'Weak' and 'vulnerable' were not among them.

"I've given it a lot of thought," Soyem continued, unwilling to give up the spotlight. "I'm pretty certain I can manage to get eaten by just about anything worth running away from. There you have it, you're always safest with me."

"Thank you Soyem," said Aralis, smiling.

Lou flashed into view, "they're here!" Then he scurried back into the bushes.

Chapter 8: Confrontation

"Why, hello there friends," a strange voice interrupted. "Mind if we join you?" Two Pichari men sauntered into the camp. One of them was tall with a bony frame. The other was round and barely taller than Soyem. Their hair was cut unevenly and their beards were dirty and scraggly.

"We'd rather you didn't," said Peltrin, standing up. His tone was even. He didn't want to sound hostile, but he couldn't imagine these two expected a warm welcome.

"Now that's no way to talk," chided the fat one. "We're just two cold, lonely travelers hoping to share food and fire."

Peltrin could hear shuffling in the forest around the camp and did his best to keep his expression blank. They were so loud he could easily identify the locations of all four of the other would-be thieves. Quickly he began planning the order in which he would take them all out.

"The night is warm enough," Peltrin answered aloud, "you won't freeze to death without our fire. And the word 'share' implies giving as well as taking. As far as we can see, you want our food and our fire, but you don't plan to give us anything."

Three of the four others had stopped moving. It was almost time. His face remained expressionless but he smiled to himself as he settled on his favored plan of attack.

The skinny one sauntered toward Aralis, grinning an ugly, nearly toothless grin. "Well look at this. A pretty little Ennai girl," he glanced at Peltrin and Soyem. "And there's no Ennai man around to get all worked up about me putting my arms around her."

"We can see that you have no intention of sharing anything," said Peltrin, getting angry.

"I think you'll find we have more to share than you think," the skinny stranger said in a low voice, his eyes still glued to Aralis.

"This one's Canbi," said the fat stranger, pointing at Soyem. "Looks to me like all three races are represented here."

Peltrin took a deep breath to calm himself. Only a few more seconds and everything would be right and he could spring into action. A little anger can heighten your strength, but too much anger leads to foolish mistakes. His father had an old Ennai saying for that, but he couldn't remember it right now.

Peltrin decided the skinny man moving toward Aralis would be first. He quickly adjusted the rest of his plan accordingly. Aralis leaned away from the intruder but didn't move. She was looking at Peltrin. Her soft brown eyes were narrow, fearless. She was poised and ready for the signal.

Peltrin slipped out two throwing knives discreetly, placing one in his right hand and one in his left. He didn't like how close the tall one was to Aralis, but he needed to wait just a little longer. Only a few days before, he had waited until Beorn and Perwin were fully distracted before he sprung the attack. This would be no different.

The lanky man moved in closer. He placed his hand on the tree behind her and leaned in. Aralis continued to lean further away, eyes glued to Peltrin. Peltrin heard leaves crunching behind him and grinned. That was what he was waiting for. The last of the thieves had finally moved to a position right behind him.

"I think you should stop," said Peltrin.

"Do you?" asked the lanky man, grinning as he reached for Aralis. The baggy sleeves of his jacket hung loose on his lanky body.

"I think you should stop…now!"

Aralis froze. Two knives appeared out of nowhere, pinning the man's sleeves to the tree behind her.

CONFRONTATION

"Wait!" Peltrin yelled. He then charged into the trees towards one of the assailants. Out of the corner of his eye, he saw Aralis turn and kick the tall man in the groin before running to her second location. The knives in the lanky man's sleeves had pinned him to the tree in a somewhat awkward position. He was unable to do anything to defend himself.

Peltrin chuckled to himself as the man whimpered loudly and his knees buckled. One of the many benefits of running all day for Bensil was Aralis was capable of delivering a very powerful kick.

Soyem was a little slow to pick up on the signal. After seeing Aralis move; however, he quickly moved to his second position as well.

Before Soyem had arrived at his second location, Peltrin encountered the first of the four thugs surrounding the camp. The man was of ordinary height and massively overweight. The man was so surprised he made no move to defend himself as Peltrin sprinted towards him. At a full sprint, Peltrin whipped his head forward. There was a loud crack as Peltrin used the hard part of his skull to bludgeon the man in the temple. The overweight bully crumpled to the ground.

Continuing with his plan exactly as he had visualized it, Peltrin then whirled to his right and charged at the second man, who barely had time to turn in his direction. The stranger swung his sword wildly, but Peltrin dropped to one knee, easily ducking the swing. It was only one of several counterattacks Peltrin had anticipated.

Still low to the ground, Peltrin continued forward, ramming his shoulder into the man's hips and causing him to double over. Peltrin then wrapped his arms around the man's thighs and stood up, lifting him off the ground. There was a hesitation of only a fraction of a second before Peltrin bent forward at the waist. The man was whipped backward, his head bouncing painfully on the ground. Peltrin released the man's legs and went on. The stranger didn't try to get up.

The third was a little quicker than the first two but fared little better. Peltrin snatched up a thick stick from the pile of firewood as he sprinted past. The would-be thief raised a sword to attack, but Peltrin swept it aside easily and clubbed the assailant over the head. There was a soft, high-pitched grunt. This one was a woman, Peltrin thought with surprise. Not that it mattered, she was just as stunned as the men.

Barely breathing hard, Peltrin reentered the clearing. He looked over at the tall, lanky one Aralis had kicked. The man was hanging from his sleeves, still whimpering. Peltrin guessed he would remain limp for some time yet.

He turned towards the short fat one, who took a step backward. There was a loud thump. The round little man's eyes crossed and he fell to the ground. Aralis was standing behind him holding the club-like stick she had used to knock the man out.

Soyem still sat by his bush, his eyes wide. Peltrin couldn't tell if Soyem was terrified of the danger or just excited to watch the fight.

Peltrin then turned to face the final man standing. The man had left the cover of the woods quietly, obviously hoping to attack Peltrin from behind. Like the others, this man was Pichari. He had dark oily hair and a dirty, scraggly beard. Unlike the others; however, he was moderately large and muscular. What's more, he held the sword as if he might actually know what to do with it.

"Looks like it's just you and me, friend," Peltrin said, drawing his relatively short sword.

"The rest will be here soon enough," the man said gruffly. "And these people are all still alive. They'll be up and about and ready to fight by the time I'm done with you. Now put your sword away before I teach you a lesson you'll never forget."

"We all know no one else is coming," Peltrin answered calmly. "And you and I both know these misfits are more than likely to run as soon as they are able." Peltrin then grinned a confident, sideways grin. There is nothing worse for a bully than to know you are not afraid.

"As for teaching me," Peltrin said calmly, "I was hoping you would offer. I've always been a quick learner."

Peltrin was back in his element now, and his usual confidence was returning. He reminded himself to not get too cocky. Overconfidence had been a problem for him in the past.

The large man took a few seconds to size up the situation. This young Pichari and the Ennai girl had incapacitated his entire crew in less than a minute. He glanced in her direction, but the girl appeared content to stay back. The little Canbi boy didn't look at all like a fighter. Despite his advantage in size, the man was sorely tempted to just walk away. The boy was too confident. No one can be that confident in the face of danger without some degree of competence with a sword. A moment of indecision went by.

"Get him, boss," called a shaky voice from the woods.

"Yeah, teach him a lesson," whined another.

That made the decision final. Leadership among these people was based on fear and intimidation. If he lost that, he would lose everything.

The man crouched down and moved forward, swaying side to side. With an evil look in his eye, he began tossing the sword from one hand to the other. It gave the impression he knew what he was doing. Peltrin waited patiently while the larger man approached.

As soon as the man was within reach, Peltrin flicked his little sword with blinding speed. He struck the man's sword just as it flew from one hand toward the other. The sword flew from its owner and clattered into the shadows.

The stranger stopped, dumbfounded. Peltrin grinned at the larger man, who now stood weaponless, completely at the mercy of the confident youth.

"Go on," said Peltrin. "Go find it and pick it up. I'm still looking forward to learning anything you can teach me."

Having no other options, the man moved in the direction of the shadows where the sword had disappeared. As soon as his eyes were averted, there was a loud smack. The large man cried out and clutched his backside. After a few seconds, he let go and checked his hands. The boy had smacked him soundly, but there was no blood.

There were several chuckles, not all of them came from the youths.

Angrily, the man retrieved the sword and strode towards Peltrin. He held his weapon firmly in his right hand. There would be no showcasing this time.

The man stepped quickly toward Peltrin, waving his sword in a wide, vicious arc. Peltrin ducked the blow easily.

In a surprising show of strength and dexterity, however, the larger man stopped the sword just after it passed Peltrin. He then immediately swept the double-edged sword in the opposite direction in a downward slicing backhand. It was his best move. Against most people, it was very effective. Sometimes it was even deadly.

But Peltrin wasn't most people. This was only one of the dozens of possibilities Peltrin had already visualized and planned for. Seeing the placement of the man's feet, he knew something like this was likely.

Remembering how his father fought against Beorn, Peltrin slid in close. He parried the blow, slamming his sword against the hilt of the other sword, right above the other man's fingers. The laws of physics took over and the sword sprung from the man's grasp. Peltrin spun away, easily dodging as the man belatedly struck out with his fists. As he put space between them, Peltrin also managed to kick the man's sword back into the shadows.

CONFRONTATION

Again, Peltrin invited the man to retrieve his sword and, again, the would-be thief was rewarded with a stinging blow to the backside. The one-sided battle resumed as Peltrin disarmed the man a third time and smacked his rump yet again. After the third time, the man hesitated, unwilling to pick up his sword only to be embarrassed again.

"Tell you what," said Peltrin, twirling his sword just a few paces away from the man he had been fighting. "I'm a fairly fast learner. Why don't we just say I've learned my lesson."

The thief raised an eyebrow. He hadn't expected it to end so soon. He was, at heart, a true bully. Had the roles be reversed, he would have continued to punish the boy until Peltrin could no longer stand. And he would have enjoyed it thoroughly. As it was, getting out of there with his skin intact was quickly becoming his only thought.

"I want you to leave," said Peltrin, still twirling his sword. "I want the six of you to head off in that direction," he pointed his sword towards the ridge where he had first seen them, "and I don't want you to stop for three days."

"Of course," the man agreed quickly. "You have my word." In reality, his word meant nothing. The man fully intended to return later that night and slit Peltrin's throat while he slept. He didn't kill at every opportunity, but it wouldn't be the first time. This boy needed to pay dearly for what he had done.

"The problem, of course," Peltrin went on, "is I don't trust you." He raised his sword and stepped forward.

"I gave you my word!" the man protested, raising his hands defensively. "We'll never come back. I swear!" The man had tears forming in his eyes. He knew he was completely at Peltrin's mercy

"Oh, very well," said Peltrin. "Let's test you, shall we?" He lowered his sword.

The man calmed somewhat. He clearly had felt as though he were about to die.

"I'm going to tell you a secret, and we'll all watch to see how well you keep it," said Peltrin.

"You can trust me, I swear it!" the man asserted wholeheartedly.

Peltrin leaned a little closer but stayed out of reach. "The three of us are protected by the forest," he whispered. He could only hope the wolves would be willing to play along with this.

"The forest?" the man repeated skeptically.

"Quietly!" Peltrin hissed.

"That's right," said the Lieutenant, strutting into the firelight. "These three are under my protection."

"You are being protected by a woodchuck?" the man asked, a slight grin tugging at his mouth.

Lou picked up a rock and threw it at the man, missing him completely. "Rockchuck," Lou said angrily. "And don't you forget it."

The stranger wasn't convinced. "You want me to believe the three of you can order around forest animals as if they were your personal lap dogs?" His mocking tone was loud enough that all could hear.

There were several low growls. Peltrin remembered Bensil had told them the wolves hated nothing more than the idea of being domesticated. "They don't follow my orders," he said hurriedly. "These animals are wild and free. For reasons of their own they have agreed to ensure our safety."

As if in answer, immediately outside of the firelight there was a long howl. The sound seemed to freeze the air around them and there was complete silence afterward.

"You think I'm a fool?" the man asked angrily, "No one is ever going to believe you are protected by wolves, just because…"

CONFRONTATION

The man was cut off by a deafening cacophony of barks, yips, howling and snarling. Lou jumped up and down, chittering and clicking his teeth. After nearly a full minute of terrifying sounds, it stopped.

By now, even the man Aralis had kicked was working his way up to his feet. Since his sleeves were still pinned to the tree, the task wasn't an easy one.

Peltrin moved in close to the leader. "There's something you should know about me," he said evenly. There was more menace in his voice than a young man his age should have been able to muster. "I never lie. If you are not running over the top of the ridge within the next hour, my friends will tear you all to shreds." There was a deep snarl from the shadows, as if to confirm what Peltrin had just said.

Peltrin grinned slightly, though his eyes remained stone cold. "If any of you come back, and the wolves don't kill you, I'll do it myself."

There was a slight stir among the six thieves.

"I don't trust you one bit," Peltrin went on, "do you trust me?"

The large man looked in Peltrin's silver-blue eyes and the answer was clear. He retrieved his sword and quickly strode into the darkness. The others followed quickly.

"Don't leave me here!" pleaded the tall, lanky man, who was still pinned to the tree.

Peltrin walked over and pulled the two knives out of the trees with two quick, powerful tugs. The lanky man fell to the ground but was immediately up again. Shamelessly, he ran after the others.

"Wow!" said Soyem after he was sure they were gone. "That was amazing!"

"You made it look easy," agreed Aralis.

"Now if that's not a confidence builder, then I don't know what is," said Lou proudly.

Peltrin blushed a little and was glad for his beard and the general darkness. "Those people were pretty pathetic," he said modestly, "only one of them knew how to use a sword at all, and even he wasn't very good."

"But there were six of them!" Soyem exclaimed. "And they were all mean to the core. You could tell just by looking at them."

"I was able to take them on one at a time," Peltrin pointed out. He glanced at Aralis and added more wood to the fire. "They didn't even try to help each other. Three of them were so intimidated after one blow that they didn't want to join in again. Besides, Aralis took out two of them."

"What a kick!" said Soyem. "He collapsed as if he'd just died on the spot."

Now it was Aralis' turn to blush. "He deserved it," she said looking down with a shy smile as she put a small pot of water on the edge of the fire.

"Well you certainly gave him what he deserved!" exclaimed Soyem, his face animated as he poked the fire with a stick, stoking it back to life. "His feet lifted off the ground and then he just hung there whimpering. Out of all of them, he was the last to get up again. I'm glad you didn't kick me like that when I was teasing you about being afraid of the dark."

"I'm sorry I got so angry," she answered, she appeared to be feeling ashamed of her earlier behavior. "I don't understand why my dreams make me so afraid."

"It's that way for me, too," Peltrin agreed. "Fighting with people doesn't make me afraid at all. But both times the devastors attacked, all I had to do was throw a knife. The second time was even worse than the first. I wasn't in immediate danger. It was a short, easy throw…."

There was a long silence. For Peltrin, it felt good to be able to talk. He was so tired of obsessing over the fact that two people were dead and three more would die soon. It was much easier to talk about his fear now they had seen him be at least a little brave.

Aralis put her hand on his forearm. Peltrin's heart jolted and his entire body felt warmer. "The day will come that you won't be afraid."

Aralis seemed to have complete confidence in him. Hearing it from her, Peltrin could almost believe it himself.

"Bet your confidence is doing good now," said Lou.

All three of the youths rolled their eyes.

"Yes, Lou," Peltrin said with a laugh, "my confidence is doing just fine."

"I should change the bandage," said Aralis, taking her hand off Peltrin's arm. "I promised your mother I would do it twice a day."

"Can I watch?" asked Soyem, "I want to know more about this family secret."

"Not yet," said Aralis.

"What difference does it make?" Soyem protested, but Aralis just answered with a cold stare.

She moved over behind Peltrin. "Um," she said uncomfortably, "you need to take off your shirt."

Peltrin removed his shirt.

Fully clothed, most would say Peltrin was a little on the thin side. Taking his shirt off; however, revealed a more accurate story. His muscles were not ridiculously bulky, but each one was well defined and toned. Everything was well developed and hard as a rock. There was no questioning the fact that he had spent his entire life training. Even Soyem couldn't help but stare a little at Peltrin's impressive build.

Clearing her throat and taking a quick breath, Aralis took the small pot out of the fire and set about changing the bandage. It was clear she had been an apprentice for the healer for quite some time. She moved quickly and confidently, removing the old bandage, cleaning the area, and applying the new bandage.

"Twice a day seems a bit much for a little scratch," Peltrin complained.

"Keeping it covered day and night is an essential part of the family secret," answered Aralis.

Peltrin didn't argue. He probably would have, but a part of him enjoyed getting a little extra attention from Aralis. Looking at the ground, he saw a small lilac between his feet. The little plant was blooming with what must have been its first set of flowers.

As Aralis worked, without giving it much thought, Peltrin plucked the top of the plant a few inches below the flowers. When Aralis finished, he presented it to her with a grin.

"Thank you," she responded shyly.

"Every flower has a meaning," murmured Soyem. "What does a lilac-colored lilac stand for?"

"The first emotions of young love," Peltrin said automatically. Then he looked at the lilac and paled. He hadn't thought about that.

"Um…I didn't mean…I…" Peltrin stammered for a way to address the awkward situation.

"I know you weren't thinking about that," Aralis assured him. "But I want to keep it anyway, if that's okay."

Peltrin nodded and put his shirt back on.

It wasn't long after Aralis put on the bandage before the conversation started winding down and they went to bed. For Aralis' benefit, the boys had collected plenty of firewood to last the night. It wouldn't be a large fire, but it was enough to give her some level of comfort.

They arranged themselves in a triangle around the fire, so they could all benefit from the heat. Peltrin and Aralis' heads were close together and Soyem was at their feet. When Soyem complained, Peltrin reminded him that his only job that night was to get eaten, so they weren't too worried about making him comfortable.

Soyem looked like he wanted to reply, but he apparently couldn't think of anything clever to throw back at them.

As he lay down, Peltrin glanced over at Aralis. She didn't realize he was looking at her. She was still holding the lilac flower he had given her.

The night wasn't terribly cold so Peltrin left one arm out of his bag, just in case it might help him get to a weapon sooner. Despite Soyem's joking, Peltrin felt very strongly that it was his responsibility to keep Aralis safe. He glanced at Soyem's bedroll. It was his responsibility to keep them all safe.

Soon, they were all fast asleep.

Hours later, Peltrin awoke with a start. A cold hand gripped his wrist. Resisting the urge to attack before assessing the situation, he opened his eyes just a crack. He recognized the hand as Aralis' and was grateful he hadn't acted too quickly.

The fire was dimmer than when he had fallen asleep, but still glowing. Grunting and turning his head he saw Aralis, whose grip tightened on his wrist. Her hair looked like it had exploded and her soft brown eyes were wide.

"Something's out there," she whispered. "In the dark."

"I'll put more wood on the fire," mumbled Peltrin. "It's probably the wolves, and if it isn't the wolves, the wolves will take care of it." Unlike his father, Peltrin was not a light sleeper. Sleeping lightly was a handy skill in situations like these, but it just wasn't something Peltrin was able to do.

"It isn't the wolves," she answered, "whatever it is, it's in the trees."

Now Peltrin was concerned. He looked around for Lou. He wanted to send the marmot on a recon mission, but Lou was nowhere to be seen.

"You have to let go of my arm," he whispered. "I need to get my weapons ready."

It wasn't entirely true. Peltrin had three throwing knives, his short sword, and a tomahawk hidden in and around his bedroll. But none of them would do him any good if she was holding on to his arm. Reluctantly, she let go and curled up defensively in her bedroll. It was interesting how she changed in the dark, Peltrin thought. When the fire was bright, she had no difficulty facing the thieves, but in the dark, she was terrified.

Peltrin focused on listening closely, trying to get a feel for what was out there and how many there were. He hoped Aralis was wrong about the noise coming from the trees. He hoped it was just a deer or an elk roaming quietly through the woods, as they often do. More than once he and Berin had woken up to find a deer practically within arm's reach of their bedrolls. Deer always ran away as soon as one of the boys moved, Elk typically did the same. Moose could be a problem; they were just as likely to attack as run away. Peltrin was fine with any of these, he was even fine with predators like mountain lions. He could deal with anything the forest could throw at him, as long as it wasn't a devastor.

It was as if his thoughts were brought to life. There was a stirring in the trees above followed by a series of hisses.

Peltrin took a deep breath. He would not let his fears overcome him tonight. His father had promised him that, if he wanted it bad enough, he could overcome his fears. Right now, he wanted nothing more than to not feel afraid. Fumbling slightly, he grabbed his throwing knives and shifted so his sword would be more convenient. He could feel all the warning signs of his body going into a panic.

"You can do this, Peltrin," said Aralis.

Peltrin felt his body calming slightly at the sound of her voice, but it didn't last long.

CONFRONTATION

There was a shuffling in the trees, and then a thump. A pair of thick, grotesque feet appeared directly in front of Peltrin's face. He looked up, directly into the black eyes of the first devastor. He froze.

"Peltrin, do something!" Aralis screamed.

His right hand quivered as he struggled to take action. He was able to move a little but It didn't amount to anything.

There was a shuffling in the trees and a series of thumps as several more jumped to the ground. With horror, Peltrin saw one of them had glowing red eyes. He stared, mesmerized. Everything but the red eyes disappeared as the devastor moved towards him. He was dimly aware Aralis and Soyem were screaming. Somewhere deep inside, Peltrin was sad it was all going to end this way.

There was a sudden flash of fur and the red-eyes were gone without a trace. The trance broken, Peltrin blinked in surprise.

"Peltrin!" screamed Aralis.

Peltrin looked in her direction, the world was in slow motion. One of the black-eyed devastors was in the air, in the middle of a pounce in her direction. If he could only move, Peltrin was sure he could throw a knife in time. Before he could even twitch; however, there was another flash of fur and the devastor disappeared just before it landed on her.

Over the next several seconds, the creatures disappeared one or two at a time. It happened so fast it was almost surreal. Finally, all of them were gone and two wolves stepped into the firelight.

One was massive, easily as large as a donkey, the wolf was so heavily muscled it would have been comical—except it was terrifying. The fact that the teeth were covered in blood made it even more intimidating. It was mostly dark gray, though there were some patches of golden brown. Seeing it up close, Peltrin was even more impressed the huge animal had been able to maneuver through the forest, silent and unseen.

The other wolf was leaner and more sleek. He seemed to be made for speed. From the cunning look on his face, this one appeared to be the craftier of the two. Like his brother, he was mostly gray, though his patches were black, rather than golden brown.

"Fang, Fangmort," said Aralis. She was still breathing hard and her eyes were still wide with terror.

Peltrin and Aralis shakily crawled out of their bedrolls. Soyem remained curled up in a ball deep in his bedroll, shaking and presumably sobbing.

"We've been watching them all day," said Fangmort, the smaller of the two wolves. "They were following you in the trees. They wouldn't come down until we pretended to leave you unprotected."

"We expected more from the tall one," said Fang. "We've watched him practice in the forest many times and we saw what he did with those thieves. He is more than capable of killing a few devastors."

Peltrin hung his head.

"It was an observation," said Fangmort, "not a criticism. We are not here to add to your shame."

"Well, thanks for saving us," said Peltrin.

Fang walked up to him until they were practically touching. The wolf's snout came to his chest. "You'll die soon enough," the wolf said evenly. "I'm not saving your life. I'm just saving you for later."

Peltrin's eyes grew wide and there were several seconds of silence. Then Fang and Fangmort made a series of coughing sounds. It was several seconds before Peltrin realized they were laughing.

"Ever since we heard you talking about getting eaten," said Fangmort, "we've been looking forward to snacking on the little one here." He nudged Soyem's bedroll, the bedroll whimpered. "But now that I see him up close, I don't think we'll bother."

"Are you sure?" asked Fang, "It isn't often you find a willing meal."

CONFRONTATION

Fangmort poked the bag a few more times. Soyem shook and whimpered each time. "Come on out, kid," he said, "they're gone. You might as well quit whining and breathe some fresh air."

Soyem poked his head out and looked at the wolves, his face filled with relief.

Fangmort watched as Soyem stumbled out of his bedroll. Lou came out as well.

"Apologies, everyone," Lou said unsteadily. He looked shaken as well. "I was trying to help little Soyem here work up some courage."

"Both of them are definitely too squirrel-like," the wolf concluded. "I've never liked the taste of squirrels."

"You just ate three," accused Fang. "Not one hour ago."

"We're on the job," huffed Fangmort. "It was a convenient snack, nothing more. It's not like I was fully distracted from our commitment by a young deer."

"He's a little jealous," Fang said, turning to Peltrin and Aralis and talking in a low voice. "I caught and ate a young deer earlier today. Once again, he has been reminded of my superior skills."

"Please," said Fangmort, "it was no accomplishment. You weren't even on the hunt. You just happened to stumble on it while we were watching the devastors."

"You like to think you're so clever," accused Fang. "You want the whole world to believe you are the superior hunter. Well, I say let the results speak for themselves. I ate a deer today, and you only got a few squirrels."

"The deer must have been blind, deaf, and had no sense of smell," grumbled Fangmort. "The way you were bumbling around."

"You ate a baby deer?" asked Soyem, who was finally composed enough to speak. "Why would you do that?"

"It was there," replied Fang. "And eating happens to be what we do for a living. If you think about it, that's what everyone does for a living."

"Anyone who doesn't, tends to die," agreed Fangmort.

"But why a baby?" asked Soyem. "Why couldn't you just eat the older ones. The poor baby deer could have lived a long, happy life, and you took that away."

"It was there," said Fang, repeating his earlier argument. "Why would I go hunting around for something else when a perfectly good meal is standing right in front of me."

"It's just wrong," insisted Soyem, "you should never eat the young."

"What did you eat for breakfast yesterday, kid?" asked Fangmort.

Soyem looked a little sheepish, "Eggs."

The two brothers laughed again.

Peltrin was unsure of how to interact with these two wolves. Bensil had made it sound like they didn't like talking to people, or that they didn't like talking at all. But here they were, chatting like a couple of human brothers.

Come to think of it, there were a lot of similarities between these two wolves and his father and uncle. Fang and Beorn were both ridiculously large and muscular. Perwin and Fangmort, though above average for size and strength, were the thinkers. The biggest difference was the men were mostly interested in talking about fighting, while the wolves were only interested in talking about food.

"Well, I suppose I should compliment you for a job well done," said Lou, grudgingly

"Ah, yes, the mastermind," said Fangmort. "You saw, of course, that we followed your instructions and didn't protect the kids when the bandits came around."

"Followed your instructions?" asked Aralis in surprise. "Lou, did you tell the wolves not to protect us?"

CONFRONTATION

Remembering what Perwin had done to Lou the day before, Peltrin quickly slipped his foot under the marmot and launched the lieutenant into the bushes.

"Ungratefuuuu…" the animal called as he sailed through the air.

"Stay out of my sight," Peltrin called angrily. "If I see you anywhere near this fire again tonight, I swear I will make you sorry."

"You might as well go back to bed now," said Fangmort, laughing at the show Lou and Peltrin had just put on. "There's no more devastors out there. You should be able to sleep for the rest of the night."

"I don't think I can sleep anymore, tonight," said Soyem. "That attack was terrifying."

"And it's over," Fang assured him. "We've learned how to track them now. We've been watching them all day. It wasn't until just now they were bold enough to come down. There are no more anywhere nearby. Fangmort and I will keep watch."

Though they all insisted they weren't tired, it wasn't long before the conversation wound down and they were all lying down again. Peltrin lay in bed, thinking again of everyone who had died, been hurt, or almost been hurt, because of his fears. He was learning to hate quiet moments like this when he had time to think about his shortcomings. It was downright embarrassing to think he was getting confidence lessons from a rockchuck.

"It's okay, Peltrin," Aralis whispered.

"No," Peltrin mumbled to himself, so quietly Aralis couldn't hear. "No, it isn't."

THE CHRONCILES OF AMYRIAD

CHAPTER 9: VALDOR

Despite Soyem's doubts, they all slept surprisingly well. For breakfast, Nirani had packed a sort of fruitcake. It was full of flavor, heavy, and quite filling. Best of all for Peltrin, it took no preparation.

Lou took the time to compliment every bite.

To their surprise, the wolves momentarily wandered into the clearing while they ate breakfast. Fangmort pointed out to Soyem the recipe for the fruitcake probably included eggs. The wolves pretended to be mortified as they talked about those poor unborn chickens Soyem had cruelly deprived of the joys of a long, happy life. After they had finished teasing Soyem, they disappeared into the forest.

Before putting out the fire, they heated some water and Aralis changed Peltrin's bandage. Again, it was clear she knew what she was doing. Peltrin shrugged his shoulders and moved his head side to side when she was done. Despite being in an awkward place at the base of his neck, the bandage was surprisingly comfortable. He hardly thought about it other than when she was changing it.

"We'd better be going soon," said Peltrin. He was anxious to get to Valdor's house as soon as possible.

Peltrin and Aralis had all of their things packed in a matter of minutes. They sat and waited while Soyem struggled to find all of his things and fit everything back into his pack. Lou was back in his pocket in Peltrin's pack. He appeared to be sleeping.

"Your bedroll is taking up too much space, Peltrin pointed out. "The rest won't fit in your pack unless you make it smaller.

"I tried," Soyem insisted. "Besides, the bedroll was the first thing I packed. I'm not going to pull everything out now."

"You're going to have to," said Peltrin, frustrated, but trying not to be impatient.

"Leave me alone!" the younger boy shouted, embarrassed and frustrated. "I can do this."

Peltrin rolled his eyes, then he had an idea. "You need more water."

"What?" asked Soyem. "I already can't fit everything, how is more water supposed to help."

"The weight of the water will help everything pack in tighter," explained Peltrin.

Aralis gave him a disbelieving look.

"Try it," Peltrin insisted.

Reluctantly, Soyem took his water flask. "I still don't see how it's supposed to work." Shaking his head, he headed over to the stream.

As soon as Soyem bent over the stream to fill his flask, Peltrin hurried over to Soyem's pack and dumped everything out unceremoniously.

Catching on, Aralis quickly came over to help.

Peltrin focused on the bedroll and Aralis attacked Soyem's pile of clothes.

"How will he learn?" asked Aralis.

"I don't care if he learns," answered Peltrin. "Today, all I care about is we get going as soon as possible. We have to be to the Fyllcarcern by tomorrow." Peltrin stuffed the tightly rolled bedroll into the pack.

Aralis stuffed the clothes on top and they quickly returned to where they were before. As Soyem approached, Aralis was lacing her shoe and Peltrin was stirring the fire ashes, pretending to make sure there were no remaining hot embers.

"Huh," said Soyem when his remaining gear fit easily into his pack. "I guess it does work."

Finally, they consulted the map and were off.

If it weren't for the terrible situation, it would have been a very nice walk. The sun was shining and there was a slight breeze. The well-worn trail sloped upwards, but the slope was gentle enough they hardly noticed.

Peltrin continually looked around for any potential hiding places where an enemy might lie in wait. After their encounters the night before with the thieves and the devastors, it seemed like a good idea to be careful. Before, practicing with his father, he generally focused on areas near the ground or in the large branches of the trees where men could hide. Realizing he was now watching for relatively smaller creatures, he started to pay attention to slightly smaller branches as well.

"What are you so focused on, Peltrin?" asked Soyem. He had been walking behind him.

"Watching for potential enemies," he answered.

"How would you know if someone is an enemy?" he wondered. "What if someone is just out hunting?"

"Always assume everyone is your enemy," said Peltrin. "That's how you stay alive."

"I don't think you need to pretend every person you meet is trying to kill you," Soyem said. "Most people in Aldayin are friendly if you give them a chance. Of course, Aldayin is the most boring place in all of Amyriad, so maybe you have to be more careful in other places."

"Why are you always complaining about how boring Aldayin is?" asked Peltrin. "You were terrified by the thieves and the devastors last night."

"I don't know how to fight," Soyem admitted, "but I don't like sitting around with nothing going on either. Maybe Aldayin would be more interesting if there were someone there who was secretly our enemy.

"You never know for sure," Peltrin pointed out. "Sometimes people pretend to be friendly so you let your guard down."

"But what about me and Aralis?" Soyem asked with a half-grin.

"What about you?" Peltrin asked.

"How do you know we're not just pretending to be friendly until you let your guard down."

"I don't think either of you is secretly planning to kill me."

"But how can you be sure?"

Peltrin hesitated. On the one hand, his training told him he could never be sure. On the other, there was no way Soyem or Aralis was a danger. "I don't think you could kill anyone," he finally answered. "And I don't think Aralis is going to try to kill me." Peltrin turned his back on Soyem to walk away.

"Stab!" Soyem shouted. He then quickly followed with, "Oof! Ouch!"

Soyem was lying on the ground, holding his ribs and gasping for breath. He had tried to poke Peltrin from behind with a stick. Peltrin had blocked the poke, punched Soyem in the ribs, and knocked him to the ground.

Aralis was laughing hysterically.

"Sorry Soyem," said Peltrin, helping him up. "You caught me by surprise."

"Something to remember for the rest of my life," Soyem gasped, "never ever, ever catch you by surprise again. I think we need to stop for a while."

Peltrin resisted at first, but he felt guilty enough he eventually relented and they all stopped for an early lunch.

"Do you think it's broken?" asked Soyem, rubbing his rib as he chewed on a thin strip of dried beef.

"I doubt it," said Peltrin. "I didn't hit you very hard. It was more of a push than a punch. I was mostly focused on trying to get you away from me before you could use a knife or something."

"What makes you think I had a knife?" Soyem complained.

"I didn't know who was behind me," Peltrin answered defensively, "all I knew was someone was trying to sneak up on me. How was I supposed to know it was you?"

"Because there's no one else here!" Soyem practically shouted.

"Quietly," Lou grumbled sleepily from Peltrin's pack. "If someone is out there, we don't want to draw attention to ourselves."

"Great," Soyem grumbled. "Now even the rockchuck is paranoid."

"Careful, not paranoid," argued Peltrin.

"Let me take a look," said Aralis. She was fairly certain the boys were only going to get more agitated if she let them continue.

She pressed and poked and prodded the sore area. She then had Soyem breathe deeply and twist and turn.

"You have some deep bruising," she concluded. "But the rib isn't broken. I have something we can put on it when we get to Valdor's house. It will help the bruise heal quicker, but you will probably be a little sore for a few days."

Soyem gave Peltrin an evil look, "What did you think I was going to do?"

"I'm sorry," Peltrin said sincerely, "you snuck up behind me and yelled."

"Let it go, guys," said Aralis, sounding irritated.

They both looked at her in surprise. They were so used to her being silent all of the time, it was a bit of a surprise for her to get involved.

They did let it go, though Soyem continued complaining from time to time as they resumed their walk.

It wasn't long after lunch when they left the main trail. They followed what looked like a game trail for another hour. Eventually, it led to a clearing. In the center of the clearing stood a small home.

The home was even smaller than Peltrin's house and was in a sorry state of disrepair. Many of the wooden shingles didn't look serviceable and the door was barely hanging in place. The shudders in the one window were closed. Just to the side of the house was a pair of graves. Each grave was marked with a stone and decorated with flowers.

"Doesn't look like anyone has been here for a long time," said Soyem.

"The house is in bad shape," agreed Peltrin, "but the flowers on the graves are fresh. They couldn't be more than a day old."

"Do we knock?" asked Aralis.

"Hello," Soyem called, "Valdor?"

Peltrin jumped to the side, crashing into Aralis, just in time to avoid being hit by an arrow. Grabbing her arm, he thrust her behind a tree and dove into Soyem, tackling him to the ground.

"Ouch! Come on! What is wrong with you?" Soyem complained. "I did NOT sneak up behind you this time. Why are you are knocking me down again?" Then, with a soft thump, an arrow appeared in the ground next to his arm.

Another arrow hit Peltrin's pack. Lou wasn't hurt but he was pinned inside his pocket.

"Oh," said Soyem, stunned.

"Wolves, help!" called Lou. "I'm trapped! The kids are unprotected!"

Jumping to his feet, Peltrin lifted Soyem off the ground with one hand and thrust him behind a tree.

"Oomph…seriously," Soyem complained, "you have to quit knocking me around. We have enough enemies. It doesn't do us any good to be fighting each other."

"Quiet," answered Peltrin. "You too, Lou, you're giving away our position."

"Why," Soyem had to ask. "He already knows where we are."

Peltrin rolled his eyes. "Because he is moving and I am trying to keep track of him. You are right, he knows exactly where we are, and we ought to be moving. When we do move, finding a new hiding spot doesn't do us any good if he hears us talking."

Soyem was able to stay quiet for almost ten seconds, "Why don't you just take him out?" he whispered. "I thought you were supposed to be good at this."

"I am good at this," Peltrin whispered as he continued to scan the area. "But you are not, so I'm not sure I want to leave you on your own. Also," he continued scanning the trees furiously, "it just so happens that whoever just shot at us is good at this as well, very good."

"He's over there," Peltrin said finally, pointing at a dense bush. "Move over a little so he can't get a clear shot at you, and signal Aralis to do the same."

"Got it," said Soyem. He shuffled noisily to where Peltrin had indicated.

"Hey Aralis," Soyem said, way too loudly. "The guy shooting at us is in that bush over there, move over a little." He waved his arms.

Peltrin sighed. This was going to be difficult. The attacker was very good at moving around silently and unseen. One on one, Peltrin guessed he could eventually capture or kill him, but that could take hours. He was quite certain if he left Soyem on his own, the boy would be dead in under five minutes.

Aralis was considerably better at hiding than Soyem, but she wasn't trained for this sort of thing. With her in particular, Peltrin wasn't willing to take any chances. Peltrin thought of his bow and kicked himself for not borrowing one.

There was a yell from behind the bush and some snarling. A few seconds later, Fang came out into the clearing. "You can come out, now," he called. "The man has been subdued."

"Get me out of here!" shouted Lou. "And let me at him."

Peltrin put down his pack and broke off the arrow. The flap opened and Lou leaped to freedom. Peltrin then reached inside. It was easier to extract the arrow from inside the pack than to pull it out the hole it had created when it entered. The arrow had only hit some of his clothing and didn't appear to have done any serious damage to his gear.

Peltrin was relieved, but still frustrated. This was the second time since they had left Aldayin the wolves had come to his rescue. He was supposed to be trained. He wasn't supposed to need saving.

Slowly, they approached the thick bushes where the man had been hiding. When they came into view, an old man of the Ennai race was lying on his back. Fangmort was sitting on the man's stomach. The man's arms and legs were stretched out, spread eagle. One finger on his right hand twitched and Fangmort growled.

The three youths and Lou moved in for a closer look. Like Aralis, the old Ennai man had brown skin and was thin and long-limbed. He had straight dark hair, a wide flat nose, and a square jaw. Unlike the Pichari, the Ennai men did not grow beards.

"You may as well end my life," the old man said quietly. There was no fear in his voice, though his eyes were closed tightly. "I prefer a speedy end, but I cannot be intimidated by pain."

"Are you Valdor?" Aralis asked.

The old man opened his eyes. "An Ennai woman?" he said in surprise. "What are you doing here?"

He then looked over at the boys. "And you're traveling with a Pichari and a Canbi? With no Ennai escort? I've never seen anything like it."

"She has lived with the Pichari all her life," said Peltrin. He was a little irritated that Valdor seemed to think an Ennai girl shouldn't be allowed to live with the Pichari. "Are you Valdor?"

"No," the old man answered, "Valdor died a long time ago."

"Liar," snarled Fangmort.

"My brother always knows when a human is lying," explained Fang. "He's never wrong."

"To lie intentionally without willingly embracing the consequences is the epitome of irrational behavior," the old man mumbled. Peltrin recognized it as one of the hundreds of old Ennai sayings his father was always quoting.

Lou came up close to the old man's face, studied him carefully, and sniffed. "Yes," he said confidently, "this is Valdor,"

"Lieutenant?" Valdor said in surprise. "What are you doing here?"

"Have you ever climbed the Fyllcarcern?" asked Peltrin. They all ignored Valdor's question.

"No," the old man answered. Peltrin looked at Fangmort.

"Lie," said the wolf.

"Oh, for heaven's sake," Aralis mumbled quietly. Peltrin was standing next to her and he could barely hear.

"I think we can let him up," said Peltrin, guessing what Aralis was frustrated about. "Valdor, we don't mean you any harm. We just need your help."

Valdor looked at Fangmort.

"True," said Fangmort. "For the girl and the tall one. The short one would like to hurt you. He is angry you nearly shot him. You don't need to worry, though, the boy knows he is incapable so he isn't going to try. I can't read the woodchuck, he's always too nervous when I'm around."

"Rockchuck," grumbled Lou.

They all looked at Soyem.

"Everything he said about me is true," Soyem admitted. "It's a little scary Fangmort can do that."

Peltrin silently agreed.

"Very well," the old man conceded, "my name is Valdor. I did climb the Fyllcarcern. I thought you were here to try to kill me, but now that I see you're not, I won't harm you."

The three youths looked at Fangmort.

"True," the wolf confirmed.

Fangmort got off of the old man and Soyem and Peltrin helped him up to his feet. There was a lot of groaning, creaking, and popping, but eventually, Valdor was standing up on his own. He wasn't particularly tall, for an Ennai. He stood just a little shorter than Peltrin, barely taller than Aralis.

"Your time would be better spent seeking other help," said the old man, who was still stretching to work out the creaks. "I cannot help you. My previous ascent was many years ago. I am no longer capable of such a feat and, even if I were, I have no intention of leaving my house."

"All true," said Fangmort. "At least he believes it's all true."

"Thanks, but you don't need to tell us anymore, Fangmort," said Peltrin, "I think we have gotten to a point where we can trust each other."

"True," said Fangmort after looking at each of them. Both wolves disappeared into the trees.

"How did you come by their assistance," asked the old man in disbelief. "I've heard of the two great wolf brothers, but I never would have believed they would condescend to serve humans."

"We're not their masters," answered Peltrin. "We made a deal with them, and they agreed to help."

"What do you pay a wolf for his services?" The old man wondered. "Especially those wolves. They can go where they want, do what they want, eat whenever and whatever they want. What could you possibly have to offer them?"

"None of your business," said Aralis and Soyem together.

"True," Fangmort's voice came from somewhere in the surrounding forest. It was difficult to tell exactly where.

"I clearly can't be free of you as easily as I would like," the old man conceded. "Come to the house and tell me why you came. Once I have heard, I can better assure you that you have wasted your time. Then you can leave me in peace."

Peltrin wasn't sure how to respond to that as they walked toward the house. Aralis and Soyem didn't say anything either.

As they approached the house, they came into an odor that convinced the three of them the front porch was as far as they wanted to go.

"Oh my," said Lou. "Your house smells more like you than you do."

"It's a nice day outside," said Peltrin, "let's talk out here."

Everyone—including Valdor—looked relieved when the old man nodded his head.

"First off," said Valdor, settling himself onto what was left of one of the porch steps, "I must inquire as to how an Ennai girl came to be traveling with a Pichari boy and a Canbi boy?"

"I grew up in a Pichari village," she answered quietly.

"How did that come to be?" the old man looked somewhat upset at the idea.

"Soyem and I are apprentices to a Canbi healer."

"Bensil?" Valdor asked.

"Yes! Do you know him?" asked Soyem.

"I knew him many years ago, during the war," said Valdor. "Quite possibly the most competent healer I've ever met."

Aralis just nodded her head.

"He's a good man," Valdor went on, "but he should know better than to apprentice an Ennai woman. Why did he not return you to your people?"

Aralis just shrugged and shook her head.

"You and I will talk more about that later."

Aralis nodded.

Valdor then turned to Peltrin. "Did you say you hail from Aldayin?"

"Yes," said Peltrin.

"You carry a tomahawk and travel with the lieutenant. That's a very unusual weapon for a Pichari, and unusual company for anyone. Lou has always been loyal to Perwin, son of Thettlemar. You wouldn't know Perwin, would you?

"Perwin is his father," said Soyem.

"Am I to assume he still lives?" asked Valdor.

"Yes," said Peltrin, "but he will die soon if we don't succeed."

"So Perwin is still around after all," said Valdor with a slight grin. "He even managed to keep his son alive all these years. Good for him!"

"You knew Perwin?" asked Soyem.

"I taught him how to use his tomahawk," said Valdor proudly. "In less than a week he went from an amateur to one of the best I'd ever seen. Then again, Perwin was good with any weapon ever invented. He could probably take down an army with a bucket of rusty nails and a broken hammer. I take it he taught you to use the tomahawk as well?"

"He did," said Peltrin with a little pride. He shifted a little and his elbow brushed Aralis' arm.

Valdor jumped to his feet, drawing a knife. "Does he have permission to touch you?" he asked angrily.

"What?" Aralis didn't seem to have noticed Peltrin's elbow had brushed up against her.

"His elbow touched you," Valdor said, pointing accusingly and Peltrin.

Confused, but unwilling to be intimidated, Peltrin put his hand on his sword.

"Does he need permission for his elbow to touch my arm?" asked Aralis, just as confused as Peltrin. "If that's the problem then…yes."

Valdor shook his head in dismay, but he put his knife away and sat down again. "It isn't right for an Ennai girl to be away from her people. Ennai women are gifted with great beauty, wisdom, and heart. To touch such a woman without permission is to recognize her beauty, without recognizing her wisdom and her heart. Such permission is given only after the man has proven first that he respects all three of her great attributes. Ideally, he should also vow to protect her with his life.

"The punishment for an Ennai man who touches an Ennai woman without permission is exile. The punishment for a Pichari man or a Canbi man who touches an Ennai woman without permission is death."

The three youths looked at the old man, dumbfounded.

Aralis broke the silence, "no one needs to be exiled or killed for me."

"Typical Ennai," grumbled Lou. "You haven't gotten any less stuffy over the years, have you Valdor? All this pomp is never good for the mission. As usual, we spend all of our time talking about rituals and traditions. We still haven't been able to explain why we are here."

Valdor didn't respond to Lou directly, but he put his knife away and sat down. Peltrin decided to move forward. He told the story of the devastor attacks and the cave. The old man listened intently, particularly to the description of the attack on the house.

"Devastors can climb trees now?" Valdor interrupted at one point. "That does change things. It was bad enough they could emerge from the ground, now they attack from trees as well."

"Wouldn't it be scarier to have them pop out of the ground?" asked Soyem. "Then they could just break into your house before you even knew they were coming."

"Perwin probably built his home on solid rock," said Valdor, "as I did. Though you should know that devastors cannot surprise you from underground. Their digging is far from quiet. Also, they move relatively slowly underground. It is no challenge to stab your sword into the ground so they expire before they emerge."

"Why don't they just dig deeper?" asked Peltrin.

"No idea," answered Valdor. "Earlier today I would have answered that they don't go deeper because it isn't in their nature. However, they now ascend the trees, which seems even more out of their nature."

"Does it even matter whether they can come up through the floor?" asked Peltrin. "If their claws are tough enough to dig, they should be tough enough to tear right through the walls of a cabin."

"A valid inquiry," admitted Valdor, "but they never do, as far as I am aware. Bear and moose are the same. Many have the strength to break down the walls. I have no notion as to why they don't. My ignorance can be interpreted only as further evidence you've wasted your time coming here."

Peltrin was beginning to see a pattern in Valdor's negative talk. He disregarded the comment and went on with the story. He did his best to be honest and unemotional about his cowardice, but from time to time he choked up and had to pause. Valdor's face hardened when he heard Peltrin's family had been poisoned, but softened somewhat as the story went on.

"So, this red-eyed bat is an old acquaintance of yours?" he asked.

"I had never seen it before," answered Peltrin.

"And it has taken an interest in making sure you succeed?" asked Valdor.

"I haven't seen it since."

"You felt completely at ease with the creature? It felt trustworthy?"

Peltrin remembered the dark little corner of his mind. The dark corner was still there, but it was far more subdued than it had been when the bat was around. He also remembered the dark and cold presence in the cave that he had never actually seen.

"No," Peltrin admitted.

"Then what exactly makes you think you can trust it? And what makes you think you can trust the mirror?"

"I don't know for sure it was trying to help me," Peltrin admitted. "But it was better than sitting at home watching them die. Nothing could be worse than that."

"Are you so sure," Valdor asked tiredly. "What if you fail? What if you can't get past the guardian? What if you can't climb the Fyllcarcern? What if you climb the Fyllcarcern and you don't get anything that helps you? What if you get back home just in time to see them die? Worse, what if you don't get back in time and they are dead before you get back?"

Peltrin just stood there silently. He had already thought of all of these scenarios. How could he not think about those things? He still believed doing something was the only way to live with himself.

Valdor took a long breath. "I indeed went to the Fyllcarcern, but what happened there only made things worse. Your family only has five days to live, and you are missing those final days. If you go to the Fyllcarcern, there is a valid chance you will have neither the cure nor the memories of your final days with them."

"I don't believe that," Peltrin said, his voice shaky.

"Do you see those two graves," the old man nodded in the direction of the graves with the fresh flowers.

"Yes."

"Then believe it. Those are the graves of my wife and daughter. I climbed the Fyllcarcern to save them, yet there they are."

"How?" asked Peltrin.

"The story is mine and mine alone," said Valdor.

"But he has to try," said Aralis.

"No, he doesn't," answered the old man. "The mirror told you a lie. Aramir sent devastors after my family. My wife and daughter were poisoned and I climbed the Fyllcarcern. But there was no cure. The Panacea, as the mirror called it, doesn't exist. If you need proof, just look right over there."

There was a long silence. Peltrin was breathing deeply, clenching and unclenching his fists. It couldn't be true. He refused to believe it. He had been so sure.

"You believed it because you needed to," the old man's voice was kinder now. "It's a cruel poison. You see your family walking and talking, eating, and breathing, but life will fade no matter what you do. Hope is gone already, there's nothing you can do about it."

Valdor's eyes grew misty and he stared off into the forest. "As a youth, you dream of conquering the coming darkness, but your courage is based only on ignorance. As a man you fight, but eventually you learn that the best one can hope for is to die before you see it all undone. Finally, in your winter years, you see that hope and vanity are one. Light is but a fleeting puff of wind, doomed to rejoin the endless darkness from whence it needlessly sprung. Warmth is even more fleeting and worse than useless, for you can't help but cling to its memory after it has left you forever. Of the few things that are truly eternal, death and decay are undoubtedly the mightiest."

Peltrin choked on his answer. "I have to try. They wouldn't be dying except I failed them."

The old man bowed his head, "Truth be told, I failed my family, too. If hope existed beyond vanity, I wouldn't hesitate to help you."

"But there must be hope," said Soyem.

"If there is, it isn't here with me," Valdor insisted.

Peltrin's shoulders slumped and his head bowed. He was in too much pain to respond. Slowly he began walking away. He reminded himself the mirror had warned him not to come to Valdor. Perhaps, in that one thing, the mirror must have been right.

Aralis followed, a pained expression on her face.

Soyem moved to follow them, but then he paused by the graves.

"You said this is your wife and daughter?" Soyem asked.

"Yes," the pain on the old man's face looked as fresh as the flowers.

"Did they know you were going to try the Fyllcarcern?"

"They did."

"What did they say when you were deciding whether or not to go?"

Peltrin and Aralis paused. They all looked at the old man and waited. He didn't answer for quite some time. A single tear broke from his eye.

"I'll go," he finally said. "But there's no sense leaving before morning. It only takes a few hours to get there from here, and the guardian won't allow you to climb the Fyllcarcern at night."

Peltrin was dumbfounded. He searched for the words to say but he was so surprised that his mind was a complete blank.

"I need some time alone," Valdor said shakily. "I'll be back." Slowly, the old man walked away into the trees.

"I'll keep an eye on him," said Lou, following after the old Ennai warrior.

THE CHRONCILES OF AMYRIAD

Chapter 10: Home Sweet Home

Soyem looked a little confused. "I don't understand why he changed his mind."

"Does it matter?" asked Peltrin, slowly working his way back to a half-smile.

"Whatever they said must have been great," said Soyem. "Now I really want to know what it was."

"I don't think we should ask again," said Aralis. "It looked like he doesn't want to talk about it."

"What do we do, now?" asked Peltrin, frustrated about the new delay. They only had a few days to begin with. Why wouldn't the old man just leave with them now? Even now that Valdor had agreed to come, he still couldn't help but wonder if the old man would be any help.

"No way I'm sleeping in there," Soyem declared, turning to the house.

"I'd rather sleep outside," Peltrin agreed.

Even Aralis looked doubtful, which was surprising, considering her fear of spending the night in the forest. "No one should have to live like this."

"Are you saying we clean it up?" asked Peltrin incredulously. "It would take a week."

"We don't have to clean everything," she answered. "We just need to make it tolerable."

"You just don't want to sleep outside again," accused Soyem.

"True," Aralis admitted. "But we need his help. Shouldn't we do something for him?"

"Fine, then," said Soyem, "you go right ahead. I'm not going in there, and I'm not helping."

Aralis looked at Peltrin pleadingly. "We can't go until tomorrow anyway."

Peltrin hesitated. Sitting around while nearly half of a day went by was the last thing he wanted to do right now. Letting Aralis down was probably the second to last thing in the world he wanted to do right now. He looked at the house with its years of grime and smells. Come to think of it, letting Aralis down was the third to last thing he wanted to do right now.

"I'm okay with sleeping outside," he said apologetically. "The wolves will keep us safe. We can build a fire so you don't need to be afraid."

"Fine," she huffed. To the boys' surprise, she stepped into the house. She lasted less than a minute before she came back out, practically gasping for breath.

"We'll help you be safe sleeping outside," offered Soyem.

"Fine," she said again. She walked in again, a determined look on her face.

A blanket came flying out the door, landing on Soyem's head.

"Aaaaah!" he screamed, throwing it off "It touched me! It touched me! I smell like a two-day-old dead chicken! I'll never be clean again!"

"Wash it," Aralis ordered.

"You want me to touch it?" Soyem's eyes were wide.

"Use a stick," she said.

Soyem looked at Peltrin for aid, but Peltrin just shrugged. Sighing, Soyem picked up a nearby stick, used it to snag the blanket, and started dragging it towards the stream. Aralis, satisfied, went back into the house. A minute later, Peltrin dodged a pile of clothes Aralis threw out the door.

Peltrin knew what she wanted, but he couldn't understand why she thought he would be willing to do it. He stared at the pile, trying to decide if he should use a stick when a bar of soap landed on top. A clothesline soon followed. The soap looked ancient. It was so covered with dirt Peltrin wondered if it were possible the poor thing would no longer be able to clean.

Then he dodged a large bucket as it came flying out the door.

Peltrin sighed. At least he didn't have to go into the house. Guessing what everything was for, he brought her water, hung the line, and then came back to the pile. He bent over to pick up a pair of pants by hand but recoiled before he touched it.

I definitely need a stick, he decided.

Holding the bar of soap in one hand, and a pair of pants on a stick in the other, Peltrin found his way to Soyem, who was already hard at work scrubbing the blanket.

"Oh, good," Soyem said, taking the soap and continuing his work. Peltrin was surprised to see Soyem so hard at work. He had been under the impression that the short, small-boned young man was lazy, but here he was hard at his assigned task.

Deciding he would rather take multiple trips than touch the clothes with his hands, Peltrin grabbed a second stick and started taking the rest of the clothes to the stream. To his surprise, Soyem was done with the blanket before Peltrin had brought all of the clothes to the stream. Peltrin did his best to wring out the blanket while Soyem went to work on the clothes. Peltrin then carried the blanket back to the house and hung it over the line.

Several more blankets were sitting on the ground just outside the house.

"Shouldn't we leave one dry?" asked Peltrin. He doubted the old man would appreciate sleeping under a wet blanket tonight.

"He'll be fine," said Aralis dismissively. "If we don't do it now, it's probably never going to happen."

Now Peltrin was surprised at Aralis. She had always been so quiet, Peltrin had assumed she was not assertive, yet here she was directing the cleaning of the old man's house. It seemed he had misjudged both of Bensil's apprentices.

Peltrin used his sticks to take the blankets to the stream. When he dropped off the last blanket, he found that Soyem was surprisingly quick at cleaning clothes. He brought back an armful of wet clothes to hang.

"Peltrin," called Aralis.

Peltrin wasn't happy about the idea of entering the house, but he was unwilling to argue. Aralis had voluntarily taken on going inside the house, which was, without a doubt, the least desirable job. He walked into the house to see Aralis had been working hard as well. The counter was clean and the newly cleaned dishes were stacked so they could dry.

She hadn't taken the time to polish the few things Valdor had sitting on the shelves, but everything had been dusted and the shelves themselves were clean. She was now trying to move the bed, which was the only furniture in the little house. The bedposts were also newly clean. The floor was still covered in a thick, smelly layer of dirt, but the rest of the house was already beginning to look tolerable.

"Lou's right," said Peltrin, wrinkling his nose. "This place smells more like Valdor than Valdor."

It's stuck," she said, tugging on the bed frame.

Peltrin took hold of the bed frame and yanked hard. The bed broke loose, dirt and grime from the floor still clinging to the legs. They both jumped as several mice scurried for the open door.

"That's disgusting," Peltrin muttered.

Aralis just nodded her head. "Move it over there," she instructed. Peltrin complied. She started sweeping, but it wasn't working very well, there was just too much dirt. Searching around the house, they found a pair of shovels and, together, they shoveled out the house.

"Peltrin," called Soyem, sounding annoyed, "come get these clothes."

Home Sweet Home

Leaving Aralis to sweep the remaining dirt out of the tiny house, Peltrin retrieved the clothes from Soyem. He was surprised to see all of the clothes were done and sitting on a rock. Soyem was now working on the rest of the blankets.

After taking the clothes, wringing them out, and hanging them up, Peltrin then saw there was a rug, half-buried among the piles of dirt he and Aralis had shoveled out of the house. Aralis threw him another length of rope.

Peltrin hung the rope between two trees, downwind of the house and the clothesline. He threw the rug over the line, found a stout stick, and started beating it. Clouds of dust filled the air around him.

"Peltrin," Aralis called.

Peltrin dropped the stick and started walking toward the house.

"Peltrin," called Soyem, "two more blankets are ready."

Peltrin hesitated.

"Peltrin!" they both yelled.

Shaking his head, Peltrin decided to go to the house first.

Aralis laughed when he walked in. "You are a mess," she said.

Peltrin looked down at himself. He was covered in a thick coat of dirt. Carrying the wet clothes and blankets had made him damp and the dirt from beating the rug had stuck to his clothes, face, and arms.

"You're a little dirty yourself," Peltrin pointed out. Aralis was also covered from head to toe in dirt. He wouldn't say it out loud, but the dirt didn't make her any less attractive.

"Peltrin!" Soyem shouted. "Come get these blankets!"

Peltrin rolled his eyes. He quickly slid the bed back to its original position, where the floor was now clean. He then jogged over to where Soyem was still doggedly scrubbing yet another blanket. Peltrin was impressed, the boy had been washing for well over an hour. Perhaps he was stronger than Peltrin had realized.

"Don't worry about me," grumbled Soyem, "I'm just sitting here scrubbing and doing all of the work while you two sit and chat."

"The house is almost clean," said Peltrin defensively, "Aralis and I haven't stopped working once." He bent over to pick up the blanket.

"Don't touch that!" Soyem shouted. "You're a complete mess! The last thing we need is for you to get it all dirty again."

"You're on your own, then," said Peltrin, turning to walk away. "Hang them up yourself."

"Fine, I'm working on the last blanket as we speak." said Soyem testily, "I might as well do all of the work since I've already done most of it anyway."

Peltrin stomped back to the rug and went back to beating it with a stick. Once again, dirt flew in every direction. It was quite some time before the colors of the rug began to show through. Eventually, the clouds of dirt began to diminish.

Finally, Peltrin returned the rug to the house and placed it on the newly cleaned floor. Soyem hung the last of the blankets and came to join them.

"It still smells a little funny," observed Soyem, "but I think we could stand to stay the night here."

"A lot of good it's going to do," said Peltrin. "The roof is useless."

Looking up, they could easily see a large number of missing and damaged shingles.

"Do you know how to fix it?" asked Soyem.

"I've helped my dad fix the roof," said Peltrin, "but we'll need tools and shingles."

"Can't you just make the shingles?" he asked.

"It takes a lot of time and some special tools," explained Peltrin. After all the time it took to clean, they only had an hour or two of sunlight left. It was still late spring. Once the sun was down, full dark wouldn't be far behind.

"Just leave it," said Soyem. He looked very tired. "Valdor doesn't seem to mind, and it doesn't look like it's going to rain tonight anyway."

"Let's look around," suggested Peltrin. "If Valdor has everything for the roof just lying around, we can fix the worst of it before dark."

It didn't take long to find what they needed. There was a pile of shingles out by the woodpile. The shingles on the top of the pile were cracked and splitting from too much sun, and the shingles on the bottom were rotting, but there were still enough usable shingles to repair the worst of the roof.

Valdor kept his tools at a workbench behind the house. They were under the roof overhang where they were partially protected from the rain. There were nails there as well. The nails and the tools were old and rusty but appeared to be usable.

They rolled a stump close to the house, and Peltrin put handfuls of nails into his pocket. Standing on the stump, he easily pulled himself up and swung his feet onto the roof. To his surprise, he found himself face to face with Soyem.

"Hello!" Soyem said cheerfully as Peltrin jumped, nearly falling off.

"Don't fool around up here," said Peltrin a little angrily. "You might fall off."

"You might fall off," Soyem retorted. "I don't fall."

Peltrin just shook his head and frowned.

"It's true," said Aralis from below, "he spends as much time in the trees as he does on the ground. He doesn't fall." She tossed Peltrin the hammer, the pry bar, and several new shingles.

Peltrin looked around to see what needed to be done. He could see that, though it hadn't been repaired in quite some time, the original workmanship had been good.

Peltrin directed Soyem to a spot near the middle where two side by side shingles had rotted and split. He showed Soyem how to pry the shingles up with the pry bar. He worked each shingle up and down and side to side until some of the nails came up. The shingle split around the rest of the nails and slid out. They tossed the rotted shingles to the ground.

As Soyem continued removing the worst of the old shingles, Peltrin found new shingles that were about the right size. He used the sharp end of the pry bar to split a little off of the edges so they fit perfectly into the empty space. After hammering in new nails, he tapped the bottom of each shingle, sliding it up into its final position.

Peltrin was no expert, but he had helped his father often enough that replacing the first few shingles had only taken a few minutes. He looked around the roof, then at the sun, and shook his head. There were a lot of bad shingles. He doubted they could replace all of them by sundown.

Realizing they weren't likely to finish, Peltrin considered telling the others it was a waste of time. After days of constant stress and anxiety, however, he found that cleaning and fixing the house for Valdor was actually somewhat refreshing. It was far better to stay occupied than to sit around worrying all afternoon.

Again, he was surprised at the way the healer's apprentices immediately went to work without complaint. Soyem continued removing damaged shingles and throwing them off the roof as fast as Peltrin could replace them. Aralis decided to split firewood and move it into the house for a warm fire for the night.

By the time the sun started to set, the worst of the roof had been repaired and all three set themselves to cleaning up the mess. There were several places they didn't have time to repair but, obviously, Valdor wasn't bothered by a leaky roof. Peltrin carefully let himself down from the roof and put away the tools and the remaining nails.

After throwing down the last of the damaged and unused shingles, Soyem ran to the corner of the roof and leaped to a nearby tree, catching hold of a branch and swinging joyfully before scurrying down.

"Wow!" said Peltrin, genuinely impressed. "Is that how you got up there?"

"Of course not," Soyem laughed, "I couldn't make that jump from a swaying tree branch. This is how I got up." He ran around behind the house and climbed a tree with a medium-size branch that overhung a corner of the house. In seconds, he was up the tree and dropped down on top of the house.

"That looks easy when you do it, but I wouldn't dare try," Peltrin admitted.

"It's probably not as hard as you think," Soyem said modestly. He then ran toward a new tree. Again, he leaped like a squirrel from the roof to a nearby branch. This time the branch bent and cracked under his weight. Without missing a beat, Soyem smoothly slipped to another branch before letting himself down.

"I've never seen anyone climb like that," said Peltrin, still impressed. In his mind, Soyem had been the deadweight of the group. It hadn't occurred to him that Soyem might be able to do something the others couldn't.

Not far from the house there was a pool in the stream surrounded by thick bushes. Exhausted and hungry, they each took a turn in the secluded area cleaning themselves and changing their clothes. They then hung their wet clothes and brought in their traveling packs and Valdor's blankets, which were now dry.

By the time it was fully dark, Peltrin had repaired the front door. It wasn't good as new, but it was functional. Soyem and Aralis had started a fire and they were preparing another stew using the prepackaged ingredients Nirani had prepared for them.

Valdor strode into the house and froze. He spent nearly a full minute scanning the tiny one-room home from one side to the other, and top to bottom.

"Well you kids have been busy," he mused. "I never anticipated seeing this place looking this good again, ever."

Lou walked in behind the old Ennai warrior. "Of course they have been working," said the marmot, "I helped train Peltrin myself. The other two are Bensil's apprentices."

"Still smells a little funny," said Soyem. Aralis kicked him.

"As do I," said Valdor with a grin. "I am uncertain I could stand to live here otherwise."

"Your clothes are clean," pointed out Aralis. "You could wash up and change."

"I'll consider it," said the old man without enthusiasm. Realizing they weren't likely to persuade him any time soon, they decided to let it go.

"Stew's ready," announced Peltrin sometime later. "There's plenty for you, Valdor, if you want any."

"I couldn't take your food," said Valdor, though his eyes were fixed on the pot over the fire.

Certain the old man was only trying to be polite, Peltrin handed him a large bowl. He then dished up a bowl for everyone else. Nirani had changed the recipe a little so they didn't feel like they were eating the same thing day after day, but it was still excellent. Once again, there was flat waybread to clean every last remnant out of the bowl. There were seconds all around and even enough for a third helping for Peltrin.

After they had finished eating, Lou sniffed the air. "The smell of food is fading," he grumbled. "This place is unbearable without it. I'll be out in the woodpile, everyone. Call me if you need me." Peltrin opened the door and Lou disappeared into the dark.

"Well, I suppose I should get my things ready for tomorrow," said Valdor. He stood up on the bed and pulled down a traveling pack and a bedroll. Much to Aralis' dismay, a large amount of dirt fell from the rafters to the newly cleaned floor. Somehow, they had missed that the old man stored many of his belongings up above.

"What's that?" asked Soyem, pointing to another object stashed in the rafters.

"It's nothing," said Valdor dismissively.

"It looks like some kind of instrument," Soyem persisted. "Will you play for us?"

"I don't play for guests," answered Valdor. "That worthless old piece is in terrible condition. Besides, I've never been any good."

"Please do," said Aralis.

Valdor hesitated as he looked at her. He took a deep breath. His eyes looked like they were threatening to tear up again. "You remind me of my daughter, a little," he muttered. He then drew in another deep breath. "She was about your age when she died. She loved it when I played, despite my lousy instrument and lack of talent."

Looking at the two of them, Peltrin could have believed they were related. They both had the same dark eyes, high cheekbones, wide noses, and straight hair.

"Please," she repeated quietly.

He hesitated a moment longer. They all looked and waited. Sighing, Valdor took down the instrument. It was clear he had lied about the quality and condition of the piece. It was beautiful and well taken care of.

"Doesn't look like a worthless old piece to me," said Soyem, eying the instrument.

"Have an interest in music, do you?" asked Valdor with a raised eyebrow.

Soyem looked away. "Not really, I mean, I've always thought it would be nice to know how to play, but there's no one in Aldayin to teach me."

"Sadly, there's no one here of any skill here to teach you, either," said Valdor. "But let's see if I can remember a tune or two."

He began plucking the instrument a little and made a few tuning adjustments. He then started with a quick, catchy tune, showcasing some complicated finger movement. It was clear he had lied about his skill as well.

"That was amazing!" exclaimed Soyem when Valdor finished. "It's exactly the sort of thing I want to learn."

"Maybe later, then," said Valdor. He smiled a little, though the smile still didn't quite seem to reach his eyes.

"Play another!" exclaimed Peltrin. All three of them clamored until the old man consented.

The playing went on for nearly an hour. The old man played a variety of songs ranging from quick and light to slow and thoughtful.

From time to time the three youths would dance to the music. Having never learned how to dance, their movements were a little random, but Peltrin's athleticism and Aralis' natural grace made them look like accomplished dancers. Peltrin particularly enjoyed when he and Aralis would join hands or arms. Each time it sent electricity through his entire body, and he found himself grinning like an idiot.

Soyem joined in as well. He tended to be quicker and lighter on his feet than his much taller companions. He generally danced alone, rarely joining hands or arms with the others, which didn't bother Peltrin at all.

"Do you sing?" asked Aralis, sitting down. They had just finished a particularly lively dance, and all three of them were a little breathless.

"Not if I can avoid it," the old man answered. Though his music had been excellent, he had not yet sung for them.

Home Sweet Home

"I don't think we're going to let you avoid it today," she said smiling.

"Very well, then," Valdor consented. Peltrin suspected he only relented because Aralis reminded the old man so much of his daughter.

Valdor started playing slowly. The tune was simple but beautiful. The music alone felt so full of memory that the song was haunting even before he started to sing.

> "Why is the sun dim, and why is the moon old?
> Why is my world so empty and cold?
> My one true love, I've searched for thee in song
> But you're taken from my arms where you belong.
> Foes by the dozen did fall before me,
> All of my battles have ended in victory.
> These have no meaning if I'm without thee…"

There was a short, mournful interlude.

> "What good are my arms if they cannot hold thee?
> Why do my years drag on endlessly?
> Each new day brings new depths to my sorrow
> As I tend your grave and long for what's below
> Years find my tears falling no more gently
> Years of my mourning have left but one hope for me,
> May death come soon and bring me home to thee."

The song ended and there was a long silence. Valdor's face was drenched in tears and there wasn't a dry eye in the room.

"It's a beautiful song," said Aralis, wiping tears from her face.

"I wrote it ages ago," said Valdor quietly. "It was different then." He wiped his face absently. If it were possible, his hand seemed too practiced in the art of wiping away tears. "It was once a song of love. But it changed when they died. I don't think I could remember the original words if I tried. Even if I could, I'm sure I couldn't sing them."

Peltrin couldn't help but be afraid he would understand Valdor a lot better at sunrise, only a few days away.

There was another long silence. It was Valdor who finally spoke.

"A good entertainer wouldn't end on such a sad song," he said. "I ought to give you at least one more to end on a slightly happier note. But I'm done for the day. My hands are tired and my heart isn't willing to pretend anymore. Unfortunate, but I never claimed to be good."

Peltrin wanted to argue, but what could he say? Nothing seemed appropriate. He also suddenly realized how tired he was. In silent agreement, they all set about getting ready for bed. They quickly cleaned the dishes and swept the floor. Valdor arranged his blankets on the bed and the three youths set up their bedrolls on the floor near the fire.

As Peltrin lay down in his bedroll near the fire, he thought about the day. He had been reluctant to help clean the house and repair the roof, but doing so had somehow helped relieve a small part of the heavy burden that had been weighing down his heart. It was almost sad to admit, but seeing Valdor's misery had helped put his own difficulties in perspective. After all that had happened, at least his parents and uncle were alive. Valdor no longer had that comfort.

Thanks to the work and the music, Peltrin felt stronger now. It had never occurred to him before that perhaps his shame had been affecting his strength.

The final song, though, still rang in his ears. Valdor had climbed the Fyllcarcern, and yet his wife and daughter were buried just outside. He had never explained how that had happened. Tomorrow they would face the Fyllcarcern. Peltrin couldn't help but think the old man had sung the final song as a warning. Perhaps the Fyllcarcern didn't hold the solution Peltrin was hoping for.

THE CHRONCILES OF AMYRIAD

CHAPTER 11: THE FYLLCARCERN

They awoke early and had another quick, cold breakfast. Peltrin's anxiety to continue the mission had spread, to some extent, to the rest of them. Even Valdor offered no resistance. Soyem actually allowed Peltrin to help him arrange his pack. The morning was chilly and the dew was still heavy on the grass when they left Valdor's newly cleaned and repaired home.

As Valdor had promised, the distance from his house to the Fyllcarcern was short. They had traveled no more than two hours when they reached the top of a ridge. There, they all stopped automatically to stare at the unnatural wonder. Peltrin was far from tired but he found himself breathless as he finally looked at the thing he had come to face.

The Fyllcarcern was an enormous stone monolith. Far too large to have been built by man, it soared hundreds of feet above the hill where it stood. It was about half as wide as it was tall and appeared to be flat on top.

The recently risen sun behind them lit up the monolith spectacularly. It appeared to be made of spires of various colors. Red, black, gray, green, orange, and yellow columns of stone wove together in fantastic patterns. All of which pointed towards the sky above. It had the appearance of solid rock—no trees grew there. The sides were scored with cracks and gaps, which increased the ancient and unnatural feel of the fantastic monstrosity.

The multicolored monolith stood upon a sparsely wooded hill, separated from the surrounding area by grassy lowlands. Peltrin couldn't help but think the place almost looked as if it had been constructed strategically. The hill and monolith, with their surrounding lowlands, gave the appearance of a fortified castle with a moat.

A small stream meandered back and forth in the grassy lowland on the south side of the monolith, supporting the impression of a moat. The nearest cover to the hill was a small stand of trees on a gentle rise just outside of the low grasslands. The stand was located to the Southwest of the hill where the Fyllcarcern stood.

Following the path, they entered the valley well to the East of the colony and across the stream. The path meandered westward between the stream and the hill, keeping the stream between them and the colony and never touching the hill.

"Don't go near the colony," Valdor warned. "Those little things are mean. They'll come after you in packs."

Looking closely, Peltrin could see dozens of small mounds dotting a section of the valley just south of the Fyllcarcern. He could see several small animals popping up out of the mounds. Each one quickly disappeared again after a short look around. As they got closer, he could see they were similar to squirrels, though larger in body and smaller in tail.

"What are they?" asked Peltrin, staring curiously.

"I don't know," said Valdor. "But they were here long before I came the first time. Little seems to change here."

"Look at those little guys," said Lou. "They look like they could be my nieces and nephews. I kind of feel like I should be looking out for them."

"Tastier than squirrels," inserted Fang, licking his chops "though not nearly as good as deer."

They all paused to look at him.

"Where did you come from?" asked Valdor in surprise.

"You categorize animals by taste?" Soyem asked with horror before the wolf could answer.

"Don't you?" asked Fangmort, appearing on the other side. "I can smell jerky made from cattle in your pack. Sometimes you eat bacon made from a pig. Do you not like one better than the other?"

"Those are normal foods," Soyem argued. "We eat those all the time. We've never seen these before."

"You've never tried new food?"

"What if these are the only ones in Amyriad?" Soyem protested. "What if you eat too many and they all die off and then they no longer exist. They live in the shadow of the Fyllcarcern, what if they are magical?"

"Not a problem if they all die off," Fang answered, "deer taste better anyway."

"Especially young deer," Fangmort agreed.

Soyem huffed in frustration. The wolves were not getting it.

Following the path, they entered the valley well to the East of the colony. They then followed the path across the stream, where it turned Westward. The path meandered between the stream and the hill, keeping the stream between them and the colony and never touching the hill.

Dozens of little heads popped up out of the ground, watching them as they walked by, but no alarm was raised. The little creatures didn't appear to feel threatened as long as the travelers kept to the other side of the stream.

The travelers grew silent as they passed near the base of the hill. The Fyllcarcern had an ancient, powerful feel—as if great things had happened there. Peltrin suspected those great things, though largely forgotten, still influenced the world.

They quickly set up camp where the trail ended in the sparse stand of trees southwest of the Fyllcarcern. Then, leaving all of their things behind except their weapons, they approached the base of the hill.

"There she is," said Valdor uncomfortably.

"Who? Where?" Peltrin asked, looking around.

"The guardian," he answered, pointing toward the base of the hill. A massive spotted cat sat waiting. Its tail swished like a snake, but otherwise, the cat was still as a stone. Her greyish-yellow coloring and dark rosette-shaped spots blended well with the surroundings.

"The guardian is a giant cat?" asked Peltrin.

"What kind of cat is that?" asked Aralis, "It looks like a mountain lion, but it's too big and the coloring is all wrong."

"Should we go around to the other side?" Soyem asked nervously.

"She's looking right at us," Lou said with a sigh, "it's a bit late for sneakiness now."

"You may approach," the huge spotted cat called. Her voice was deep but clearly feminine. "I cannot leave the hill. You are safe from me as long as you do not try to set foot on the hill without my permission. The proper name for my current form, by the way, is jaguar. Mountain lion wasn't a terrible guess; they are among the jaguar's distant cousins."

The four of them approached, stopping several paces from the base of the hill. Though the jaguar did not make any specific effort to be intimidating, intimidation was inevitable. In a sitting position, the jaguar's nose was almost higher than Peltrin could reach.

The two wolves held back. They appeared to feel their agreement did not obligate them to approach the Fyllcarcern, much less the guardian herself.

"Am I to assume you wish to approach the monolith?" the jaguar asked when they were close enough for conversation.

"My family was poisoned by red-eyed devastors," Peltrin answered. "I was told I could find a panacea on top of the Fyllcarcern." Peltrin took several minutes to recount what had happened to his family and his journey into the cave. He left out the same parts he hadn't told the others, as well as the part where the mirror told him the guardian wasn't trustworthy.

"You were misled, I'm afraid" the jaguar said regretfully when he had finished. "You are not the first to come here looking for a magical solution to an impossible problem. Sadly, no panacea exists here…or anywhere, for that matter."

"But the mirror told me…" Peltrin protested.

"The mirror—as you call it—deceived you. The red-eyed bat you spoke of followed you here, though it has now fled, no doubt intending to cause further mischief. Perhaps it will send someone else to annoy me further."

"But what do we do?" pled Peltrin. "Even Bensil doesn't understand this poison."

"The source of the poison is a magical object, combined with some quality of the creature who currently holds it. The only cure for the poison is to destroy the creature who created it."

"How can you know for sure," asked Peltrin. He was a little offended the jaguar would dismiss him so readily.

"I have guarded this place for thousands of years," the jaguar answered, "all magical objects are attracted to it. Most that are not currently joined to this place have been or will be at some time or another. Over time I have gained a level of understanding of such things."

"Can you tell us the source?" asked Soyem. "And how we can destroy it?"

"I am familiar with the object," answered the jaguar, "but not its current owner. Some creature is using it to create the poison."

"Aramir," Peltrin mumbled to himself angrily.

"Once the creature is destroyed," the jaguar went on, "the poison's hold over its victims will be broken."

"How do you know so much about it?" asked Soyem skeptically. "Are you saying that particular magical object used to be here?"

"Magical objects exist only in pairs," the guardian answered, "The two wolves who keep you company, for example, consumed a pair of complementary objects. Similarly, the object used to create your poison has a partner. The pair to that object is one of many currently bound to this place."

"Can we…" Peltrin started

"No, you may not have it," the jaguar interrupted. "Even if you were to obtain the object, you lack the knowledge and skill to use it. Here, it serves a valuable purpose. With you, it would be of no benefit to anyone, including yourself."

"But can you not help us?" Soyem asked. "Lend us the item and teach us to use it. Or use the item to make a cure. They will all die in less than two days if we do nothing. There's no way we can kill Aramir in two days. Can you not find a way to give us more time?"

"It would take more than two days to extract the object," answered the huge cat, "and more than two days again to teach you to use it. As for making a cure or giving you more time, I do not have that ability without significant outside assistance. Your companion already knows this." She nodded towards Valdor.

"Was something given to Valdor when he came here before?" asked Peltrin. Valdor inhaled sharply and Peltrin suddenly wished he hadn't asked. Valdor had made it clear he didn't want to share the story.

"Yes," answered the jaguar, "though he didn't receive exactly what he desired. Such things are possible under the right conditions when I permit someone to approach. Valdor convinced me he had the courage, motivation, and ability, so I allowed him to make the attempt. I know he feels the results were unsatisfactory, but that is not within my power to remedy. The courage he demonstrated, though great, was not sufficient to obtain what he hoped for."

Valdor's face fell and his shoulders slumped. Peltrin felt sorry for him.

"Thank you for answering our questions," said Peltrin, "But we need more than words. How can I get help from the Fyllcarcern?"

"You cannot," answered the guardian. "I will not permit it."

"You climb the monolith," answered Valdor stiffly, "as the mirror told you. But it isn't enough to just climb. You will need the help of the guardian to direct the magic."

"Why won't you help me?" Peltrin asked the jaguar. He was beginning to lose patience.

"My reasons are my own."

"Her reasons are selfish," Valdor said angrily. "She has her own personal battle she is fighting. She'll only let you climb the Fyllcarcern if you can convince her it serves her purpose."

The guardian sighed. "Very well, I'll tell you my reasons, since Valdor insists on misrepresenting me. I don't blame you for your bitterness, old man, but I must remind you that your failure was not my doing."

Valdor turned away bitterly. Peltrin glimpsed tears on the old man's face.

"First, you should know the name Fyllcarcern does not refer to the monolith of stone. The correct name for the monolith is Mihtighof. Long ago, the name meant home of the great power. The other thing you should know is the Mihtighof is not a force for good or evil. It is a gathering place of knowledge and power. As you interact with the Mihtighof, over time you can eventually gain a portion of this knowledge and power. How you use it is left to you alone."

Peltrin listened closely. This was definitely not the same story the mirror had told him. On one hand, Peltrin remembered the mirror had told him not to trust the guardian. But on the other hand, he wasn't confident he could trust the mirror, either.

"Many thousands of years ago," the jaguar went on, "my people lived in the shadow of the Mihtighof. Our lives were spent praying to the source of the power, protecting its home, and learning its secrets. I was human at the time. I was about your age and very attractive. I was also particularly gifted at learning the ways of the Mihtighof. Many of the young men of my village sought my attention.

"One young man, in particular, I detested. He was obsessed with only two things: powers of destruction, and making me his possession. He was, unfortunately, also quite gifted. Over time, he discovered new ways to interact with the Mihtighof, and his powers quickly became formidable. At first, he shared his secrets with me, hoping I would join him in his twisted ways, but I rejected him.

"After I turned him away, he became bitter and sought revenge against me. At first, his attacks were relatively subtle. Suitors and loved ones would disappear, my home burned down three times in a single season, and accidents befell those who were friendly to me. I told him repeatedly we would never be together, but still, he persisted. Though he often harmed those around me, he never once tried to harm me.

"In his lust for power, he eventually learned to transform himself into a terrifying beast of destruction, known as the Fyllen, meaning the fallen one, or the bringer of death. It was a new manifestation of a beast that anciently nearly destroyed the entire world. Joined to him, the beast was even more powerful than before. He and the beast believed, correctly, that once my people were destroyed, the rest of the world had no hope of stopping them.

"By day he walked in human form, by night he took the shape of the Fyllen. Many warriors attempted to destroy the beast, but weapons were no match for it. Even in human form, he was unnaturally powerful. One by one, the great warriors and wise men of our people were destroyed.

"One stormy night, in a fit of rage as the Fyllen, he destroyed all that was left of the village. Only he and I remained. He was so bent on destruction that, without my people to contain him, I was certain the entire world would soon be destroyed.

"He was in the form of the beast, and I cowered before him. I filled his ears with all of the flattering words he had always dreamed of hearing from me. I talked of his unequaled powers, his insurmountable will, his infinite wisdom. I told him the world was his for the taking and, in exchange for my life, I would submit myself to him.

"He returned to human form and we embraced. Only then did he learn the extent of the knowledge and power our village elders had helped me to obtain. Holding him in my arms and knowing his heart belonged to me, I absorbed him into myself. I made myself the Fyllcarcern, the prison of the fallen one, or death's prison. Since then, the term has been applied to the monolith, rather than to me, and the name Mihtighof is all but forgotten.

"Realizing he was betrayed; he used his last ounce of will to transform into the beast. My human form was not able to fully absorb and control the Fyllen, so I transformed myself into the mighty jaguar you see now.

"Even as a jaguar, there are times I cannot fully contain the beast. Sometimes, on stormy nights, the evil takes over. I take the shape of the Fyllen and prowl this hill surrounding the Mihtighof. I can keep the Fyllen from wandering beyond the base of the hill, but any who venture here during those times are destroyed."

"It's a terrible story," Peltrin said sincerely, "but I don't understand why you say I cannot approach the Fyllcarcern, or Mihtighof, or whatever it's called." He was still unsure whether he believed the guardian or the mirror.

"The Mihtighof gains power from your inner strength," the jaguar explained, "which in turn empowers one of us. The Fyllen feeds on fear, selfishness, hate, and despair. I am strengthened by courage, selflessness, love, and hope.

"Think of the Mihtighof as a ship of the sea. The hearts of men are the wind that powers the sails. The Fyllen and I are captains with the ability to steer the power of the Mihtighof in the desired direction. As the power of your heart fills the mighty sails, the captain you choose is given the power to grant your request. If you choose me and demonstrate attributes associated with me, I am strengthened. If, however, you choose the beast and your heart is aligned with him, the Fyllen is strengthened."

"You see," Valdor accused, "the only reason the guardian does not allow you to approach is because she is not confident you will help her cause!"

"You can give one of us power, but you cannot force us to help you," the jaguar contested. "If I allow you to appeal to me, and you succeed, I am bound by my nature to help you. If, however, you appeal to the Fyllen, the beast may choose to apply the power it gains to escape me, rather than help your cause. As a creature of selfishness, that scenario is very likely. If released, the Fyllen will destroy everything: you, your families, your towns and cities, even your enemies."

"The real issue, then," Peltrin surmised, "is you think I'm not brave enough or selfless enough to face the Mihtighof in a way that serves your cause."

"It is the cause of all," the guardian reminded him, "but yes, you are correct. When he came before, Valdor was a man of great renown, known far and wide for his courageous and selfless accomplishments. Now he returns a broken man, full of misery and regret. The wolves do not have the ability to climb, even if they were so inclined. The marmot and the rest of you are untried. Your hearts are unknown even to yourselves. I would have as much luck flipping a coin."

"But we have no great hero to do this for us," Soyem protested. "If you won't let us try then they are sure to die."

"You may not approach," the guardian answered with finality. "For the good of all, I cannot take that chance. Now go back to your camp and rest. Tomorrow, return to your homes to seek what joy you may find in your few remaining hours. I wish you well. Know now if you attempt to approach the Mihtighof, I will know the instant your feet touch this hill and your lives will be forfeit."

The giant jaguar inhaled deeply. She then opened her mouth wide, revealing heavy, pointed teeth.

"Get back!" said Lou, quickly scurrying away. The rest of them didn't move, paralyzed by the view of the powerful jaws and massive teeth.

The guardian exhaled, sending a warm breath over them. The air from the jaguar's mouth was filled with peace and relaxation. Peltrin was suddenly tired. So tired he could barely walk. Looking around he could see the others' eyes were drooping as well. Unable to resist the guardian's suggestion, they wandered back to camp and quickly fell asleep.

THE CHRONCILES OF AMYRIAD

CHAPTER 12: THE FYLLEN

Peltrin awoke to hot panting. Opening his eyes, he found himself looking straight into a mouth filled with pointed, drool-soaked teeth. Peltrin gagged and rolled away.

"Fang!" he choked, "get your mouth away from my face!"

"Relax," Fang replied. "I just ate. Besides, I'm still not convinced I am interested in you as a meal. I've never cared much for squirrels."

"What makes you think I would taste like a squirrel?" asked Peltrin. The idea offended him slightly, though it was hard to say why. "And what is that smell?" Peltrin was still struggling to keep from throwing up.

"It's the smell of fresh blood," Fang retorted, "which is nowhere near as bad as the smell of a man."

"If you ever decide to eat me," Peltrin answered, sitting up, "do me a favor and start with my face. Nothing you do to me could be worse than making me smell your breath again."

"Funny," Fang answered, though there wasn't a trace of humor in his voice.

"How long have I been asleep?" Peltrin asked, rubbing his eyes. It was full daylight but he was still feeling disoriented from whatever the jaguar had done to them.

"Only a few hours," Fang answered. "Fangmort and I used the time to eat some of those little critters. A few had wandered from the colony."

"I think Soyem is right," Peltrin murmured, scratching his left arm. "You should eat something else. You and your brother could wipe out the entire colony in a matter of weeks.

"Don't get distracted," Lou interrupted. "You need to get up the monolith tonight. If you don't, you'll never make it back before the others die."

"But the jaguar won't allow it," Peltrin answered.

"Which is why we are not asking," Lou answered. "She claims we need her help to make it work, but she refuses to aid us, meaning we lose nothing by climbing without her permission. We won't have her help either way. Besides, for all we know, this story of the Fyllen is just something she made up to try to frighten us."

"Should we wake Valdor?" asked Peltrin, shivering a little at the thought of the Fyllen. He had no real concept of what the creature might look like, but the Jaguar's description had been enough to get his imagination going. He didn't like the possibilities.

"We've been trying to wake all of you ever since you went to sleep," said Lou. "No one has been responding until you woke up just now."

"Besides, look at him," Fangmort said disdainfully. The old man was splayed out awkwardly. Only half of his thin, skeletal body was covered by his blanket. A thick steady stream of drool had formed a considerable puddle below his half-open mouth.

"Once he was great," Lou said, "but he's lost something. I don't think he can help us now."

The rockchuck's lack of confidence seemed a little harsh, but Peltrin had to agree. There was no possibility the old man could manage the climb.

Peltrin emptied his pack of everything and debated carefully what he should take on the climb. In the end, he settled on taking as little as possible. He packed only a single water flask and enough food for a single meal. For weapons, he took two throwing knives and one of his short swords. Even the tomahawk would be left behind this time.

"I'm ready," he said, throwing the pack over his shoulder.

"Now," Lou said, "let's plan your ascent."

"It's not something that takes much planning," Peltrin replied. "I keep going up until I get to the top."

Lou rolled his eyes, something Peltrin had never realized a rockchuck could do.

"There's nothing to plan," Peltrin insisted. He was getting agitated with Lou's obsession with planning every detail.

"Humor me a little," said Lou. "Ever since I learned to talk, my colony doesn't accept me anymore. You and your family are all I've got. Planning is all I can do to help. What could it hurt?"

Peltrin just sighed in frustration and looked at the monolith.

"Ok then," Lou prompted, "just answer this question for me. Is the Mihtighof identical all the way around?"

Peltrin thought about it for a minute. He hadn't paid much attention. From a distance, the monolith had seemed so symmetrical, so perfect. He hadn't thought to consider the different sides as they got closer.

"What difference does it make?" Peltrin protested. "The top is the top. It doesn't matter how I get there."

"Not that I care," said Fang, "but if I decided to kill you…"

"What?" exclaimed Peltrin.

Fang continued, "I could approach it like a human. Give you a formal challenge, wait until you are fully armed and ready to fight, and then kill you slowly, one small injury at a time until you finally bleed out. That kind of killing gives you a chance to injure or kill me before you die."

Peltrin didn't answer. The image was disturbing, but an accurate description of the way humans often fought.

"Or," Fangmort inserted, "I do it like a cunning wolf, and rip out your throat before you even realize I am there. I could then step back and watch you bleed out until you die. That way you have no opportunity to defend yourself or cause me injury."

Peltrin was beginning to doubt he could sleep outdoors anymore.

"The meal is the same either way," Fang went on. "It's just a question of how much you risk."

Peltrin took a minute to consider. The proposal still sounded more like a threat than sound advice, but as he thought about it, he could see the logic. He could also visualize himself bleeding to death while the two wolves sat back and watched. He could almost hear them discussing how he would taste after he finished bleeding out. He quickly pushed the thought aside.

"What do you think I should do?" Peltrin asked Lou.

"What did you do to prepare for the forest training scenarios?" asked Lou. "What did you do while you waited for those thieves to take their positions around your camp?"

"I made a plan of attack," said Peltrin.

"Then make a plan of attack," Lou said. "Make a plan of attack for the climb."

Peltrin gazed at the Mihtighof, or Fyllcarcern, or whatever it was. Now that he was looking for it, he could see there were, indeed, subtle imperfections that could be used to aid the climb. From this angle, he could also see that, unlike the north side, the south side was not perfectly vertical. There were huge boulder fields on the East and West sides of the hill, but the North and South sides were mostly grassy slopes. He also noticed the valley that surrounded the monolith was much lower on the south side than on the North.

Peltrin moved to his left, hiking up a small hill until he had a better view directly from the West. From here it was even more obvious the north side would be far more challenging than the South.

"Plan it from beginning to end," Lou instructed, "step by step."

"I don't want to climb the north side," Peltrin began. "The south side will be far easier."

"Go on," Lou prompted.

"I don't want to climb the north side," Peltrin repeated, "but the hill that surrounds the Mihtighof is not nearly as steep on the North. Also, the hill touches the base of the monolith higher than the south side. It looks like I should approach from the North, and work my way around the West side of the monolith until I get to a good starting point."

The marmot and the wolves said nothing, letting Peltrin work out the problem for himself.

"It would be too slow to go over the boulder field," Peltrin's natural ability to visualize problems and solutions was finally starting to kick in, "but there is a flat area at the base of the monolith. It forms what looks almost like a path around the west side." He moved to his left a little more to get a better view of the area. "I will have to climb or go around a few boulders leaning on the base of the monolith, but it shouldn't be very difficult compared to going over the entire boulder field."

He continued to stare. "I should start climbing somewhere around there," he pointed to the Southwest face. "There's a high point where the hill meets the monolith almost as high as it does on the North side. It will be much less climbing than if I started climbing the south side."

"Good," said Lou, "that puts you relatively high on the southwest side, which looks like a good starting location for the actual climb. Where do you go from there?"

Wanting a better view, Peltrin moved to his right, back down the slope where he could see the Southwest side straighter on.

Looking closely, he could see that the many columns that formed the Mihtighof varied in height, as well as width and color. The tops of the columns appeared to be flat, possibly forming platform areas where he could stop. He realized that, if he planned it well, he might be able to use these platforms as resting places, breaking the long climb to the top into a series of shorter climbs. It would still be difficult, but it would be far less difficult than climbing from bottom to top without a single rest.

"I would start climbing there," Peltrin began, indicating a column whose top was not far above the base. "It looks like there is a gap between that column and the one next to it that I can use. By the time I get to the top of that column, I should be out of reach of the jaguar."

He continued to study the area, indicating three more platform areas where he would be able to rest on the way up. Near the top, there were a series of columns along the south side ending at about the same height, forming a ledge. Moving to his right so he could get a better view of the south side, he saw that the columns forming the ledge were somewhat taller on the east side.

"After I get to the top of the fourth column, I'll climb to the ledge," he indicated the area. "From there, if I walk on the ledge toward the East, it slopes upward to the Southeast corner. By the time I get to the far end of the ledge, it will just be a short climb to the top."

Peltrin went over the entire route again. With a rush, he realized that, if he could get past the jaguar, the plan gave him a much better chance to reach the top.

"Okay," Peltrin said, "I think I can do it."

By this time Valdor had finally awoken and had wandered over to join them.

"Not that I think this is a good idea," Valdor grumbled after Peltrin described the planned route for him, "but that is very nearly the same route I took. I didn't pay attention to the north side so I didn't notice the approach would have been easier if I had started from the North and came around the base of the Mihtighof."

Valdor pointed to an area on the south side. "I started there."

The area Valdor pointed to was down and to the right from Peltrin's starting point. The climb from there was longer than Peltrin's climb.

"It's difficult to see from here," Valdor said, "but there is a good crack that starts there and goes all the way to the top of your first column."

"Do you think your way is better?" asked Peltrin, doubting his planned route.

Valdor studied the differences between the two climbs intently, seeming to forget for a moment his determination to be glum and generally useless.

"No, your way is better," he finally said. "Partly because the climb is shorter. But the biggest advantage is it puts you out of reach of the Jaguar sooner. The run around the base of the monolith should be pretty quick. My route is near that pile of boulders leaning against the Mihtighof. The Jaguar would be able to stand on one of those boulders and reach over and take a swipe at you, even after you have been climbing for a while."

Peltrin nodded his head. He hadn't thought about that, but it was a good point.

"Now for the next problem," said Lou, "the guardian has refused us. How exactly do you plan to get to the start of the climb?"

"How fast are you wolves compared to a jaguar?" asked Peltrin, turning to the wolves.

"We're a lot faster than ordinary wolves," answered Fang, "We may be as fast as a jaguar. They don't live in the Pichari mountains so we've never chased one down before. We've chased mountain lions. The two of us are faster, but they're pretty quick to go up a tree or a rocky area where we can't go."

"We might be as fast as an ordinary jaguar," Fangmort pointed out, "but I would guess the guardian is much faster. If anyone's wondering, I'm faster than Fang, but I don't like my chances against the guardian."

"I think it would have to be Fang," said Peltrin. "I don't doubt Fangmort is normally the fastest, but I'm worried my weight will slow him down too much."

"You want me to play pony?" Fang made no effort to hide his disgust.

"It would be our best chance of getting me to the start of the climb," said Peltrin hesitantly. He had been worried about whether or not the horse-sized wolf would be willing to do this.

"We agreed to get you here safe," the wolf growled, getting right into Peltrin's face. "Which is exactly what we did. Now you want to ride me like one of those worthless pack animals you keep at the farm. Were you hoping I would make the climb for you as well?"

"Those animals are not worthless." Peltrin protested. "We couldn't run the farm without them."

"No, you couldn't," Fang fumed. "Every farmer needs his mules, every butcher needs his pigs, every general needs his horse. Even now, when you are on a quest to save your parents, you find yourself helpless without an animal to do the work for you."

"And what of the Fyllen?" asked Fangmort. "You cowered away from the devastors and left your parents to face them alone! How could you face the Fyllen if you can't face devastors?"

Peltrin dropped his head.

To Peltrin's horror, Fang and Fangmort turned and started walking away.

"Wait!" Peltrin cried, "you promised. We can't do this without you."

Valdor could only stare dumbfounded as the two wolves continued to walk away.

"We promised to protect you," Fang called back, "not to climb for you. We kept our bargain, don't expect anything more."

"You had better find some shelter to cower in," Fangmort inserted, "a storm is coming."

Peltrin and Valdor were still staring at the empty forest long after the great wolves had disappeared.

"Well...that's the end of our little adventure," said Valdor with a sigh, "I never thought much of our chances anyway."

"You're giving up too?" Peltrin protested.

"It's time to cut your losses, kid. I don't mean to be cruel, but your family never had a chance to begin with. The wolves said there's a storm coming, and the guardian said the Fyllen destroys anyone who comes during a storm. My climb was terrifying, and the Fyllen wasn't there that day. If it had been, and if it's as terrible as the guardian says…"

"I'm going," said Peltrin. "I'd rather face the Fyllen than give up. This is probably better; the mirror said my best chance of success is to go alone. I've had too much help already."

Valdor paused for a while, breathing slowly and looking at the ground. To Peltrin's eyes, the old man seemed even more weighed down than usual.

Aralis and Soyem joined them, still sleepy-eyed and groggy.

"I know what it's like," Valdor said quietly. "I lost my wife and daughter to red-eyed devastors. Aramir sent one after each of them, and two after me. A lot of devastors died that day. We all survived, but my wife and girl were both poisoned. I came here hoping for a cure and I succeeded in climbing to the top."

Valdor paused again.

"The Mihtighof wasn't as impressed with me as I had hoped it would be. I returned to my home with a single stone. The stone has the power to freeze someone in time and keep them alive. I could have used it to freeze one of them, giving me time to find and kill the source of the poison. Once the source was dead, I would be able to return and revive the one who was frozen in stone."

"Only one stone for both your wife and daughter?" asked Peltrin, confused.

"That was the problem," Valdor answered. "It would only work for one of them. My performance was sufficient for one stone, but not for two.

"My daughter wasn't a child. She was about your age, so we talked about it together. In the end, they both refused to take it. Neither of them could live with the thought that she had sent the other to her death. I couldn't persuade them. I pleaded and waited and watched while they both died before my eyes. You've seen their graves."

"What did you do with the stone?" Aralis asked softly.

"I buried it with them," he answered, "what else was I to do?"

It was several minutes before any of them spoke. "The point is, Peltrin," said Valdor, "you need to consider this more thoroughly. If your parents were here right now, what would they tell you to do?"

Peltrin shook his head. He had no idea what they would say.

"They would tell you thanks, but no thanks," said the old man, answering his own question. "Think about it. Your chances of success were so small. Now the guardian won't let you approach and the wolves are gone and a storm is coming. Let's be honest, you have no chance whatsoever of even making it to the base of the monolith.

The old man paused to compose himself before he continued. "I would have gladly given anything to have died in the place of my wife or daughter. I don't doubt you feel the same way, but there's nothing to be gained."

Peltrin paused to ask himself if he could do this. Was it possible? Was it even within his abilities?

"I have to try," Peltrin finally said. "They gave their lives for me. They didn't even hesitate. It had nothing to do with whether or not they expected to win. They did it because they love me. They never even thought about the consequences. Should I love them less than they love me?"

The words seemed to have come from someone else. Peltrin was almost surprised to hear them. But the answer was crystal clear.

"I'm going to try," Peltrin said with conviction. "Even if I have to do it alone and there's no chance of success."

Valdor and the others lowered their heads as he walked away.

"We have to do something," said Soyem. "I don't believe for one minute his chances are better without us."

"I'm sorry," Valdor said as he shook his head, "I can't help you with this. I'm still dealing with deaths in my own family, I won't add your deaths to the list."

"Do it for your family, then." Soyem knew he was reaching for anything that might work. "What would they have wanted?"

There was a moment of silence before the old man answered.

"What destination awaits us, my love, if fear and doubt are our guiding stars?" the old man murmured.

"Did you just call me, 'my love'?" asked Soyem, looking annoyed.

"It's what my wife said," Valdor said quietly. "Just before I left for the Mihtighof."

"Wow!" said Soyem, his eyes wide. "I knew it would be something amazing."

"She was everything anyone could expect of an Ennai woman...and so much more." There was a long pause. "What do you want me to do?"

"I don't know," Soyem admitted. "I just think we should do something."

"Peltrin is going to approach from the North," said Lou, "and then go around the base of the monolith on the west side and climb up the Southwest side. As soon as he sets foot on the hill, the jaguar will come for him."

"He needs a distraction," said Valdor.

Lou nodded. "His best chance would be for you to pretend to approach the monolith from the opposite side so the jaguar is distracted when he approaches."

"I'm going to help, too," inserted Soyem.

"So am I," said Aralis. Her voice was quiet, but her eyes were fearless and full of determination.

"If all of you are willing," said Lou, our best chance would probably be to spread out around the hill. The jaguar will be preoccupied with you, allowing Peltrin to get past. Don't put yourselves in danger, just step onto the jaguar's territory. As soon as she gets close, you can get out of her territory and the Guardian won't be able to harm you."

"I like it," said Soyem. He started to do a little dance. "Distractions… diversion…illusions."

"That might work at first," said Valdor, "but eventually the jaguar will figure out that only one of us is going for the climb. By then Peltrin will be too far into her territory to get out again."

"By the time the guardian figures out what's going on," said Lou, "it will have to run almost all the way around the Fyllcarcern to get to him. It will have to go over at least one of the boulder fields, which should slow her down. Peltrin doesn't have to get to the top before she gets there, he just has to get to the top of the first column."

"He will have to be amazingly fast," said Valdor. "My guess is jaguars are a lot faster than we think. And I have a feeling this one runs much faster than most."

"I am the fastest runner," said Aralis, "maybe I should go."

"I'm the best climber," said Soyem.

"I don't think there's any stopping Peltrin," said Valdor. "I know how he feels right now. The best thing we can do is to make sure he succeeds."

"Just do everything you can to delay the guardian," said Lou.

Soyem still looked like he was about to argue, but eventually, he nodded his head in agreement.

They took several more minutes to work out exactly how they would distract the guardian, then they all left for their assigned positions.

Away from the others, Peltrin took his small pack and headed for the north side of the Mihtighof, or Fyllcarcern, or whatever. He still was unsure who to believe. He desperately wanted to believe the mirror. If the mirror was right, all he had to do was climb the monolith and the magical cure would be waiting. On the other hand, the guardian's story seemed to fit better with Valdor's experience.

As he walked, he was careful not to step onto the base of the hill that marked the guardian's territory. Often, he looked over at the bare rock of the monolith, rising hundreds of feet above the ground where he now stood. The first time he had seen it, it had looked impossible. Now, thanks to Lou and the wolves, he could see the flaws. The thousands of individual columns that gave it such beautiful symmetry were also its flaws. Between some of those columns were cracks. Those cracks provided a place to wedge a hand or a foot, one step at a time until he reached the top.

When he finally reached his starting point at the base of the north side of the hill, he sat next to a large boulder to rest for a moment. Over and over again, he visualized exactly how he would make his approach. He was so focused on the mental preparation that he jumped when Aralis sat down next to him.

"What are you doing here?" he asked with surprise.

"Do you want me to leave?" she looked directly into his eyes. The intensity made him a little squeamish, though not in a completely bad way.

"No," he admitted. "I'm glad you came."

"We're going to distract the guardian," she said quietly, "wait half an hour for everyone to get to their positions."

"I'm doing this alone," Peltrin insisted.

"No, you're not." She said as she scanned the hillside. She said it softly but it was clear from her tone that she wasn't going to argue or negotiate.

"Thanks," said Peltrin, giving in. It felt woefully inadequate, but it was all he could think of. He gazed at the base of the monolith, willing his eyes to catch some detail that could help speed him along his way.

The unexpected wait gave Peltrin a chance to review his plan for the climb over and over again. He had a plan—one that seemed like it might work—but he couldn't help but think something must inevitably go wrong. He remembered the last time he had gone through a pretend attack with his father and his uncle. The unexpected rabbit and the change in the wind had nearly gotten him shot in the leg.

As the time to begin the climb approached, he saw the jaguar coming around the East side of the Fyllcarcern. It glided along casually, muscles knotting and flexing in perfect rhythm. Each step showcased its amazing power. Its shoulders were at least as tall as Peltrin and each of the claws were longer than his hands.

Peltrin couldn't help but think the jaguar's strength and size were a bit excessive. With one swipe of her paw, the great animal could take out any other animal Peltrin had ever seen. Even a moose or a bear, Peltrin guessed, couldn't stand up to a blow like that.

His one advantage, he realized, was the help of his friends. The jaguar could only be in one place at a time. He could only hope the guardian wouldn't guess he was the one who planned to climb the monolith until it was too late.

The jaguar stopped for a moment and sniffed the air. She crouched slightly and her massive head began scanning from one side to the other. Cursing himself, Peltrin realized they were upwind. He had been so intent on making sure he started in the best location that he failed to think about keeping his presence unknown from the jaguar.

The huge cat began to prowl towards them.

Peltrin and Aralis had been hiding behind a large rock. They ducked and pressed themselves together, side to side. Peltrin would have enjoyed the contact, but the fact they were hiding from a gigantic jaguar made the scenario much less appealing.

There was no sound whatsoever. Even the birds had stopped singing and the squirrels had stopped their chatter. It was as if all of nature could feel the tension between the predator and its prey. Peltrin was almost certain the sound of his breathing and his heart thumping had already given them away.

The jaguar continued to approach. Peltrin could hear the soft crunch of the ground as it moved towards them. He held his breath as the heavy paws grew closer, padding the ground one by one. Eventually, the jaguar stopped at the edge of its territory, only a few feet away. The three of them stayed still for what felt like an eternity. Only the rock Peltrin and Aralis sat behind and a few insignificant feet of distance lay between them and the jaguar.

Peltrin could only hope as he listened to the long, deep breathing that they had guessed the boundary correctly. Their lives depended on the fact that the jaguar could not take those final few steps and swipe at them with one of those enormous paws.

Finally, the jaguar took in a sharp breath and growled menacingly. The sound of crunching leaves quickly fading into the distance. As the sound diminished, Peltrin eventually dared to look out from behind his rock. The jaguar's motion looked lazy, casual even, but it covered the distance with astonishing speed.

Peltrin moved to the edge of the hill and waited. It was several seconds before the jaguar disappeared behind the Fyllcarcern. Peltrin waited a little longer until he guessed the Guardian must be near the Southeastern edge of her territory. He could only hope Valdor and Soyem would be able to delay her for a while.

Just as Peltrin was about to start running, Aralis took his hand, sending a bolt of lightning through his entire body. He turned and looked at her. She looked him in the eye and squeezed his hand.

"You can do this," she whispered.

For a short moment, he was certain he could.

Adjusting his pack one more time, he grinned confidently at Aralis, released her hand, and sprinted away. The second he touched the slope of the hill, there was a roar. The jaguar knew he was there! Throwing caution to the wind, he sprinted for all he was worth. Part of him worried he would burn away all his energy in a few seconds and be too tired to climb, but the thought of the giant cat coming after him left him no choice.

Peltrin had reached the monolith and was only a fraction of the way around the west side when he heard the jaguar roaring. It was no longer on the opposite side of the monolith.

From the sound it made, it was running with a fury, now. Peltrin looked back over his shoulder and nearly stopped to stare as it came around the corner. The massive creature was moving with incredible speed. It looked wrong, somehow, for something so large to be moving so fast.

Peltrin's heart dropped. Even riding a horse, he wouldn't have made it to the Southwest side of the monolith in time. And now, so far from the edge of the hill, Peltrin didn't have time to return to the safety of the woods either. Fang was right.

Peltrin continued running. What other option did he have?

The Guardian was still some distance away when, inexplicably, she wheeled around and sprinted in the opposite direction. Guessing the others had found a way to distract it, Peltrin redoubled his effort. He ran desperately, mindlessly, with no thought for anything but staying alive.

He gave up on the possibility of getting to his planned starting position. He knew he would never get that far. Desperately he searched for another way up the monolith. The situation looked grim. He was so close to the monolith itself it was impossible to have enough perspective to plan a route.

As he searched the cliffs above, he also saw the wolves had been right about the storm. The thin wispy clouds that had filled the sky earlier were quickly being replaced by thunderheads. A rumble in the distance confirmed the storm was not far away.

There was a whisper behind him. Before Peltrin could react, a fanged mouth snatched him by the belt and tossed him into the air. To his surprise, Peltrin landed in a saddle. "Fang," he panted in surprise, "you came back."

"Fangmort is with the others, distracting the guardian," he answered. "We made a promise, kid," he answered without looking back, "to look out for you. The final decision to attempt the climb had to be yours alone. Nice work, by the way, using the others to distract the jaguar. You still would have died without our help, but at least someone tried to think things through."

"That was Lou," Peltrin admitted. "Where did you get the saddle?"

"I persuaded a nearby farmer to put it on me," said Fang.

"He just gave it to you?"

"I may have had his throat in my mouth when we agreed. And Fangmort may have threatened to eat a lamb or two when the farmer hesitated. You people get too worked up about eating the young."

Peltrin decided that, somehow, he would repay the unfortunate farmer for his trouble. But the thought was lost to the wind when Fang put on a new burst of speed. It was amazing! The fastest horse Peltrin had ever seen couldn't have come close.

When the first column of Peltrin's planned climb finally came into view, they heard a roar behind them. Peltrin glanced back to see the Guardian bound over a pile of boulders.

"Hang on tight," Fang ordered as he jumped to the top of a large rock. Peltrin clutched the saddle with all his might as the wolf bounded from one rock to another, quickly covering the ground at an exhilarating pace.

Hoping for a miracle, Peltrin chanced a look back but his heart sank. With unnatural agility, the jaguar, too, was leaping from rock to rock. The Guardian was easily gaining. Heedless of the rockslides she was causing, she glided effortlessly from boulder to boulder in furious pursuit.

Peltrin could practically feel the beast breathing behind them when the jaguar stopped and charged in the opposite direction.

"Aralis," Peltrin said with a smile.

Finally, they reached the first column. "Go, kid, now!"

Still winded from his run and the exhilarating ride, Peltrin threw himself at the wall. It was easy enough to get to the base of the column, but the Guardian would be able to do that as well. Desperately, he climbed for all he was worth.

The jaguar arrived only seconds later. Leaping easily to a high rock, it stood up on its hind legs and swiped. Peltrin did his best to dodge, pressing his body into the crack he was using to climb, but the jaguar still grazed his left leg. He cried out as the tips of the claws ripped his flesh, nearly tearing him from the wall.

He clung helplessly, struggling to steady his breathing and keep his grip both on the wall and on reality. As he watched the blood dripping from his leg, he realized the jaguar wouldn't have to do much more. If she chose to, she could swipe him once or twice more and then simply sit and wait patiently while the blood drained his life away.

In a flash of black and brown fur, the jaguar disappeared.

Peltrin blinked in surprise, it took him a few seconds to piece together what had just happened. Fang had rammed her, running at full speed. The two animals then fell off the tall boulder together. Twenty feet below, their bodies crashed to the ground. Fang immediately fled, narrowly avoiding a swipe that probably would have broken half his bones.

In the distance, Peltrin could see Fangmort and Valdor at the edge of the guardian's territory. There was also a small shadow on the ground just outside the guardian's perimeter. Peltrin assumed the shadow must be Lou.

The sight of his friends gave him a fresh wave of determination. Repositioning his body, he resumed the climb until he finally reached the top of the first column. Thankfully, the top of the column was large enough and flat enough that he could almost lay down. Once there, he tore strips off his shirt to use as makeshift bandages to slow the bleeding in his leg.

As he worked, a shadow fell over him. Peltrin started reaching for the weapons in his pack until he realized who it was.

"Soyem!" he said in surprise. "How did you get here? What are you doing here?"

"The guardian wouldn't chase after us anymore once you got close to the Fyllcarcern," Soyem explained, "so I started climbing Valdor's route. Boy that got her attention. I thought I was dead until Fangmort got here."

"You can't be here," Peltrin said angrily. "I have to do this alone."

"Well I'm not going back down," said Soyem, pointing below.

Peltrin looked down. The jaguar had returned to the base of the column. To Peltrin's surprise, the fury seemed to be gone. The Guardian sat calmly, perhaps sadly.

"You did well boys," she said quietly. "I doubted your hearts, but I have never seen friends sacrifice themselves so willingly. If you are worthy of such friends, perhaps I was mistaken about your potential."

"I didn't ask them to do that," Peltrin answered. "But you cannot stop us now."

"Correct," the jaguar answered. "You have succeeded in getting to the Mihtighof. My only consolation is, after what your friends just did, I don't believe you are here for selfish reasons. The only question now is whether you are strong enough to finish what you have started.

"If it were only the climb, I would be less concerned, but tonight the Fyllen will be on the prowl, and there are other creatures approaching. I pray to the source of the great power you can stay out of the Fyllen's reach until you reach the top. Now that you have passed my test, I would like nothing more than to see you succeed."

"You're doing that all wrong," said Soyem, looking at Peltrin's poorly bandaged leg. "I'm not as good as Aralis or Bensil, but I can do better than that."

Peltrin sat back and let Soyem work on bandaging his leg. As usual, he was impatient to get going, but he knew he wasn't likely to make it to the top with his leg bleeding.

"Now I can only beg you to see this through to the end," the guardian went on, "the Fyllen will likely overcome me soon. If you turn back now, or if the Fyllen devours you before you reach the top, it would be an act of cowardice and the Fyllen will gain greater strength. Perhaps enough that it will be able to leave the Mihtighof."

An explosive crack of thunder shook the ground. The guardian groaned and shimmered unnaturally. "Climb on, boys—as fast as you can—climb on!" She cried in anguish. "The Fyllen is here! His strength and size will only increase throughout the night. Face the monster with courage and you may survive."

She lowered her head and groaned again, "The balance is so fine, and tonight the Fyllen will be particularly strong. I fear the destruction of all is upon us if you fail."

The jaguar lay down at the base of the monolith, groaning and mumbling with her eyes closed. Presumably, she was fighting to hold back the Fyllen.

THE FYLLEN

Rain began to fall and lightning struck. It occurred to Peltrin that the top of the monolith might not be the best place to be during a lightning storm.

The groaning below grew louder as Soyem finished bandaging Peltrin's leg. The two of them quickly resumed the climb but they couldn't help but pause from time to time to look at the jaguar.

It began to change. They watched in horror as the already massive creature grew to twice its previous size. Its skin bubbled and broke. Its thick yellow and black fur was replaced with brown, reptilian skin.

"The Fyllen," Soyem said to himself in awe.

Peltrin was stunned. The enormity of the creature alone was terrifying. Like the Jaguar, it was a four-legged animal. Its earth-toned skin was heavy and armored with random spikes projecting in odd directions. Its face was flat with bulging, multicolored eyes. It had a wide mouth with heavy, stout teeth. Its tail was thick and long, like a scorpion's tail, with a solid spiked bludgeon at the end.

For the moment, the Fyllen hadn't noticed Soyem and Peltrin. In a fit of rage, it attacked a nearby tree, reducing it to splinters in a matter of seconds. As he watched, Peltrin began to understand the guardian's urgency to keep the animal contained. It seemed to be consumed with an unquenchable, senseless fury. When the tree was no longer worth attacking, the creature tore at the ground, shredding stones like butter, destroying the grass, and tossing dirt in all directions.

There was no longer any question that the guardian had been telling the truth and the mirror had not. The monolith was the Mihtighof and the jaguar herself was the Fyllcarcern. Realizing the truth, Peltrin questioned the wisdom of what he was doing.

He loved his parents and uncle more than anything but was it worth potentially releasing this beast on the world? There was a chance he could save three, but what are three compared to the countless people this beast would kill if it were released? Was it possible the mirror wanted this beast released? Unsure of himself, he hesitated, clinging to the side of the cliff as the Fyllen prowled below.

Lightning struck and Peltrin blinked his eyes in disbelief. The creature had grown! Hoping he was mistaken, Peltrin watched a little longer. Sure enough, the creature was growing even as he watched.

"Come on, Peltrin," Soyem insisted. "We have to go!"

Then the Fyllen locked eyes with the boys. Peltrin paused as he stared into the multi-colored, cat-like eyes. In a single bound the creature jumped much higher than Peltrin would have guessed possible, missing the boys by mere inches.

Soyem reacted immediately, climbing with remarkable speed and dexterity. Reflexively, Peltrin shimmied up behind the smaller boy. He looked down at the Fyllen, wondering if there was any hope of finishing the climb before it reached them.

Surprisingly, he saw the fire in the Fyllen's eyes fade just a little.

"You must go on," the jaguar's voice came from the mouth of the creature. "If you fail to reach the top and face the demon from there, he will devour you."

"We shouldn't have come," Peltrin answered, his voice was shaking, "I would rather fail than free the Fyllen."

"It's too late now. By touching the Mihtighof, you have challenged the beast. The Fyllen has accepted your challenge. As the night goes on, the Fyllen will continue to grow in size and power until you reach the top and face him. If you are devoured, I will be weakened and he will be strengthened—perhaps enough to escape."

The fire in the creature's eyes resumed and it was clear the guardian was gone.

Only the Fyllen remained.

CHAPTER 13: THE MIHTIGHOF

Peltrin and Soyem hung on the side of the Mihtighof, momentarily distracted by the view of the growing Fyllen. The beast was shredding the ground below in another fit of rage. It was still growing and could pounce again at any time. Giving up—or even resting—simply wasn't an option.

Peltrin's one consolation as he looked at the Fyllen was, somehow, the eyes of the Fyllen didn't paralyze him with fear like the eyes of a red-eyed devastor. The Fyllen's eyes were wide with an all-consuming madness to destroy everything in reach. The devastors, on the other hand, were focused. Once it focused on you, its only purpose in life was to destroy you at any cost. Considering the raw power of the massive—and still growing—demon, Peltrin couldn't think of any other reason why the smaller creature's eyes had so much more of an effect on him.

Taking a deep breath, he turned and began climbing again.

Even on the south side, the climb up the Mihtighof was very nearly straight up. Their only way to hold on was a small gap between a blue column and a red column. Soyem showed Peltrin he could flatten his hand and slide it into the crack. He then cupped his hand slightly, wedging his fingertips against one column, and the back of his hand on the other. Although the rain poured down, soaking him through, the rock was rough enough he didn't slip. While the hand wedging worked well to keep him from falling, the angle was too awkward to lift himself effectively using his arms. Most of the upward thrust came from his legs and feet pushing on whatever they could find on either side of the crack.

Soyem seemed to have no difficulty at all with the climb, but Peltrin's progress was slow and the climbing technique, although effective, was extremely painful for his hands. It wasn't long before the backs of his hands were bleeding.

At one point, Peltrin started to complain, but then he saw Soyem's hands. The smaller boy was faring no better.

They kept climbing. Looking at the fell beast below, they knew their lives depended on it. Thinking about the events of the past few days Peltrin also knew his family's lives depended on them getting to the top.

The creature roared again. Peltrin now fully trusted the guardian had been telling the truth. Many lives depended on their perseverance.

"What are those?" asked Soyem as he and Peltrin reached one of the planned rest areas on top of a column. Below, dozens of small shadows rushed up the hill toward the Mihtighof.

"Devastors!" Peltrin answered in dismay. Even at this distance, he was sure of it. Because of the darkness, he could see that several of them had red, glowing eyes. He gulped. At this distance he could keep his head, but it was only a matter of time before they started to climb.

As soon as the devastors touched the hillside, the Fyllen went ballistic. Roaring in fury, it attacked left and right. Devastor bodies flew in random directions as the demon tore through them tirelessly.

To Peltrin and Soyem's relief, the Fyllen lost interest in them for a short time. It charged from one side of the Mihtighof to the other, tearing up the ground and spraying rocks and boulders as it ran. For some time, they could hear the beast roaring from the other side. From the sound of the beast, it must have been growing as the guardian had predicted.

A few minutes later, the ground rumbled.

"Could that be the Fyllen?" asked Soyem. "Could it have grown so large that the ground rumbles when it jumps?"

He didn't have to wait long for an answer. Soon the Fyllen reappeared. Impossibly huge, the animal's temper appeared to have grown even more than its size. Screaming and raging, the Fyllen pawed and pounded the ground. Boulders flew in all directions, many of them cloven in pieces. Lightning flashed and the animal roared in reply as if the chaotic storm and the feral demon were somehow connected.

There were no more devastors the boys could see. There had been several dozen, but the Fyllen appeared to have ended them before any could reach the Mihtighof.

"Why wouldn't the Fyllen let them through?" Peltrin wondered aloud. "Wouldn't the devastors and the Fyllen help each other?"

Soyem was climbing ahead and didn't even hear him.

It didn't matter, Peltrin realized. He returned his focus to the climb.

Finally, Peltrin reached the next resting place. Exhausted, he collapsed on the ledge next to Soyem. He closed his eyes while the rain poured over his face.

Lightning crashed above them and the Fyllen roared beneath. Despite the dangers above and below, they were relatively safe for the moment.

As his breathing slowed, Peltrin recalled in his mind the route to the top. The section he had just completed was by far the longest. By now they were nearly a third of the way up and the resting places would be more frequent. He was tempted to stay. The momentary relative safety was much more appealing than pushing on to the top.

"What exactly do we need to do to conquer the Fyllen?" asked Soyem. "The Guardian wasn't very specific."

"I don't know," Peltrin admitted. Saying it aloud made him feel foolish. How could they have come this far and still not know what to do when they arrived at the top? Destroying the creature was out of the question. No weapon Peltrin knew of could make a mark on that beast.

Maybe I just have to climb, Peltrin thought to himself. Maybe stopping here is good enough to count as beating the Fyllen. But even as he said it to himself, he knew it wasn't true. Besides, even if the beast remained contained, stopping here wouldn't get him the panacea. The guardian had claimed there was no such thing as a true panacea. But if the Mihtighof could give him something that could slow or stop the poison—like Valdor's rock—that would be more than enough reason to continue to the top…if he could manage it.

Tearing more strips from Peltrin's shirt, the two boys wrapped cloth around each other's bleeding hands. The backs of Soyem's hands, in particular, were not doing well.

Peltrin couldn't help but think there wouldn't be much left of his shirt if this kept going. It was not a comforting thought as the cool night air continued to get colder. He considered suggesting they use Soyem's shirt in the future, but one look at the tiny shivering boy convinced him Soyem wouldn't do well if he got any colder.

More to reduce the weight of his pack than anything else, Peltrin removed the food and they quickly ate. After taking a long drink, Peltrin passed the flask to Soyem, who did the same. It felt strange to drink water when their entire bodies were already completely drenched from the rain.

Momentarily, Peltrin closed his eyes to focus on getting himself ready, mentally and physically, for the next leg of the climb. Just as he was about to fall asleep, however, a roar from the Fyllen brought him back to the present. Doing his best to ignore the intensifying lightning above and the growing beast beneath, Peltrin reluctantly arose and set himself to the next part of the climb.

Numbly, he followed Soyem's lead. Soyem had been unusually quiet during the climb, but Peltrin had to admit his chances would not have been good without the little Canbi. Soyem seemed to know instinctively which way to go. He also naturally found ways to navigate the more difficult sections, and would then patiently show Peltrin the technique. Sometimes

Soyem had to try two or three different techniques before they found something Peltrin was able to do.

Later, there was yet another crack between two columns. This time, however, the crack was so wide they could each put their entire body into it with a room to spare. Moving his body into the crack, Soyem placed his left hand and foot on one wall and his right hand and foot on the other. Moving one hand or foot at a time, he slowly worked his way up.

Peltrin followed Soyem's example. It was exhausting, but he was able to climb this section without additional help or guidance.

More and more, the increasing size and ferocity of the Fyllen were beginning to concern Peltrin. How in the world would he be able to contend with such a beast? Didn't the guardian say the beast had destroyed her entire people? Didn't she say it had killed many great warriors in the process? She had been able to contain the Fyllen only because of magical abilities she had spent years to learn and develop. Peltrin and Soyem had nothing of the sort.

Sometime later, they reached the top of yet another column. This one was adjacent to the ledge. Unlike the tops of the individual columns, which had been mostly flat and mostly clear of debris, the ledge was covered in debris that formed a short, steep slope leading directly to a huge drop-off.

The column on which they stood was the same height as the ledge, but the two were not connected. The distance wasn't far but it was easily more than either of them could ever hope to jump.

"Aralis probably could make this jump," said Soyem.

Peltrin only nodded. Aralis wasn't there. It wasn't very important what she could or couldn't do.

The light of the sun was completely gone now and the storm would admit no light from the moon or the stars. In the darkness, Soyem strained his eyes, studying the wall between the top of the column where they stood and the larger ledge ahead. Using his hands as much as his eyes, he crouched down and searched. Eventually, he found a small horizontal indentation near their feet that would serve as a foothold. It was difficult to tell for sure whether it went the entire way, but it went on for as far as he could reach.

Standing up and feeling with his hands, Soyem eventually was able to find another small horizontal indentation near his face.

Against his better judgement, Peltrin looked down. This stretch of the climb was exposed. The slightest slip would send them plummeting to certain death. They could only hope there would be enough friction, despite the pouring rain.

Below, the Fyllen turned its fury to the Mihtighof itself, roaring and clawing at the huge rock structure. The stone monolith must have been made of tougher stuff than the surrounding rock. As far as Peltrin could tell, the rage of the Fyllen wasn't doing any damage.

Doing his best to keep his breathing slow and even, Peltrin followed Soyem as he began the sideways climb. Thanks to the roughness of the rock, he wasn't slipping. Not at first, anyway. Peltrin's legs, however, were strained to their limits. His right leg began shaking uncontrollably, bouncing up and down to the point he was afraid he would fall off. Not knowing what else to, he stopped his progress and stood on his left leg. He removed his right foot from the wall and worked his right leg in every possible direction, hoping that stretching it would help the blood flow and stop the bouncing. It was only a few seconds before Peltrin's left leg started bouncing as well and he had to put his right leg back on the wall.

Without thinking, he looked down. He quickly clenched his eyes closed but it was too late, he had seen it. Hundreds of feet of nothing but freefall. At the bottom, the glowing cat-like eyes of the Fyllen awaited.

Peltrin closed his eyes again and put his forehead against the wall. His entire body was shaking now.

"Don't stop," Soyem yelled from the ledge. "You have to keep moving. The shaking is only going to get worse. It won't stop until you make it across."

Peltrin tried unsuccessfully to breathe deeply and calm himself. It didn't help. His body, both mentally and physically, was approaching its limit. Soyem was right, the longer he stayed, the more his energy drained.

"Move!" Soyem shouted between thunderclaps.

Realizing that time was not his ally, Peltrin forced himself to be in constant motion. To keep from getting overwhelmed he focused on one limb at a time—one arm, one leg, another arm, another leg.

Eventually, he collapsed shakily to the ground. Soyem grabbed what was left of his shirt to keep him from rolling down. The ledge was not as big as he had expected. It surprised him that he had been able to see it so well from the valley. He removed his flask from the pack and he and Soyem emptied most of the rest of its contents.

Below, the Fyllen roared and pounced. When it jumped, the Fyllen pounded the ground with its monstrous tail. The spiked bludgeon decimated the ground where it struck and propelled the creature to a fantastic height. To their surprise, the Fyllen was able to grasp hold of the ledge.

The two boys pressed their backs against the wall. The claws were so long that the tips were close enough to touch. But even at its current colossal size, the Fyllen was not able to quite reach him.

"I hope you have a plan for defeating that thing," Soyem shouted, his eyes wide.

With a roar of fury and frustration, the beast slipped down to the ground. It then charged to the other side of the Mihtighof again.

Peltrin was confused. Why did the Fyllen keep going to the other side?

Opening his flask again, Peltrin gulped down one more swallow. He handed it to Soyem, who drank the last of the water. The worst of the climb was over, but they still had to face the Fyllen at the top of the Mihtighof. As time went on, it seemed like the night was getting even darker, if darker was even possible.

"I have no idea what to do when we get to the top," Peltrin admitted.

Soyem only nodded, the concern on his face was obvious.

After taking a minute or two to catch their breath, they began to slowly make their way across the ledge. The ledge crossed the entire south side of the Mihtighof, climbing towards the top. More out of caution than out of necessity, Peltrin kept his left shoulder against the cliff. It gave the illusion of safety. He could almost convince himself it would give him something to hold on to if he started to slide. He did stumble from time to time in the darkness, but never in a way that caused him to start the deadly tumble down the short, steep slope and off the edge of the cliff.

At the far end of the ledge, it took only a few minutes to scramble the rest of the way to the top.

Soyem hung back while Peltrin peeked tentatively over a large boulder to get his first look at the top of the Mihtighof. At first, there was nothing but darkness.

Then, a flash of lightning momentarily revealed the top. Though it had looked perfectly flat from a distance, the top of the Mihtighof was slightly rounded, with the highest point perfectly in the center. A variety of rocks and boulders littered the area, but nothing grew there. It was completely barren.

Peltrin hesitated and watched. Lightning continued to strike here and there, giving him more short opportunities to study the barren area. He had hoped the storm would lessen before he reached the top. If anything, however, the storm was intensifying and the lightning was becoming even more frequent.

THE MIHTIGHOF

Deciding he probably wouldn't need his pack, Peltrin removed his short sword and the two throwing knives. After several minutes, Peltrin took a deep breath, there was nothing to be gained by doubting, he decided. For better or for worse, he was committed to face whatever there was to be faced on the top of this mountain.

"Stay here," he instructed Soyem. Although the small boy had been invaluable during the climb, it seemed unlikely he would be of much use on top.

Soyem just nodded. He looked more than a little relieved.

Peltrin gave himself a moment to gather his courage. Finally, breathing deeply again, he leaped over the final rock, sword ready.

Nothing happened. The Fyllen still roared. The lightning and thunder still flashed and crashed all around, but there was no immediate threat. Peltrin felt almost foolish to have worked so hard to gather his courage, only to find himself alone. Keeping his sword out, just in case, he began walking up the gentle slope towards the top. As he approached, the lightning increased in frequency and intensity, striking the mountain on both sides of him. One, in particular, was so close it knocked him to the ground.

Dazed, he waited a moment to get up. Maybe it would be wiser to stay close to the ground, he wondered. His head was aching and his ears were ringing. He considered going back to the large boulder and waiting for the storm to pass but quickly discarded the thought. The guardian had made it clear the Fyllen would continue to grow until he faced it. If that was true, it would be foolish to wait.

Finally, he stood on the very highest point. Lightning struck all around, often forming spiderwebs of light across the sky above him. The rain continued to come pouring down.

"I'm here," Peltrin shouted. He wasn't sure if the Mihtighof had any way of listening. But he was at a loss for what to do next.

"My family was attacked by devastors. Some of them are dead," he shouted to the storm. "My mom, my dad, and my uncle have all been poisoned. I need something to stop the poison or they will die."

He decided not to use the word panacea. The mirror in the cave had said all he had to do was climb and a panacea would just be here for him. That clearly wasn't the case.

At first, there was no response. Then, in one of the rare quiet times between crashes of thunder, he heard a familiar hissing.

He nearly dropped his short sword when the first devastor approached, its eyes were the color of the night. He felt the paralyzing fear taking over his body.

He should have known some of the devastors would have made it past the Fyllen. Why did he have to be so afraid of devastors? Even now, he was barely keeping his sword up.

It leaped towards him. Surprisingly, he had enough presence of mind to put his sword between them. Almost without realizing it, he struck the creature down. Peltrin almost felt good enough to congratulate himself. It was the first time he had killed one.

There was a flash of red above. Peltrin swept his sword in the air, but striking a bat midair is nearly impossible in the best of conditions. Still, he felt a light connection and watched as the bat flew awkwardly away. It wasn't likely he had killed it, but it appeared to have been injured.

Distracted by the bat, he very nearly didn't see the second devastor and he barely dodged as the unexpected claws swept through the air. He had difficulty seeing the creature between lightning strikes, but he could tell easily the eyes were not glowing red. He felt a surge of relief. He leaped forward and the creature stepped back.

In the light of the next lightning strike, he caught a shadow in the corner of his eye and swept his sword around, slicing the third devastor in the torso only a fraction of a second before it wrapped its deadly claws around his throat.

The creature clutched the wound and stepped back. It fell and lay still. Spinning, Peltrin fended off several others who were attempting to sneak in behind him. Peltrin worried how many there would be. He was proud of himself for killing two so far, but if he were attacked by dozens, as had happened to his father in the house, he expected they would overwhelm him very quickly. He was good, but he wasn't nearly as good as his father.

Peltrin counted four devastors surrounding him. So far, he had been able to keep his fear under control and two were dead. A colossal achievement considering his previous failures. Whenever he held still, his hands would start shaking, but he was surrounded, there was very little time to hold still.

Remembering when his father had fought these creatures by the dozens, he tried to imitate the technique, staying in constant motion. He intentionally favored long sweeping strokes that kept them out of reach.

Eventually, he hoped, their ferocious nature would overcome their fear of his sword, as had happened with his father. That way he could kill them one at a time as they voluntarily moved into his range.

Finally, the red-eyed devastor arrived. It was slightly taller and more muscular than the others. As it drew near, there was no doubt who was in charge. Wherever it went, the others kept their distance. When it grunted and spat, the others responded as if obeying its commands.

At the sight of the red-eyes, Peltrin's head spun with fear, his sword lowered and his defense began to falter. He felt the same feeling that had paralyzed him only a few days ago. Silver-blue eyes locked with red and he felt sanity slipping away. In those eyes, there was only one thought, one goal…his death.

Just as he was about to slip into oblivion, there was a mighty roar of thunder. Lightning struck again and again in the same place. Peltrin and the devastors alike turned to the source of the sound and the target of the lightning. An impossibly huge, ugly face appeared on the horizon. Peltrin was stunned. It was the Fyllen. The creature appeared to have grown to the point its head was higher than the Mihtighof itself.

A blinding bolt of lightning struck the creature and it burst into brilliant red and orange flame. Though the ethereal flames surrounded the creature, it was not consumed. The flames were so bright in the growing darkness that Peltrin could barely see the living creature inside.

The creature roared. Peltrin fell to the ground from the sheer force of the resulting wind. All five of the devastors were sent tumbling as well.

Now that he could see the power of the Fyllen, he understood why the guardian had been so afraid for the welfare of everyone. If this creature ever escaped the Mihtighof, what in the wide world could ever challenge it? His own problems seemed so small and insignificant. What good would it do to save his own family if everything was destroyed? He couldn't imagine it would make any difference, but he had to try. He had to face the Fyllen!

With that thought, Peltrin jumped to his feet. The devastors around him were beginning to recover. Fighting every instinct, Peltrin forced himself not to look at the red-eyes. One look, he knew, and he would succumb to the terror.

This was the moment. Somehow, he knew. This was the moment to decide if he would fight or flee.

After the blast of the Fyllen's roar, only two of the five devastors stood in his path. They had been knocked down with the rest of them, but they were beginning to rise.

Charging, Peltrin cut the two down. Disregarding the remaining three, he ran toward the demon. Remembering the devastor's unnatural speed, he could only hope he could stay ahead of them long enough to face the Fyllen—the bringer of death.

Switching the sword to his left hand, Peltrin reached into his belt and drew the first of his two throwing knives. He remembered his cowardice the first time a devastor attacked him. He had been holding this very knife at the time. In a burst of lightning, he could see the white claw marks on the black metal. If he had only dared to use it days ago, none of this would be happening.

Summoning his strength, he threw the knife with all his might. Sailing through the air end over end, it pierced the Fyllen in its left eye. The Fyllen blinked but appeared uninjured.

Dimly, he was aware a devastor had caught up to him. Without looking back, he swept his sword with his left hand, relieving the creature of its head. The body collapsed to the ground though its head rolled alongside him for a few seconds.

Still sprinting, Peltrin reached into his belt a second time and withdrew the second knife. This was the knife he had been holding during the attack on the house. Again, he could see the familiar white claw marks. If he had been brave enough to use it at the time, Nirani and father likely never would have been injured by red-eyed devastors. He threw the second knife at the right eye. Once again, the Fyllen only blinked.

Peltrin stabbed backward, ending the last black-eyed devastor without even giving it a full second's thought.

Peltrin moved the short sword from his left hand back to his right. This was the sword his father had thrown to save him and his mother from the red-eyed devastor. It had been Perwin's last weapon at the time. Throwing it had exposed him to the claws and teeth of the creatures that surrounded him.

Peltrin could hear the hissing of the red-eyed devastor behind him, it would be on him in seconds.

Peltrin was also dimly aware of something else running behind the devastor. He glanced over his shoulder just enough to see whether it was another devastor. It was Soyem! Despite his claim a few days before that he was nowhere near as fast as Peltrin, the short boy had somehow caught up.

The Fyllen was moving forward now, jaws gaping wide open as if to consume Peltrin and the devastor and Soyem together in a single bite. It wouldn't have been difficult. The three of them combined wouldn't make half a mouthful. They each were smaller, even, than the demon's individual teeth.

As the mouth closed in on them, Peltrin released the sword, exactly as his father had only a few days ago. The short sword sailed like a javelin into the mouth of the beast. Out of the corner of his eye, he could see that Soyem was throwing something at the Fyllen as well.

This time the Fyllen responded. It withdrew its head and its mouth snapped shut. The red and orange flames that surrounded the creature dimmed somewhat. Peltrin couldn't imagine his sword had caused any more damage than a pinprick. The Fyllen was motionless for a second, seeming more stunned than injured.

The lightning stopped. The rain stopped.

The fury in its eyes seemed somehow subdued, and the demon began to shrink. The flames began to sputter and die and the brownish skin beneath began to show in fleeting patches.

Peltrin moved toward the edge to watch the Fyllen as it continued to shrink, but a furious set of teeth and claws tackled him from behind. Rolling over when he hit the ground, Peltrin faced his attacker lying flat on his back. The red-eyed devastor pounced on his chest, straining for his throat. Peltrin caught the creature by the wrists just before it scratched the skin on his neck. He knew the slightest scratch from the red-eyed devastor would guarantee his death, even if he somehow survived the day.

The creature drove towards him. Despite all that had happened, Peltrin was still strong enough to push the creature off of him. If he could only control the paralyzing fear. Little by little the claws and teeth and eyes got closer and closer. Eventually, its face was just inches from Peltrin.

Peltrin stared into those mindless, deadly eyes and the familiar fear returned in full fury. All thought of his family and the rest of the world faded from his mind. He wanted to quit—to give up. All it would take is one little scratch and he would be dead, if not now, then in a few days. What difference did it make as long as this horrible, terrible fear was gone? Finally, Peltrin closed his eyes and relaxed, succumbing to the darkness.

There was a thump and the devastor went limp. Peltrin opened his eyes to see Soyem standing over him, a large rock in hand. Soyem kicked the unconscious creature's body off of Peltrin and off of the edge of the Mihtighof. Then he fell to the ground beside Peltrin.

Peltrin closed his eyes and all went dark.

THE CHRONCILES OF AMYRIAD

Chapter 14: Awakening

Peltrin's eyes fluttered open in the early morning light. He was lying on the ground under a small tree. Blinking and confused, he looked from side to side. He started slightly when he saw a massive yellow and black jaguar. He then relaxed somewhat when he realized it was the guardian.

"You aren't going to attack me now?" he asked.

The jaguar's eyes narrowed slightly. "If I wanted you dead, would you not be dead already?"

Accepting the answer as obvious, Peltrin sat up and looked himself over. His body was covered from head to foot with scratches and bruises. His hands looked terrible, but none of his injuries were life-threatening. Looking around, he realized he was on the ground at the base of the Mihtighof. He was on the southeast side, just south of the boulder field. Even lying down, the place gave him a great view of the rising sun.

"Did any of these come from the red-eyed devastor?" he wondered aloud.

"You were not poisoned last night," the Guardian answered.

"I didn't release the Fyllen?" he asked.

"Thanks to what happened, I am as strong as I have ever been," the joy in her voice was obvious.

"But it doesn't make any sense." said Peltrin, "There's no way my knives and sword could have hurt the Fyllen. Especially when it was so huge."

"For you, it was never a battle of strength," the jaguar explained. "As I told you when you first arrived, and again before I was overtaken, your task was to face the Fyllen with selflessness and courage. At the crucial moment, you deliberately chose to forsake your mission and sacrifice yourself and your family to stop the Fyllen. Many would agree it was a reasonable choice, but very few have the selflessness and courage to carry it out."

"So, you stopped the Fyllen?"

"You didn't see me, but my power was always present. Once you fully committed to setting your own needs aside and facing the Fyllen with everything you had, the magic I use to contain the Fyllen was activated. For me, it was a battle of strength. For you, it was a battle of the heart. Together, with the aid of the power of the Mihtighof, we were victorious."

The jaguar shook and a pair of knives and a short sword fell to the ground, "Speaking of which" she said, "I won't be needing these."

Peltrin picked up the weapons. The knives he put in his belt and the short sword went into his small pack, which had magically been moved to the ground as well.

Peltrin looked around at the hill that surrounded the Mihtighof. "Nothing looks damaged from the Fyllen," he said with wonder. Remembering the Fyllen's fits of rage and the incredible destruction it left behind, he had expected every rock and tree on the hill, maybe even the Mihtighof itself, to be filled with the scars of the Fyllen's fury.

"It is part of the magic that contains the beast," the jaguar answered, "until he fully escapes me, any damage he does to the hill will disappear by morning." She looked a little smug. "It is most frustrating for him. For thousands of years, he has only been able to escape at rare periods, and anything he accomplishes during that time is instantly undone."

"Did you see what happened up there?" Peltrin asked.

"Because the Fyllen and I are joined. I was able to see everything that happened through the eyes of the Fyllen," she answered. "It's a terrible thing to see the world through its eyes. From the perspective of the Mihtighof, what you accomplished was very well done."

"How can you tell?"

Because it gave me sufficient power to create gifts." The jaguar nodded toward a large flat stone.

Peltrin approached to see. On the stone was a small metal vial that appeared to be made of silver. Next to the silver vial was a bulb about the size and shape of a tulip bulb.

"What are these?" he asked.

"Generally, it is left to the receiver of such gifts to discover their virtues," the jaguar answered. "However, since your time is short and you helped my cause, I will explain. The silver vial contains three drops of an elixir. The elixir will pause the effects of the poison for two days."

"Only two days?" he moaned.

"The bulb," the guardian went on, "you must plant as soon as you get home. The day after you plant it, the bulb will sprout, forming a single flower. Beginning the next day, you must squeeze the flower every morning. Each time you do, a few drops of a similar elixir will come out. The elixir from the flower, however, will only last a single day. You will need to extract elixir each day in order to stave off the effects of the venom."

"Thank you," Peltrin breathed, "thank you so much." The fact that there was a way for his family to live was almost too good to believe.

Then he remembered Valdor. "Why am I getting everything I need, but Valdor only received a single stone?"

"The difference was the test that you passed," answered the Guardian. "I allowed Valdor to pass without a challenge. The Fyllen was not free that night. There were no devastors last night. The challenges you overcame were great, therefore the reward was great. The sacrifices of your friends worked in your favor as well."

Peltrin smiled to himself. "I didn't think Soyem would much help."

"But in the end," said the Guardian, "he contributed almost as much as you did. It is possible that Valdor was brave enough to gain the reward he desired, but even he will never know, because he was never truly tested to that extent.

"It is often only in retrospect that we see the value of our trials.

"It is only in overcoming such trials that we learn our true potential."

Peltrin nodded his head thoughtfully. Were it not for the depths of his trials, he never would have had the opportunity for such a victory.

Using a thin rope cut from his pack and another piece from his shirt, Peltrin quickly created a simple necklace with a pouch and placed the silver vial and the bulb inside. By now his shirt was in a truly sorry state.

"I would like to make a request, if I may," the jaguar said tentatively.

"Of course," said Peltrin. At this point, he was feeling good enough to agree to anything, though he couldn't imagine what the powerful creature could want from him.

"I would like to request that you exercise a degree of caution in sharing your experience and the knowledge you have gained. Many would see only the possible gains and would fail to consider the required sacrifice. If all of Amyriad knew of the possibilities, I fear this place would be accosted day and night."

"Of course." It was easy to see why the guardian would be concerned about that. "I need to go now. I have to get this to my family before tomorrow morning. Thank you!" With that, he set off running towards the camp where he supposed his friends had spent the night.

The jaguar watched as he jogged away.

"You should probably go, too," she said, turning to Soyem, who was still lying on the ground nearby. "He's gone and I doubt he'll look back. His only thought now is of getting home."

Soyem slowly sat up. "Did we succeed?" he asked groggily.

"You both faced the Fyllen admirably," the jaguar said.

"How many drops did you say there were in the vial?" asked Soyem.

"Three," answered the guardian.

"That should be enough," Soyem confirmed.

"Can I count on you to keep this place a secret?" the guardian asked. "I cannot force you to keep your silence, but I assure you it is for the best."

"Of course," Soyem said. He then ran to catch up with Peltrin.

As Peltrin and Soyem entered the camp, Peltrin had never been happier, despite his injuries. He had succeeded when it would have seemed impossible.

"Well, well, well," said Fang. "Look who is back all happy and smiling. You look like you just took down and ate your first deer." Fang was still wearing the poor farmer's saddle.

"We did it," Peltrin gushed. Excitedly, he and Soyem recounted the events on the Fyllcarcern. Getting out of his bed painfully, Valdor congratulated him, patting them on the back and shoulders.

Lou stood up on his back legs. He proceeded to jump up and down, punching the air and chanting their praises.

"You need to get back now," said Aralis, getting up from the fire she had been tending. "You have to get them the cure by morning."

"Where have you been all night," asked Soyem.

"I stayed on the north side of the monolith until it was almost dark," she answered. "I was doing my best to distract the guardian so Peltrin could start the climb. Once it started to get dark, I came back here."

"What about all the devastors," asked Peltrin.

"They ran right past me and didn't even try to attack," she said with a shrug.

"She wasn't stupid enough to get herself injured like you two," said Lou.

Soyem and Peltrin looked at each other. They both looked pretty bad.

"You saw the Fyllen?" asked Peltrin.

"I don't see how anyone could have missed it," Aralis answered. Her face looked haunted. "By the end, it was so huge it could stand on its tail and reach the top of the Mihtighof. It was the most horrible thing I have ever seen. I hope to never see anything like it again."

"It was a nightmare," Peltrin agreed.

The others nodded in agreement.

"You need to get going," Aralis repeated. You have to get the cure back to your house today or they will all be dead by morning.

"I can get you there in half a day," Fang said, indicating the saddle. "On the condition that you get this thing off of me as soon as we get there, and you never mention this to anyone as long as you live."

"Absolutely," Peltrin agreed quickly. He had been tempted to make a joke or tease the wolf, but he was fairly certain Fang wouldn't appreciate it. Fang only seemed to like jokes that included blood or eating helpless animals.

"I need to change the bandage on your neck before you go," said Aralis.

She turned to the others. "The rest of you can watch this time, I think Nirani wouldn't be opposed to me sharing the family secret with all of you now."

Peltrin took off the remains of his shirt. He was still wearing the hopelessly shredded rag he had torn to pieces on the Mihtighof.

Aralis went to work quickly. Peltrin still felt a rush of electricity whenever her hands touched his skin.

Soyem gasped when Aralis removed the bandage, "But that's a…"

"Keep your mouth shut," Aralis commanded, "that's the family secret and I don't want any of you saying it out loud."

"Then how am I supposed to know," Peltrin complained, "I can't see what you're doing back there."

"You'll have to wait until your mother explains it to you," Aralis answered.

"Why am I the only one here who can't know my family secret?" he complained.

For an answer, she just glared.

Frustrated, but unable to do anything about it, Peltrin grumbled under his breath.

"I'm not a packhorse," said Fang when Aralis was done and Peltrin had a new shirt on, "you'll have to leave your things behind."

"Everything?" Peltrin exclaimed.

"Everything. You can take the elixir, the bulb, and your clothes, nothing else."

"Even my weapons?"

"Especially your weapons. The last thing I need is one of those things poking me along the way. Trust me, my teeth will be all the weapons you will need."

Peltrin was again tempted to tease the wolf, telling him horses never complained so much, but he was afraid Fang would withdraw the offer. It was pretty clear the wolf felt that carrying Peltrin on his back like a horse was far beneath his dignity.

"I'll stay here with the pack and watch over the rest of the people," said Fangmort.

Aralis, Valdor, and Soyem all looked relieved at the offer.

Before long they were loping through the forest. Peltrin had hoped the wolf would run as he had at the Mihtighof, but Fang refused.

"Running too fast burns too much energy, too quickly," Fang had said, "At that pace, I'll tire out in less than an hour. We'll move faster overall if we just go at a quick walk."

Aralis, Valdor, and Soyem had said little as he rode away. Soyem seemed unusually solemn considering the mission had succeeded. He supposed they were just tired.

Regardless, Peltrin was feeling on top of the world!

Chapter 15: Home Again

Peltrin studied the house from the cover of the brush. There were a dozen or so black-eyed devastors—not nearly as many as the first attack. There had to be at least one red-eyed devastor somewhere, but there were none to be seen from where they were hiding. Peltrin could only assume it was—or they were—hiding somewhere nearby.

He looked at his assets, which wasn't encouraging. Fang was strong as a horse, and fierce as…well…a wolf. But there were too many opponents to just go charging in recklessly, even for Fang.

"Could you call your pack to help us?" asked Peltrin in a low voice.

"They stayed with Fangmort. Speaking of my pack, get this saddle off of me. If I still smell of it when they get back, I will never be respected again." Sensing this was still a touchy issue, Peltrin quickly removed the saddle.

"If I could get to the weapons cabinet," said Peltrin, "I would have something to fight with, but I don't see how I can get close, those things will go nuts as soon as they see me."

"No," answered Fang, "those are devastors. They will go nuts as soon as they smell you."

Peltrin smiled. That was it!

"Fang, what can I use around here to mask my scent?"

The wolf thought for a moment, "I'll show you." They circled wide around the house until they came to a muddy meadow fed by a small stream.

Peltrin stepped in the muddy stream and nearly vomited. "Yuck!" he exclaimed, "this stuff smells horrible."

"Anything trying to track you will agree," answered Fang. "Trackers don't worry as much as humans about whether or not the smell is pleasant, but they will definitely get the messages 'this is not food,' and 'this is not Peltrin.'"

Peltrin removed all his clothing except his shoes and a pair of shorts that served as his underclothes. Taking a deep breath, he began rolling in the cold mud.

The cold was uncomfortable, but the stench was unbearable. He gagged over and over again as he covered himself in the putrid filth. Putting it on his face was enough to make him dry heave. He felt like he was about to vomit everything he had ever eaten since the day he was born. He tried holding his breath, but even when he wasn't breathing the smell still somehow found its way through.

Finally, Peltrin emerged, dripping the awful, smelly stuff. He took the bulb and the bottle and put them around his neck again.

"Finally," Fang said, "now let's get out of here. My nose is practically burning."

"It's probably good for your sinuses," Peltrin answered. "But now I need your help again with my clothes."

"Now you're thinking of me like a pack animal again."

"A pack animal couldn't handle this," Peltrin answered, "for this, I need a hunter. One that can outrun devastors without letting them lose the scent."

"I see," Fang said testily, "now I'm just bait."

"Exactly," Peltrin answered unapologetically.

"Fine," the wolf answered, "but this won't work if you leave your scent all over the place. Make sure you don't touch anything."

Home Again

"I doubt devastors coordinate as well as a wolf pack," Peltrin pointed out, "aggression seems to be their only thought. If you can get them separated from each other, you can kill them one or two at a time."

Fang smiled a crooked smile, "now you are starting to sound like Fangmort. Separating one from the herd and cutting it down is something I was born to do." Without waiting for any more instructions, Fang took Peltrin's clothes and disappeared into the forest.

The walk back to the house wasn't far, but it was surprisingly difficult. Peltrin was shivering from the cold, which only added to the noise he was making. In the dense forest, Fang's instruction to not touch anything was difficult to follow in some places. Everywhere else, it was impossible. Tree branches and bushes barred his way at every turn. Eventually, he took glops of mud off of his shorts and used them to push branches aside as he went by. It was the best he could do, given the thick forest around him. It had taken only a few minutes to walk to the meadow but he took nearly an hour to get back. In that time, he was seriously beginning to doubt his plan.

"This has to be done today," Peltrin reminded himself. "All three of them will die when the sun rises." He grabbed a couple of short thick sticks to use as weapons. This would have to do until he could get to the cabinet.

Peltrin moved toward the house. He stayed downwind but the large clear area around the house was working against him now. Surprisingly, there were no devastors behind the house so he ventured out of the trees. He felt exposed and vulnerable, standing in the open wind with almost no clothing on. There was no response so he kept moving forward.

There was nothing he could do about visibility, but he stayed silent and downwind. He remembered the fateful day only a few days ago when a change in the wind nearly got him shot in the leg. Later that day, a change in the wind had carried his scent to the trees, which started the devastor attack on his home. He prayed the wind would stay steady. If possible, the stakes were even higher this time.

As he neared the house, there were a series of hisses and a troop of devastors left the front of the house and sprinted into the forest, their eyes black and greedy. Peltrin froze in place. They continued without even looking in his direction.

Fang was right. They relied on smell far more than sight.

Peltrin crept around the house, slowly and silently. Only a few days ago, he had been almost bored with the self-control required for creeping around unseen. Today, it served a more visible purpose and he was far more willing to be patient.

When he reached the door, he attempted to open it. It wouldn't budge. The window shutters were all closed. The door and shutters were covered in scratch marks. In some places, the shutters were broken, but the opening was blocked with wood Peltrin recognized as the countertop. Smiling to himself, Peltrin realized his family had barricaded themselves in, reinforcing the openings with anything they could find in and around the house.

Looking around to make sure the coast was clear, he called out quietly. "Mom…Dad…Beorn? It's me, Peltrin."

There was no answer.

"Hey, can you hear me?" he said, a little louder this time.

Peltrin heard a hissing sound.

He turned just as the devastor pounced. All he saw was claws and eyes…terrible, ferocious red eyes. Crying out, he dropped the two sticks and caught the creature by the wrists. The force of the pounce was enough to make him lose his footing. Desperately, he tried to regain his balance but his head crashed against the side of the house.

Dazed, he hit the ground, landing on his back. He was vaguely aware he had somehow managed to keep hold of the creature's wrists. It strained against his hold in every possible way, screaming in fury.

Finally, it gave up on breaking free and just drove its claws towards his throat. Little by little its claws and teeth got closer and closer. Eventually, its face was just inches from Peltrin. Peltrin stared into those mindless, furious eyes and the familiar fear returned in full fury. He wanted to quit, to give up. All it would take is one little scratch and he would be dead, if not now, then in a few days. What difference did it make as long as this horrible fear was gone?

As the endless seconds ticked by, the world seemed to slow down. He was breathing. His heart was beating. The devastor was breathing. Nothing else seemed to exist. The rest of the world had simply ceased to exist. More seconds ticked by.

He hadn't given up.

The thought almost surprised him. The fear was there, as real and as tangible as it had ever been but, somehow, he was still fighting.

His family needed him to live.

From the depths of his fear, a coherent thought seemed too foreign for immediate action. Could he hope to survive this? Did he want to?

Father, mother, and Beorn needed him to act now.

He blinked. It was such a little thing, but it was a command he had given his own body. And his body had obeyed.

Next was a movement of his arm. Barely a twitch, but the movement meant something. It meant he had found a way past his fear.

Next was a deep breath. Finally, the world began to expand again.

Then he began to push it away. Inch by inch, he increased the distance between his neck and the creature's claws.

The fear was still there, still threatening to crush him, but it no longer consumed him. He noticed it, but it didn't control him anymore. He narrowed his eyes and increased the force against the animal until he finally regained his feet.

Out of the corner of his eye, Peltrin saw the door open just a crack.

Having created a little space between them, Peltrin kicked the devastor in the chest, sending in sprawling off of the porch. Dashing into the house, he retrieved three throwing knives from the weapons cabinet. Nirani moved to close the door but it was too late. The red-eyed devastor pounced triumphantly through the doorway.

Thunk! Thunk! Thunk!

With three knives protruding from its chest, the creature fell—first to its knees, then flat on the floor. Turning its head to an awkward position, the dying devastor glared at Peltrin and made one final attempt to push itself back to its feet. Peltrin snatched a short sword from the cabinet and stepped forward.

Then the creature collapsed, releasing its final breath in a long, soft hiss. Peltrin watched the red glowing eyes as they slowly faded, eventually becoming pale and lifeless.

"Peltrin!" Nirani cried, rushing to him. "You're back!"

Peltrin embraced her tightly. "We did it, mom! We did it. I have the cure."

When the embrace finally ended, she looked him in the face, tears forming in her eyes. "I'm just glad you're back and you're okay. I was so afraid I wouldn't see you again."

Then she looked at the rest of him. "What happened to your clothes? And what is that awful smell?"

"I had to mask my scent to get past the devastors," Peltrin explained.

They embraced again, Peltrin's mother was so happy to see him she ignored the smell. Peltrin hugged her back, wanting to forget everything that had happened, but he happened to glance at the body on the floor. Even now, this wasn't over yet.

"Are there any more?" he asked, pulling out of the embrace.

"I don't know," she answered, reluctantly letting go. "As soon as you left, Bensil gave us a supply of herbs and I barricaded the windows and door. I also blocked the opening near the loft that the devastor got in through last time. They came the night after you left, but they haven't been able to get in."

Peltrin remembered what Valdor said. Most animals never try to force their way into a house. It still seemed strange to Peltrin that an animal with claws built for digging wouldn't think to claw its way through the wood walls of their home, but he was glad to see that was the case.

Peltrin dragged the dead devastor outside. He wasn't sure if the claws were still poisonous after death, but he stayed well away from them, just to be safe. He removed the knives from its body, cleaned them on the ground, and went back inside and closed the door.

Worried the other devastors might come back, Peltrin replaced the logs Nirani had used to block the door. He grunted with the strain of moving the heavy logs. He was impressed she had been able to lift them at all with her injured leg.

His mother then handed him a fresh set of clothes, which he accepted gratefully.

"Did you say you have the panacea?" Nirani asked as Peltrin dressed. He would have liked to have bathed first, but he could only see one barrel of water in the corner. Cleaning himself was going to have to wait until later.

"Sort of," Peltrin answered, "the mirror lied. I learned at the Fyllcarcern that a panacea—a cure-all—isn't possible."

"What did you get from the Fyllcarcern, then?"

"Two things." He showed her the silver vial and the bulb and quickly explained what had happened. He left out many of the details. He would share the rest with all of them later. Right now, he just wanted them to take the elixir.

"You each have to take one drop from the bottle," he concluded. "It will keep you alive for another two days. We plant the bulb today and it will sprout the day after tomorrow. It will create a few drops of the elixir every day. You have to take a drop of the elixir from the flower every day or the poison will kill you."

"Why don't you go give your father the elixir right now?" Nirani said with a tired smile. "This has gone on long enough. It's time to start healing."

Peltrin approached his father slowly. The man lay ominously still. Peltrin had to look closely to see the man's chest move ever so slightly with his shallow breathing. He was pale and looked weak.

Surprisingly, Perwin's face and neck were nearly unharmed but the rest of him was covered with a mixture of gashes and bandages. Peltrin guessed Nirani had conserved bandages by only dressing the worst of his injuries. Some of the injuries Peltrin could see looked pretty bad. He was glad he couldn't see the rest.

Peltrin dropped to his knees by the side of the bed.

Perwin put a bandaged hand on Peltrin's shoulder. "I'm proud of you son."

Peltrin didn't answer. He didn't know what to say.

"I saw you," Perwin went on, "just a moment ago, when you killed the red-eyed devastor with those three knives." He paused to take a few shallow breaths.

Still unsure of himself, Peltrin said nothing again.

"I know the feeling," Perwin went on. "I know what it's like when fear clutches your heart and paralyzes your body. I know you felt it again today, and I saw you have learned to overcome your fear."

Perwin stopped for a moment to catch his breath before he went on.

"I can teach you many things: how to farm, how to hunt, even how to fight. But everyone has weaknesses. Often, there is one particular fault that prevents a man from becoming what he was meant to become.

"My fault, like yours, was fear. Overcoming that fear was the hardest thing I have ever done, and it has made all the difference in my life. Seeing you overcome the same weakness was the proudest moment of my life. If I'm going to die in the morning, the two things I would want the most would be to hold your mother and to remember that moment."

Peltrin choked, but couldn't answer.

"I don't know what happened while you were gone," he went on, "but I know you have changed."

Peltrin took in a shuddering breath but refused to let himself cry. "I have changed," he said, "and I found the cure." He unstopped the bottle and tipped it over his father's mouth. A single, pure drop fell and landed on Perwin's tongue.

Perwin swallowed. "Oh my," he mumbled, taking a deep breath "that feels wonderful!"

He then closed his eyes and began to breathe deeply. After a moment, some color returned to his face. After another moment, he opened his eyes, sat up, and the two embraced. Perwin used only his right arm. Even after receiving the Panacea, his left arm still was too injured to move.

Peltrin handed the precious silver vial to Nirani. "I gave some to dad. There are two drops left!"

"Two drops?" she repeated. Something seemed to catch in her throat.

"One for you and one for Beorn."

"What about you?" She asked, looking him over, "you should use one of those drops for yourself." Peltrin was, indeed, in a pitiful state. Every inch of his body was covered in bruises, cuts, and scratches.

"I'll be fine," Peltrin responded, "besides, the mirror lied. This isn't a true panacea. All it does is counter the poison of the devastors so you don't die from the venom itself. It doesn't heal wounds. I was never poisoned so I don't need it."

There was a brief moment of silence. "I'm so proud of you," Nirani's voice trembled as she pulled him into a tight embrace. "You have done the impossible. Who would have believed we would all be together and safe tonight? Tonight, we will celebrate!"

And they did. Nirani claimed the honor of giving a drop of the panacea to Beorn. "I've been keeping him alive for days," she asserted, "It's only right I should end it."

She stared at the huge man for nearly a full moment, breathing softly. Her hand shook a little as she raised the silver vial. "Aramir has found us," she said softly, "more than anything else, Peltrin will need protection and training. And there is no one else I would trust that to, besides his father and his father's brother." Taking a deep breath, she steadied her hand and tipped it just enough to allow the miraculous drop to fall.

The change was certainly nothing less than magical. The cursed injuries covering Beorn's body had been black and swollen, surrounded by purple veins. In a matter of minutes, the unnatural coloring and even most of the swelling was completely gone. His body was still covered in dozens of injuries, and he still looked pale from the loss of blood, but the difference was remarkable. Slowly and painfully Beorn arose and began to laugh and embrace everyone.

Peltrin showed everyone the bulb. They marveled as he explained it would produce a few drops of elixir every night. Amazingly, it was still intact after everything Peltrin had been through since the Fyllcarcern.

Peltrin removed the logs from the door and they all went outside. He selected a spot in the garden and planted the bulb in the ground.

Home Again

"And now, let's be done with this poison," Perwin demanded. "Take your drop," he said, putting his arm around his wife. There was a cheer of approval from Beorn and Peltrin.

"Not yet," she answered, stuffing the silver vial into a hip pocket. "I will take it later, in a quiet moment." Perwin wanted to press the matter, but a look from his wife silenced him. With a deep breath and a quick wipe of a tear, she went back inside and set about directing the preparation of the food.

Peltrin barricaded the door again. As he looked at his mother he was bursting with pride. For days now, Nirani had been caring for her husband and his brother, knowing her only son was out on a dangerous search.

Though she still had a limp, she was back to normal life again, laughing and chatting away as if nothing serious had ever happened. What an amazing woman she was! He came to her side and they worked together, laughing and joking as they prepared the food.

For Peltrin it was a nearly perfect celebration. He sincerely wished Aralis, Soyem, Lou and even Valdor could join them. He would have liked Fang and Fangmort there as well, though he doubted the wolves would have been willing to join such a gathering. While the rest of the world felt uncertain, Peltrin's parents and uncle were, for the moment, safe. No one would die in the morning and, for the time being, that was enough.

Throughout the evening, Peltrin found himself gravitating again and again to Nirani. She marveled at his stories of their travels through the forest and their trials at the Mihtighof. Again and again, she reminded him of how proud she was of who he was and what he had accomplished. Peltrin knew Perwin was the strength of the family, but Nirani was the heart and soul. Her presence, more than anything else, was what made this place home.

"I still don't understand the bat and the mirror," Peltrin admitted later that night. "They sent me in the right direction, telling me to go to the

Mihtighof. But they lied about the help I would need, and they lied about the Panacea. Why would they do that?"

"They seemed to have wanted you to suffer Valdor's fate," guessed Perwin. "They wanted you to try, but fail."

Poor Valdor," said Nirani, "he has suffered so much over the years."

Peltrin remembered when he had cried secretly in the cave and the bat had somehow enjoyed his pain. He could only imagine how it would have reacted around Valdor.

"Food is ready," announced Nirani, interrupting Peltrin's musings.

All three of the others quickly moved in to help prepare the table. The food looked and smelled absolutely delicious!

As they ate, they heard the howling of several wolves in the surrounding forest. Some of the pack had returned. The house would be safe tonight. It was odd how the long, mournful sounds could be comforting.

Hours later, when all three of the men had finally succumbed to their exhaustion, Nirani sat quietly at the table, deep in thought. She listened as they breathed deeply, or in Beorn's case, snored like a bear with a broken nose. Beorn was still sleeping on the makeshift mattress in the middle of the floor.

"It's time to finish this, I suppose," she said to no one in particular.

Removing the silver vial from a pocket in her dress, she stared at it thoughtfully for a moment.

Then, moving slowly and quietly, she limped over to the ladder and went up to the loft. At the top of the ladder, she sat quietly on the floor next to Peltrin's mattress. Grasping the vial in her hand, she leaned down so her face was on the same level as his, only inches away.

"It was a brave thing you did, my son," she whispered. "We're so proud of you." Her voice caught and she wiped another tear from her eye. There had been many tears that evening.

Gently enough to avoid waking him, she caressed his face. After a slight hesitation, her hand slid down his neck and pushed aside his collar. Using a small kitchen knife, she carefully cut away the bandage Aralis had recently replaced. There, at the base of his neck, where Peltrin would never be able to see it himself, was a tiny scratch that stood apart from his many other injuries.

"Thank you, Aralis," she murmured to herself. "There are so few who could be trusted with something like this."

Even after watching Perwin and Beorn's deteriorating states, it shocked her how the wound had changed over the last few days. When it had first happened, it was little more than a scratch surrounded by an unnatural greyish hue. Now, though the wound had mostly closed, the entire area was completely black. The black decay was surrounded by grotesque purple veins.

She knew her boy had been poisoned from the moment she saw it. Thinking only to spare her son from the fear of death for a little while, she had lied. She had been planning to tell Perwin and Beorn the truth later that day when Peltrin wasn't around. Peltrin would have been told as well, eventually. Little did she know that, within hours, they would all be suffering from the same poison.

"There are some women who play a direct role in the war," she told her sleeping boy. "Some are healers, some prepare the food, some even join the men in the fighting. I respect them and admire their contributions, but I've always known that wasn't my calling."

She paused to stroke his hair. "This is my calling. I know you better than anyone else. With your natural skills and your father's training, you could be the key to ending Aramir's terror."

She hesitated a moment to take a shuddering breath, "what I do tonight might save countless lives and end more than a century of terror and heartache."

She touched his face again, not bothering to wipe away her tears anymore. In all the world this moment was hers and hers alone. She had a right to let them flow.

"But I won't do this for the war, and I have no desire to be remembered as a hero. All I care about tonight is protecting my little boy. My precious, precious son, who perhaps isn't so little anymore, but who needs his mother to protect him just one last time."

Suppressing her sobbing just enough to keep from waking him, Nirani removed the top from the silver vial and tipped it directly over the wound. The others had taken the elixir by mouth, but somehow, she knew that this would work just as well. The last drop of elixir hung for a moment on the edge of the vial, giving her one last opportunity to change her mind.

But the decision was already made. The decision had been made from the moment Peltrin had told her how many drops were in the silver vial. She wouldn't question it now.

She watched and waited patiently until the final, precious drop fell, shimmering like a diamond in the dim light until it landed on his neck. She then watched and waited while his poisoned wound all but disappeared. His body relaxed and he took a deep, cleansing breath.

Only then did she allow herself a few tears for her own regrets of things that would never be: the things she hadn't said and done, the plans and dreams that would never be fulfilled. They were petty things, mostly, she told herself. Nothing that should give her cause for any real grief. But they mattered to her, nonetheless.

Finally, when there were no more tears to cry, she kissed her son on the forehead and slowly came down the ladder. At the bottom of the ladder, she leaned heavily on the table. She was tired now. So tired in fact that the thought of falling asleep and not waking again did not frighten her in the least.

It is an effective poison, thought to herself, but not cruel. If she fell asleep now, she was certain she wouldn't wake. Now that it was both inevitable and imminent, she was grateful it would not be painful.

But not yet. From the feel of it, she knew she still had several hours to live. Slowly, she made her way over to the bed and sat down. Perwin stirred, pulling her close as she lay down. She settled into his arms, feeling the closeness and security she had always treasured.

She loved the man, totally and completely. And she knew he loved her just as much. Buried in the strength of his arms, she listened to him breathing deeply and fully for the first time in days. Here in their bed, with Peltrin safe in his loft, it was hard to imagine anything could possibly be wrong in the world.

She knew she needed to wake Perwin and tell him what was happening, but she waited a moment. He would understand why she had given the elixir to Peltrin. He would agree with her the moment it was out of her lips. His only regret, she knew, would be that he could not have died in her place. They had loved each other so completely. What could she say that could give him the strength and comfort he would need? She hesitated a little longer, temporarily lost in the comfort of the moment.

"Perwin," she ventured.

"Hmmm?" he mumbled sleepily.

"We need to talk."

THE CHRONCILES OF AMYRIAD

CHAPTER 16: NIRANI

Peltrin awoke the next morning feeling better than he had in days. It was as if a huge burden had been lifted from him during the night. He rolled over luxuriously, moaning a little as his body reminded him of the events of the last week.

He had, literally, saved his family. Considering the fury and power of the Fyllen, he might have prevented the destruction of all of Amyriad. The devastors were dead, his family was alive, and his friends were alive. They would have to do something to avoid further attacks from Aramir—Peltrin wasn't looking forward to that—but it was a small price to pay after all they had gone through.

Groaning, he sat up, stretched, and dressed. A few minutes later, Peltrin came down from the loft and went out the front door. The bed was empty but Beorn was still snoring on his makeshift mattress on the floor. On the way out, Peltrin noticed the silver vial on the floor near the door.

He found his parents sitting on the bench on the front porch. Perwin was slouched low, staring blankly into the forest, his face tired and expressionless. Nirani was leaning on her husband's chest, sleeping comfortably under his protective arm. In her hand were pansies. Somehow, she managed to keep hold of them as she dozed. Her face was peaceful and relaxed, more so than Peltrin had ever seen before.

"Every flower has a meaning," Peltrin mumbled to himself automatically. His father gave his mother flowers regularly, that was not unusual. What was unusual was the type of flowers. Pansies usually represented thoughtfulness and remembrance. Among the Pichari, they were often planted on and around graves.

Peltrin couldn't help but stare at his mother. Something was fading. He couldn't quite place it, but her face looked empty. A light he had always subconsciously associated with his mother was not there. Not completely gone, but fading. As he studied her face, searching for what had changed, Perwin started, suddenly aware Peltrin was there.

"She nearly made it through the night," Perwin said blankly. "She's never been one to stay up all night for anything. But tonight, she almost made it. She finally fell asleep less than an hour ago."

Peltrin looked at her again. Perhaps that was the change. Perhaps it was the effects of exhaustion playing on her face. Somehow that didn't seem right.

He reached out and placed his hand on his mother's. It was surprisingly cold, even colder than the chill of the morning. Peltrin slipped back into the house and returned with a blanket, which he softly set over her.

Perwin nodded his approval but said nothing. He returned to staring into the empty air, apparently exhausted from the events of the last week and from staying up all night.

Nirani stirred and looked around. "I told you not to let me sleep," she chided her husband. "How long until the sun comes up?"

"Just a few more minutes now," Perwin answered. Peltrin was surprised to hear his father's voice shake. He couldn't remember ever seeing his father cry.

"Come sit by me, Peltrin," Nirani requested. Her face was so strange. So peaceful, yet somehow fading. Peltrin sat next to her.

"Peltrin," she said, "the devastor that scratched your neck had red eyes."

Peltrin rubbed the back of his neck. "I thought it might be poisoned, but it's almost better now."

"Your mother healed you, son." Perwin was still staring into the distance. "There was only one drop of elixir left. She was the only one who knew you both needed it. She chose you."

Peltrin's chest locked. There was no wind, no birds or insects chirping. The world stopped. He wasn't sure if he was breathing. He no longer cared if he was still breathing.

"Call it selfish if you must," she whispered. "One of us had to bear the guilt of living. I chose you. I could have told everyone last night. I didn't because I knew we would have spent all evening arguing and worrying over who should be the one to die."

Peltrin wanted to disagree, but he knew it was true.

She took a few raspy breaths, "I made my decision the instant I knew there was a decision to be made. Once I knew I was going to die, I just wanted a few final hours of peace. I wanted my last evening to be one of joy—a few precious hours with my husband and my only son. Maybe it was my final gift to you. Maybe it was a dying wish just for me. Keeping the secret last night gave me one last evening of love and peace and warmth. It meant more to me than anything else in the world."

"The plant," Peltrin murmured.

"You can't harvest until tomorrow," Perwin reminded him. "She has only until the sun rises today."

"The time has come," she murmured. "I love you both far more than life itself. Never forget that." Her voice was barely a whisper. She looked as if she might have said more but she needed the energy to breathe.

Peltrin was in shock. He, like his father, found himself staring into the woods. He stared without blinking, but he saw nothing. He reached under the blanket and grasped his mother's hand.

The cool touch of his mother's hand was the only thing that kept Peltrin from collapsing on the spot. Unconsciously, his breathing slowed until it matched hers. Perhaps his breathing would stop when hers stopped. Part of him hoped it would.

To their left, a bright point of light peeked over the mountain and touched the top of the house behind them. The moment had come. Peltrin felt it more than he saw it. He knew that once the light touched Nirani, it would all be over.

He continued to look at the trees. Part of him wanted to see Nirani breathing one last time. But that would mean watching as the last spark of life left her face. He knew he couldn't bear it.

Dimly he became aware of a distant mournful sound…Crying? Was it his own voice? His father's? Both? He wasn't sure.

There was a flurry of motion as someone sprinted from the trees. The person was running faster than he had ever seen anyone run before. Odd that something so unimportant would even occur to him at a time like this.

His eyes focused somewhat and he realized it was Aralis. He was glad she was here. Other than his father, she was perhaps the one person in the world he most wanted to be with right now. Her quiet, friendly presence would be welcome.

Her arms were pumping and her long legs were a flurry of motion as she continued to run faster than he would have believed possible. She crashed hard into the porch railing, reaching out to Nirani just as Peltrin's mother took in a long, final shuddering breath. Aralis then fell hard to the ground.

Just as the sun's first rays touched them, Nirani was no longer moving. She didn't exhale her final breath. She was cold, stone cold. Her softness was gone and she was hard as stone.

Confused, Peltrin looked at her face. She was actually made of stone. The blanket was unchanged, but Nirani's face and all that he could see of her clothes were made of greyish stone. The details were more perfect than any artist could have managed. In her mouth was a small, red crystalline rock. Peltrin removed his hand from hers and pulled the blanket off. The rest of her body and clothing was made of the same greyish stone, though the pansies in her hand were unchanged.

He turned to Aralis, still baffled by what had just happened. She was lying on the ground clutching her ribs, which were probably bruised deeply from the collision. It was possible something was broken.

Aralis looked Peltrin briefly in the eyes. Then she rose to her hands and knees, gasping for air and shaking violently.

Reluctant though he was to leave his mother, Peltrin got up and moved to see if Aralis was okay. He arrived just as she started throwing up. Not knowing what else to do, he put his hand on her right shoulder. It was drenched. He removed his hand and looked at it. It was covered in sweat and blood.

He looked at her shoulder. The sleeve was torn and there were deep claw marks across the back of her shoulder.

"What happened?" Peltrin managed.

Aralis didn't answer at first, she was still throwing up and struggling for air.

Perwin, who had some difficulty extracting himself from the statue of his wife, went into the house and quickly returned, still limping heavily. He handed Aralis a rag and a towel. He also pressed a cloth to her shoulder to slow the bleeding.

Aralis used the rag to wipe the sick from her mouth. With the towel, she began to dry her face and arms. She was still shaking violently and tears and sweat were still streaming down her face.

"I almost didn't make it," she said unsteadily.

"It was close," Perwin said hoarsely, his face still streaked with trails of tears. "I don't doubt she was breathing her last breath. What is this stone you gave her?"

"It has stopped the poison," Aralis explained. "After Peltrin left, Soyem told us there were only three drops in the vial and Valdor suggested we use the stone."

"Valdor told you how to use it?" Asked Peltrin.

"Nirani is frozen in stone until we take the rock out of her mouth, turn it around, and put it back in again," she responded, "but we have to destroy the source of the poison first, or she will die as soon as she is no longer frozen."

"What's the source of the poison?" Perwin asked.

"Aramir," Peltrin answered.

"Possibly," Aralis corrected tiredly.

"It took us three days to get there," Peltrin said with awe, deciding not to argue, "you ran all the way back in one night?"

"We weren't traveling for most of that time," Aralis reminded him. "Also, I was alone with no gear or distractions."

"The stone was buried with his wife and daughter," Peltrin said, remembering. He looked at Aralis, "you robbed a grave?"

"Not really," she said a little defensively. "Valdor told me to. He said his wife and daughter would be pleased."

Just then they heard Beorn noisily grunting as he struggled to work his way up to his feet.

"I'd better tell him what happened," said Perwin. Peltrin took over holding the bloody cloth to her shoulder as Perwin disappeared into the house.

"You were alone," Peltrin said, remembering Aralis' recurring dreams, "all night in the forest and something attacked you."

"It was a mountain lion," she said it with no fear in her voice. "It followed me for what felt like hours and attacked just as morning was beginning to break."

Peltrin was flabbergasted. As they had traveled to the Mihtighof, she had been willing to do anything rather than spend the night outside. Being alone in the forest and attacked by a predator was exactly what she had always feared the most.

"Why didn't the wolves run with you?" he asked, remembering Fangmort and the pack.

"We realized that devastors would be here at the house. Fangmort and the others came ahead of me to clear the way for you and Fang."

"You were right, but Fang and I were able to get through," said Peltrin. He quickly explained the strategy he had used to get to the house.

"How did you survive the mountain lion?" Peltrin asked.

"When I thought about my dreams, I always pictured myself as the prey," she answered, still working to slow her breathing. "But once I decided to take the risk, I had time to think about those dreams for what they are. It occurred to me that, in my dreams, I always saw the world through the eyes of the predator. I knew then that my dreams were showing me my strength, not my weakness."

Peltrin nodded for her to go on.

"I knew the mountain lion was there before it attacked," she said, her eyes fierce. "I felt fear, but not enough to stop or hide. I couldn't afford to stop or hide; your mother would die if I did.

"There was even a part of me that hoped it would attack. When it did, I killed it using only my knife. Part of me was happy when it happened. It gave me a chance to prove to myself that I am not the hunted."

She then looked him straight in the eye. "I am the hunter."

Peltrin felt a chill as he looked into her intense, dark eyes. It was the most he had ever heard her say in a single conversation. He found it difficult to reconcile this girl's extremes. One minute she seemed too afraid to add a few words to a normal conversation. The next she was fighting bandits and taking on a mountain lion alone in a dark forest.

"You knew all along I was poisoned," said Peltrin.

Aralis looked away. "I made Nirani a promise." Peltrin waited for more but there was no further explanation. She was back to her usual, quiet self.

"You wonderful, brave girl," said Perwin, coming to the door. "What a terrible night you've had. Come in and warm yourself."

Peltrin put his arm around her to help as Aralis entered the house and collapsed gratefully into a chair.

***

"You've saved Nirani's life!" Beorn boomed happily.

"I didn't save her," Aralis reminded them sleepily, "I have only bought you time." She was looking considerably better than she had that morning, though her hair was still a mess and she looked like she needed a lot more sleep. It was late evening and she had only recently awoken.

"It was a gamble," said Bensil, "You will have some serious scars on your shoulder, but it paid off."

Peltrin had retrieved Bensil that morning. The old healer had come quickly to tend to Aralis' shoulder. He and Aralis had remained at Perwin's home while she slept.

"We will use our time well," Perwin said, his voice was steady and his face was full of determination.

"I will help you," said Valdor quietly. Perwin, Beorn, Peltrin, Aralis, and Bensil all looked at the door in surprise. Valdor and Soyem stood in the doorway. They both looked very tired.

"It would be most welcome, my old friend," Perwin limped over to embrace his old mentor. "We're grateful you came, killing Aramir isn't going to be easy."

Soyem hurried over to embrace Aralis. Though very different in appearance, the two were like brother and sister.

"What happened," asked Soyem, looking at her bandaged shoulder.

Aralis explained to Soyem and Valdor her travel through the night and the wound on her shoulder.

"We tried to keep up with Aralis," said Valdor. "But these old bones just weren't up to it. We hadn't talked for five minutes after Peltrin left before she went running to my house. By the time Soyem and I got there, she had just dug up the stone and she was off again. We walked until well after dark and we started early this morning but we never would have made it in time."

"Never underestimate Aralis," said Bensil proudly. "There's more to her than anyone would guess."

Aralis ducked her head shyly.

"Aramir underestimated all of us," Perwin pointed out. "It will be his undoing."

"Trying to kill us will be the biggest mistake Aramir ever made," growled Beorn. "All I need is a little time to heal and an afternoon to sharpen my ax. As soon as that happens, I'll go tell him myself."

"Years ago, we were among his greatest enemies," Perwin added. "We would have been perfectly content to hide for the rest of our lives and raise our families. His attack destroyed Beorn's family, and my only hope of getting my wife back is to seek his destruction."

Perwin then walked out the door, slowly and painfully. They all watched Peltrin's father as he removed the pansies from Nirani's hand and replaced them with gorse from a bush at the corner of the house. The gorse wasn't as pretty as pansies, but its meaning was significant.

Undying love through all seasons, Peltrin thought to himself. He couldn't agree more.

"Then we will seek his destruction," Peltrin said, his face filled with determination.

"We hoped that your training would only serve to defend yourself and your family," Perwin said sadly, "But attacks like these likely mean Aramir is preparing for another war. Only a few days ago you said you didn't want to go to war, but I don't suppose we could stop you now."

Peltrin turned to the Northeast, where he knew the fortress of Krakmai stood. "It's the only way to save mother. Aramir himself couldn't stop me now."

Peltrin narrowed his silver-blue eyes. "Soon he will be very afraid."

His hands clenched. "Because I'm not…not anymore."

ACKNOWLEDGEMENTS

No matter how hard one tries, writing a book with any semblance of quality simply isn't a one-person endeavor. I'd like to give a special thanks to my wife and kids, who have always been supportive of my endless projects and dreams. My wife, in particular, spent many long hours reading and rereading various drafts of the book as my primary content editor. I implemented the vast majority of her recommendations and the book is unquestionably better because of it. I also have to thank Melanie Ketcheson, who was willing to provide her valuable time and considerable talent to the editing process. Finally, I must thank the many friends and family who gave encouragement, particularly those who read the original draft of what later became The Chronicles of Amyriad. That was over thirteen years ago.

COMING 2021!

S.R. JENSEN

See www.srjensenbooks.com for the latest updates!

About The Author

Scott R. Jensen has a Bachelor's degree in Mechanical Engineering from BYU-Provo and a Master's Degree from Utah State University. Scott also lived for two years in Colombia, which he still claims was the most important part of his education. For the past 13 years, Scott has been working as an engineer while he endlessly writes and rewrites the novels he has finally decided he likes well enough to start publishing.

Scott currently lives near Rigby, ID with his wife, four children, and overly energetic dog. Scott and his family enjoy hiking, camping, spelunking, rock climbing, whitewater rafting, and ridiculously long walks.

The Panacea, Book 1 of the Chronicles of Amyriad is Scott's first fantasy publication.

www.SRJensenBooks.com

www.ingramcontent.com/pod-product-compliance
Lightning Source LLC
Chambersburg PA
CBHW031716170626
46808CB00005B/1769